EMMA AND THE SILK THIEVES

TALES OF WIDOWSWOOD BOOK 2

MATTHEW S. COX

DIVISION ZERO PRESS

Emma and the Silk Thieves
Tales of Widowswood Book Two
© 2016 – Matthew S. Cox

ISBN (ebook): 978-1-949174-52-6

ISBN (print): 978-1-949174-53-3

CONTENTS

SIR TAM

*S*omber and quiet, Emma stood on tiptoe to reach the rope strung across the back porch of her family home. She tugged a fold out of the bedsheet and shimmied left to the nearest spot of empty line. Kimber, at her side, handed up one of her mother's dresses, a sopping wad of dark green cloth. Emma smiled at her little sister as she took the bundle of fabric.

The girl had changed much from the dirty, bruised waif who'd shown up at her doorstep selling pitiful apples three weeks ago. Had Emma not known better, she'd never have believed them the same person. Waist-long curly red hair fluttered in the breeze, framing a pale, freckled face covered in a broad grin, and her bright green eyes glimmered with happiness. Kimber clutched a basket of damp clothes to her chest, creating a spreading wet spot on her white cotton dress. Water dripped from the bottom of the basket, pattering around the girl's toes.

Somewhere out in the rolling patch of meadow behind the house, Tam roared and yelled war cries amid the crunches and whiffs of tall grass dying in valiant battle.

"I'll beat alla goblins!" yelled Tam. A wooden sword rose out of the green and chopped downward out of sight. "Yah! Take that!"

Despite Nan's assurances the Banderwigh's curse would've killed that man anyway, Emma couldn't help but feel Da had somehow made a mistake. She busied herself hanging two of her brother's tunics while trying not to think about the look on the poor man's face. Carefree humming to her right made her glance at the big grin on her sister's face. Soon, the shroud of gloom hanging on Emma's shoulders receded under Kimber's cheerful light. After giving the younger girl a conspiratorial grin, she turned to the line, hurled Mama's dress up and over, and smoothed it out to dry.

"Wha's wrong?" Kimber sidled closer.

A cold drip of water landed on Emma's right foot and trickled to the wood. "I feel sad for that man."

Kimber handed her one of Tam's tunics. "Nan a'said he'as dead an'way."

"Yeah." Emma tossed her head to clear hair from her eyes as she hung another of her brother's shirts.

The hiss of wind amid the boughs of Widowswood caught her attention. Emma paused, one hand on a pair of Da's pants, and stared into the forest. The occasional *snap* of a running deer or flash of a cruising bird caught her eye, but nothing at all seemed scary about the dark.

"Is we bein' watched?" whispered Kimber, leaning so close her chin hovered at Emma's shoulder. "You's starin' a' the woods 'gain."

"Aaah!" yelled Tam. He came running out of the meadow-grass holding his side as if he'd been stabbed. "Em!" The six-year-old did a pratfall on the little two-step stairway between the porch and the path to the privy. "Goblin arrow! I needa potion or Im'a die!"

Emma grinned. She hurried to him, pretended to open a satchel on her side, and poured the contents of a nonexistent bottle into his mouth. Tam sprang upright and ran back into the meadow, waving the wooden sword overhead.

Kimber handed over another of Mama's dresses. "Em?"

"I'm being careful." She returned to the line and swept her gaze across the forest, all the way from the left corner of the house around to the right, where the patch of meadow behind their home opened out into rolling plain. "There's nothing scary."

"Whew." Kimber exhaled. "I's don' wanna be put inna cage."

Emma hugged her. "No one's putting you in a cage. The monster's gone."

A few minutes, and six pieces of laundry later, Kimber darted inside with the empty basket while Emma fussed at one of Nan's dresses on the line. The rope didn't have quite enough room left for it, but she arranged it as best she could to let the air have at it. She went inside and took up the broom while Kimber ran about dusting. Nan sat in her chair at the corner nearest the hallway leading to her bedroom, knitting. Emma returned to the back porch and swept it before heading around to the front and repeating the process.

She stood the broom on its bristles and twirled it back and forth while stealing a glance at the woods. A momentary feeling of being watched came and went, but it didn't carry the same strange dread it had before the Banderwigh appeared.

"Probably just a trapper or something." She looked around for a moment, found nothing, and hurried the broom to the left side of the porch.

Mama appeared on the road leading to town, walking home from her morning rounds. Emma rose up on tiptoe and waved to her before hurrying to the top of the stairs and waiting for her mother to reach the house.

"Is Mr. Parr okay?"

"He's fine." Mama patted Emma on the shoulder. "He fell into a bit of Creeproot is all."

Emma's skin crawled at the memory of when she'd discovered the irritating plant, itching bright red patches from the tips of her toes halfway up her thighs. Mama's salve had made the itching stop, but even air blowing across the spot hurt for a few days. "I don't like Creeproot."

Mama pushed the door open and went inside, Emma behind her. "The root itself won't bother anyone. It's the sap inside. If the root doesn't break, it won't hurt you."

Emma set the broom against the wall by the door. "Sweepin's done. Clothes are hanging."

"I'as finnish a' dustin'," chirped Kimber. "C'we play?"

Tam's war cry echoed out back.

Mama laughed. "Go on. Don't get too far away. It's almost time for lunch."

Kimber cheered. She took Emma's hand and led her out to the meadow. After a little less than an hour of 'faerie tea party,' Mama called them inside to eat lunch. With a belly full of warm bread and jam, they returned to the meadow for a while more.

"Let's find faeries!" said Kimber.

Emma drew in a breath to declare no such things existed, but bit her tongue. Even if they didn't, she couldn't crush Kimber's eagerness. As the girls headed toward the woods, Tam scurried up behind them, wooden sword hung on his belt.

"It's dange-rous inna woods. You need a knight."

Emma smiled. "Oh, how foolish of us. Will you be so kind as to protect us?"

Tam puffed up his chest. "Aye." A few steps later, he turned his head to her. "What be your quest?"

"We'as gonna find faeries," whispered Kimber.

"Oh." Tam's face collapsed with a look of severe disappointment for a few seconds before he grinned again. "Goblins eat faeries. I'll pa'tect them too."

"Eww!" whispered Kimber. "Tha's bad!"

Emma couldn't help herself and giggled.

They came to a halt near the stream where they usually swam, and hid in the bushes.

"Where a' faeries?" asked Tam.

"Shh," whispered Kimber. "Donn'ae make loud. Scare 'em 'way. We keep quiet, 'an they come out."

Patience gave way to fidgeting before long. Kimber's eagerness faded to sorrow, but Emma pulled her upright before she could cry.

"Wanna swim?" Emma pointed at the stream.

Not waiting for an answer, Tam flung off his tunic and ran headlong into the water.

"I'as cann'ae." Kimber looked down. Her posture stiffened and a hint of a tremble took her. "Donn'ae like water."

Emma remembered Old Man Drinn holding the girl underwater in the horse trough as punishment for not bringing home enough copper from begging. *Oh no...* Without thinking, she grabbed on and hugged her tight. "I'm sorry. I forgot."

"Is okay." Kimber sniffled.

"Let's just sit in the grass." Emma led Kimber a little closer to the stream and plopped down where she had a clear view of Tam.

Kimber relaxed and watched the boy splash about. The stream came up to his armpits at the deepest point. The girls studied the forest, still on the hunt for faeries, but spotted only a small boar and a pair of badgers.

"I'as sorry for keepin' yas from swimmin'." Kimber glanced at her lap. "You 'kin if you want."

Emma smiled. "I don't mind."

The redhead gave her a sidelong glance, shifted her eyes toward the water for a few seconds, and back to Emma. "Do I'as 'ave ta put m'head unner?"

"You don't have to put one toe in if you don't want to." Emma squeezed her hand.

"'Kay." Kimber stood. "I'as try little."

Emma let her lead to the edge, and stepped in with her until the water hovered within an inch of the younger girl's dress. Since Kimber hadn't pulled a Tam and flung her clothes off, Emma figured she had no intention of going much farther into the water than shin deep. She stood quietly at her side, holding her hand.

"Kimber, look." Emma pointed up at a blue bird with a long shimmery green tail glinting like metal.

"Faerie?" asked Kimber, wide-eyed. "Oh... bird." She smiled. "E'es pretty."

Tam, spotting the girls standing in the water, pivoted toward them with *that* look in his eyes.

Emma shot him a stare and shook her head 'no.' He tilted his head in confusion. Emma indicated Kimber with a flick of her eyes and shook her head again. Tam shrugged and dove under. Over the next half hour or so, Emma pointed out the occasional bird, deer, or passing fish. They walked a little and picked at submerged rocks with their toes. She let Kimber decide how far off the bank to go, but the girl never strayed deep enough to have to hike up her dress. Emma kept holding her hand and talking about anything and everything she could think of other than swimming. Kimber's trembling ceased, but she still seemed stiff... until a small silver fish nipped at her foot. Squealing, Kimber tried to leap away, but slipped in the muck. Emma caught her, and they both burst into laughter.

"I'as not a nibble!" Kimber pointed at the retreating fish. "Donn'ae eat me!"

Emma managed to sneak a few words in between laughs. "Fish just wanna tickle us."

When the giggling died down, Kimber appeared more relaxed. They stood for a while more in the shin-deep water before she pulled her dress up enough to squat without getting it wet. Emma hovered protectively over Kimber as the girl swished a hand back and forth in the water, as if trying to measure if the stream would hurt her. The redhead eyed Tam, looked up at Emma, and bit her lip with a sudden hint of fear or guilt.

"Okay. I'as safe wi' you." Kimber managed a weak smile. "But I'as don't wanna duck under."

Emma nodded.

Kimber threw her dress onto the grass past the water and lowered herself to sit, emitting a squeal as the chilly water rose over her ribs. She looked up with a strange unsettled expression. Emma removed her dress as well and threw it onto the bank, then sat next to her. Emma grimaced at the sensation of sitting on cold, squishy mud, and understood the weird look on Kimber's face. She scooted a few feet to the left until she found a mossy rock to perch on. Kimber followed, squeezing up against her so they could both fit on the same stone. Emma put an arm around her, holding her close in an effort to be reassuring. Kimber's shivering lessened as she occupied herself playing with her hair where it became a cloud of bright red below the surface.

Flowing water glided around her middle, refreshing if a bit too cold. Wind carried the fragrance of leaves and forest, and added a faint whisper to the branches overhead. She couldn't have asked for a more peaceful moment. She smiled at Kimber, hoping to chip away the bad memories the girl had about water.

They spent a few minutes burying their feet in the mucky bottom and lifting them out, making wispy trails of mud that carried off in the current. Tam kept giving Emma the 'come and play' look before resuming his quest to find treasure at the bottom. It took a little while for Kimber to relax her death grip on Emma's hand.

"Tam wann'ae play wif you. I'as gonna stay here." Kimber's smile still held a bit of worry.

"Are you sure?"

Kimber nodded. "I'as onna rock. I okay."

"Okay. I won't go far." Emma slipped into the middle of the stream to swim around a bit with her brother. She initiated a brief splash war, which she could tell Tam had been dying for. Every time they went swimming, at least since he'd been old enough to swim without someone holding him, he adored throwing water everywhere. They traded splashes and sprays for a little while before Tam jumped back.

"Aah!" yelled Tam. "A black water dragon is trying to eat me! I'm t'rowing a fireball!" He jumped up and fell to the side while slapping his hand at the surface, throwing a big wave at Emma.

She frowned at being called a 'black dragon.' "Aren't you a knight? They don't use fire magic."

"Imma knight-wizard now." Tam jumped left, sending another big splash her way.

Emma snarled, spreading her arms wide. She roared and lunged forward, burying him with a massive splash.

He bobbed to the surface a second later. "Shield spell! You dinna kill me."

She growled as if annoyed, but couldn't stop grinning.

Kimber remained seated on the small submerged boulder, but smiled at the two of them kicking up a ruckus. Now and then, she screamed or squealed when curious fish got too close, but her shouts always broke into giggles afterward.

Emma glanced upward, noting the afternoon would soon be evening. She herded Tam to the bank. "We'll need to go home soon. Time to dry."

Kimber wasted no time moving back to dry land. They lay in the grass for a while, picking animal shapes out of clouds. Eventually, Mama's voice carried over the field, beckoning them back.

"Come, Tam. It's time to go home," said Emma. "It's going to be dark soon and Mama wants us close enough to see."

Mostly dry, they dressed and hurried back across the meadow. Once home, Emma and Kimber helped Mama prepare dinner while Tam weaved around them in an effort to sneak an early taste. Perhaps twenty minutes later, Da hurried in, grumbling about the upcoming feast. He pulled the boy away and occupied him with sword lessons out back for the time it took the food to cook. Much to Emma's disappointment, no sooner had they finished eating than Da offered the briefest of hugs and ran back out to attend to his duties with the Watch.

Emma helped clean the table and dishes, then went straight to the porch and sat while Tam resumed his knightly quest of goblin slaying in the meadow a short distance from the house. Kimber raced up behind her, holding a hairbrush. After handing it to Emma, she sat on the edge of the porch.

Emma scooted up behind her, both their legs dangling, and proceeded to work the brush over the tangled mass of red in front of her. She took the younger girl's hair in portions, holding a clump until it brushed smooth to keep the tension from pulling too hard at her head. Kimber clutched the floorboards between her knees, squirming and gasping with each knot that snagged the bristles. She spent a good fifteen or so minutes working on her sister's hair before the snagging ceased.

Fiery orange spread across the clouds at the level of the black treetops and streaks of yellow-green appeared in the meadow from fireflies zipping about. Tam had been quiet for too long. Emma's breath caught in her chest. Still drawing the brush through Kimber's hair, she searched the area for any sign of motion.

Her mother's face appeared in the window. She smiled at Emma and spent a moment trying to locate Tam in the grass. Emma pointed. Mama gave her a look that bade her bring him in soon and vanished back into the house.

Tam burst out of a mass of thick weeds taller than him in pursuit of a particularly large firefly. The insect outpaced him with ease, though he showed little sign of giving up. Soft thuds in the floorboards at her seat suggested Mama had returned to the window.

"Tam," called Emma, "it's getting dark. Time to come in."

She drew the brush down Kimber's lush hair in a series of easy passes. "I know you heard me, Tam." Emma scooted back, pulled her feet up, and stood. "Tam, don't make Mama come out here."

"'Kay," yelled the boy, sounding less than happy about it.

Emma sidestepped as Kimber crawled backward. She sat on the edge and handed the brush over her shoulder. Fortunately, the eight-year-old had learned the fine art of hair brushing with less difficulty than bathing. A brush, at least, she could practice on dolls. Emma kept her knees tight together, a death grip of floorboards on either side of her legs. She braced for it to hurt, but Kimber took gentle care and broke into a whispery rhyming song. Something Mama usually sang to herself, though the babble behind her made it clear Kimber had no idea what the words really were.

Tam barreled out of the grass and took a seat beside her. Coupled with the quiet song, the continuous tug of the brush down Emma's silken black hair started to lull her to sleep. Tam bumped her awake a moment later, stabbing his wooden sword out at the meadow.

"Goblins are hiding." Tam slipped the weapon into his belt. "I scared 'em off."

"You sure did." Emma put an arm around his back and patted his shoulder. "Silly goblins should have known not to challenge a knight."

The boy puffed up his chest, nodding.

"I's a'done," mumbled Kimber. "I's do okay?"

Emma swiped her fingers at her hair once on either side before she smiled over her shoulder at her. "It's perfect."

Kimber grinned so hard her eyes shut, and handed back the brush.

The door opened with a faint *squeak*. "All right you three," said Mama. "Time for bed."

"Yes, Mama," said Emma and Kimber at the same time.

"Is too early for knights ta sleep," muttered Tam.

Mama padded out onto the porch and picked him up. "The dragons are all sleeping. If they get more sleep than the knight, they'll be too strong to vanquish."

He stuck out his bottom lip, but offered no more protest than a sour face as she carried him to the privy. Emma stood and took Kimber's hand, following. She became nervous at the sight of the forest behind the outhouse. Ever since the Banderwigh had taken her, she'd been afraid to be near it without Mama or Nan close by. Of course, she acted brave for Tam, but he had to know.

She ducked into the little wooden booth at her turn and wasted no time, eager to be inside the house before full dark. Mama held Tam's hand on the way back to the porch, Kimber and Emma running astride in front of her. Emma slowed to a walk as soon as she reached the porch, and left a trail of grass-damp footprints across the little rear alcove. She went the long way around the table, looping past the front door, and headed to the left. Kimber pulled her dress off over her head before they reached the bed, folded it, and traded it on the shelf for the pink nightgown Da had bought her.

While Emma changed into her plain white nightdress, Tam made a drawn-out show of hanging his wooden sword on the wall in a place of reverence. He flung his tunic to the floor and climbed into bed after them in his skivvies.

Perched on his knees, he twisted left and right, searching the room. "Mama, where's Nan? Story?"

Mama pulled a nightshirt down over his head. "Nan will be back soon. Even as a bird, the Griffondark Wood makes for a long trip."

"Aww." He whined while wriggling his arms loose.

Emma rolled onto her side, back to the room, the wall inches from her face. Nan hadn't said much about why she'd gone to visit another group of druids in the east: only that the trip was nothing to worry herself over, and she would be gone for a few days. Emma clasped her hands at her chin, fussing with the thin silk ribbon at the neck of her nightdress. *Why does Nan have to be old?* Fear that her grandmother might not return made her eyes wet, but she kept still and quiet.

Mama twisted the lantern, plunging half of the house's main room into darkness. Kimber scooted close behind her and Tam threw his arm over both of them. They didn't have to cram against the wall like that until Mama and Da went to bed, but she didn't mind. Having her siblings close eased her worry over Nan.

"Sleep tight." A soft kissing noise came from behind.

"Night, Mama," whispered Tam.

"May the faeries guard your dreams." Another kiss.

"Night, Mama," said Kimber.

Hair tickled the side of Emma's face as Mama leaned down close, looking into Emma's ear. "I don't see any spiders hiding in those dreams."

Emma smiled as a kiss landed atop her head. "Night, Mama."

The house hung in quiet for a few minutes after her mother went outside to the front porch. Once again, Da had a late night with the Watch, though it had to be something boring, as Mama didn't seem worried.

Kimber's fingers dug into Emma's side. A sniffle broke the silence at the back of her neck.

Emma reached up and grasped the girl's hand. "What's wrong?"

The younger girl clung tighter. "I'as happy."

"Happy doesn't cry," grumbled Tam. For all his complaining about having to go to bed, he sounded exhausted.

Kimber sniffled again and put her chin on Emma's shoulder. "I'as don' wan' me bad Papa tae show up an' take me 'way." Fear and urgency elevated her whisper to a voice. "I'as wanna be wif my family."

Did she forget?

Emma patted and squeezed the girl's hand. "Kimber…"

Sniffle. "Yeah?"

She squirmed enough to make eye contact, their noses almost touching. "He can't take you away from your home. He's dead."

Kimber's tears stopped. Her emerald eyes widened. "Dead?"

"Dead, dead," muttered Tam. "Dead like the Bandy-wee."

"Tam," snapped Emma in a whisper. "Don't say such things. That man is *not* going to come back."

"I hadda ni'mare." Kimber shivered. "You's right. He's gone."

Emma wriggled around to put her back to the wall, facing her. "I'm sorry."

"Mmm." Kimber nodded, wiping her eyes. "He didn' wan' me."

"Dead like the Bandy-wee," muttered Tam in his sleep.

Much to Emma's surprise, Kimber giggled. "Like th' Banderwigh."

"Yes." She tried not to think of the last mournful stare the poor man had given her when Da killed him. Something told her she'd picture that face in her dreams for the rest of her life. As horrified as she'd been, the cursed man collapsed with a contented look on his face. "Dead like the Banderwigh."

Emma rolled flat on her back and closed her eyes. Kimber snuggled close.

Uruleth, if you're listening, please help that man find his way in the spirit world.

She resigned herself to sleep, hopefully without dreams of spiders, cages, or monsters sneaking up on her in the dark.

2

THE SILKEN ACCORD

*E*mma awoke squished face-first into the wall. The house sat dark and silent, a trace of wood smoke in the air from the fireplace. Kimber's breaths puffed into the back of her head, and Da's snoring resonated in the room. Despite a rather desperate need to use the privy, being pinned to the wall by the weight of her family *and* the weight of her fear kept her from squirming. She shut her eyes, but made no effort to go back to sleep. Leg twitching, she tried to concentrate on anything but the pressure wanting out. She could wait until her parents woke up in another few minutes. Going outside, alone, in the wee-early morning didn't have to happen. She didn't *have* to go out to that horrible little building where that creature grabbed her.

I'm being silly. She exhaled. *It's dead.*

The down-stuffed mattress shifted and the pressure squeezing into her lessened. Tam yawned. Sensing an impending wet finger in her ear, Emma opened her eyes and looked up. Sure enough, the boy perched on his knees and hovered over, reaching for her. At the sight of her watching him, he grinned.

"Have'ta pee."

She drew in a breath, intent on telling him to wait for Mama, but exhaled without a word and pushed herself up to sit. Kimber's mouth hung open, her body limp. *She'd sleep through a goblin war.* Emma slipped out from under the blanket and scooted off the foot end of the bed. Tam climbed over Mama, then Da, and jumped to the floor.

Emma took his hand and walked him into the rear alcove, past all of Da's things hanging on the pegs. As always, Tam stared at the swords with adoration, though he didn't dare touch them. He'd made that mistake once, and the way Da bellowed scared them both. That his anger came from worry Tam would hurt himself took the sting from the shouting. She reached up and unlatched the back door, opening it with a firm shove.

The early sun blued the horizon in the east, the light too far away to yet lift the gloomy night from their home. The back door faced west. Widowswood resembled a smear of black paint across a canvas beneath an indigo sky. Pale wood on the face of the outhouse caught the glow of the morning rising behind the house, making it appear charged with magical energy.

Emma froze, staring at the little outbuilding. The Banderwigh's dire glare returned to her thoughts, followed by the memory of her scream, and the lantern she'd thrown in panic.

"Ow," said Tam.

She relaxed her grip on his hand. "Sorry." *It's gone. It's dead.*

Freezing stones underfoot hastened her steps. She managed to resist the urge to break into a full run, but did slip inside with him before he could lock the door in her face again. He didn't even try, content to deal with his morning needs while she stood with her back turned, one eye hovering over the little moon slit in the wood, watching for threats.

By the time he finished, Emma bounced in place.

"Why are you scared? It's dead." Tam tilted his head.

She hugged him. "I know. Just bad dreams."

He stood by the door 'on guard' while she sat. Fear and unease leaked out with her discomfort. A distant cry of a dying bear (Da's yawn) made her smile. He came tromping down the stone path and rattled the door.

"Almost done," said Emma.

A moment later, she stood and adjusted her nightdress. As soon as she got up, Tam unlatched the door. Da put a hand on both of their heads, ruffling hair, and stepped in. Emma dragged Tam to the water pump on the way to the house to rinse their hands.

Inside, Mama puttered about with Kimber, setting the table for their morning meal. It felt strange not having Nan here, but Emma refused to let herself think about it. *Everything returns from whence it came,* said Nan's voice in her mind. She knew the day would come, but she wanted to at least be grown up first.

"Why the face?" asked Mama.

Emma took a seat at the table. "I miss Nan."

"That woman's going to outlive me," said Mama. "She's got a few tricks up her sleeves."

"Nan's got big sleeves," said Tam.

"I hope she doesn't join the spirits until I'm someone's mama." Emma looked down. "I'll be too sad if I'm still little."

"Oh, Em…" Her mother walked up beside her and stroked her hair. "When you grow up, some things become easier to understand, but it doesn't hurt any less. Don't worry so much. Ralithir's watching over her."

"Who?" asked Emma.

Mama smiled. "The Raven Spirit. You've heard of Uruleth, Ylithir, and Strixian, but there are many others. Nan's close to Ralithir. He's quite tenacious, a survivor, just like your grandmother."

Kimber set a basket of rolls on the table. "He'a trickster, an' he brings omens. Like ta warn 'bout death 'an he comes."

Emma shot her a look. "What?"

The outhouse door clattered closed.

"To some, yes." Mama took Kimber's hand.

"The men who'd come 'round 'da house'd always talkin' 'bout him." Kimber looked down as if she'd done something wrong. "Ia's sorry."

"It's okay." Emma smiled. "I thought only druids knew about the spirits."

"Oh, that man knew about spirits alright," said Da as he tromped inside.

Mama gave him a scolding look. "Come on, our turn."

Emma kept quiet as Mama took Kimber out to the privy. Da fell into his seat at the head of the table. He collected a few slices of bread, some cheese, and a bit of fruit on his plate, but didn't move to eat anything yet. Emma followed suit. Tam as well, though Da rapped on the table when the boy stuffed an apple wedge in his mouth.

"Wait for your mother and sister."

He nodded, but kept chewing.

Within a few minutes, the entire family—aside from Nan—gathered around the table for the morning meal. Mama and Da chatted about their plans for the day, which consisted mostly of her making the rounds in town to offer what help she could here and there while Da grumbled about having to stand watch for the upcoming festival. People from tiny outlying villages had already started arriving in the town of Widowswood in anticipation of the Feast of Zaravex. Eoghn's Inn had only three rooms left, and his barn had filled with other travelers too poor to pay for a real bed. The town elders worried about pickpockets and thieves, so Mayor Braddon had ordered the Watch to keep patrols at all hours.

Emma bit her lip. She'd mentioned it once within hours of returning home from that awful night, but in all the excitement of being found alive and unharmed, her parents had forgotten. When a lull came in Da's grumbling about Braddon, she spoke up. "I need to go into the woods today."

Da almost choked on a bit of bread. "What's that, Em?"

Kimber glanced at her with a mixture of curiosity and worry while Tam grinned from ear to ear, seeming under the belief he'd be going with her.

"Remember I said I'd made a deal with the Spider Queen? I have to visit her and collect silk to bring to Marsten." Emma turned a bit of cheese in her fingers, staring at it. As much as she had to keep her word, the *last* thing she wanted was to be anywhere near enormous green spiders.

"You're not going into the woods, Emma." Da bit off a hunk of bread and chewed it. "After everything that happened, how could you even think about wanting to go off into the woods? Absolutely not."

Mama smirked at him.

"But, Da… I have to. I gave my word. You always say that a man's only as good as his in… umm, int-eg-ri-tee." She quirked her eyebrow at him, wondering if she'd said it right. At his bemused grin, she smiled. "I know I'm a girl, but I have integrity too."

"Do I have a teg ritty?" asked Tam.

Mama covered her mouth, laughing.

Da fought the urge to smile as he fixed her with as serious a face as he could summon. "That is very noble of you, but the simple fact is that I am not going to permit my ten-year-old child to wander into the woods in search of emerald creepers large enough to cart her off for a mid-day snack."

She shivered. Her mind leapt back to the moment the Spider Queen had started to cocoon her out of instinct.

"See, look? You're shaking at the mere mention of the word 'spider.'

Enough of this talk." Da picked up a bit of apple, and tossed it in his mouth with some cheese.

A sense of purpose welled up within Emma, chasing away her fear. She grabbed the table and leaned forward. "Da, the queen thought I was lying to get away. I promised her I would keep my word. Bringing silk to the town will also keep the spiders from attacking people."

Kimber and Tam munched on apples and bread, their gazes shifting across the table to Da.

"If these spiders can be reasoned with, why hasn't anyone done so before?" He shot a sidelong glance at Mama before sighing at Emma. "Don't be naïve. I haven't the faintest idea how you got away from their nest in the first place. I'll not risk losing you to that again."

"Spiders are tricky, Liam." Mama nibbled on a bit of melon. "Even Iskarun has little sway over them. Neither Mother nor I ever considered trying. I never thought the Wildkin Whisper would work on them."

Emma blinked. "Why wouldn't it?"

"The magic for speakin' to animals," said Tam. "Spiders are bugs."

"They're not 'spiders,' Mama. They're emerald creepers." Emma held her fingers about an inch apart. "Spiders are this big. Maybe the creepers are something else an' just *look* like spiders."

Da blinked at her, impressed.

Mama smiled. "You needn't worry about it. I'll bring them once I'm back."

"Oh, wait just a moment." Da raised a hand at her. "You're going to bring all *three* children into Widowswood to"—he coughed—"talk to spiders? Those creatures have been a menace since before my father was Tam's size."

"They're only mean because no one tried to understand them." Emma leaned back in her chair and gnawed on a bread crust. "The Spider Queen was surprised I talked to her."

Da drummed his fingers on the table. "I... No. Not all three of them. Emma, you are serious about *wanting* to go near those things? You've been terrified of them since you were five."

She sat up and steeled herself. "Yes, Da. I have to keep my word. They won't hurt me."

He waved a hand about in resignation. When Mama smiled, he threw half a slice of bread back on his plate and clapped the table. "Alright then. We'll go first thing after we eat." He pointed at Tam. "You're staying with your mother today."

Tam frowned at his plate. "I'm not 'fraid of spiders."

Emma closed her eyes, forcing herself not to tremble. *You haven't seen one up close.*

"Ia's stay wif Mama?" asked Kimber.

"Aye. I know you've spent a lot of time in the woods, but those spiders live deeper in than you've gone."

Kimber nodded. "They'as carry me off inna bundle as easy as pie."

Emma squeezed the sides of her chair. Nerves prickled at her belly, but she forced herself to finish off two more apple slices and a piece of melon. Soon, she helped collect plates. Kimber took the scraps out back for birds and animals to forage while Tam flopped in front of the fireplace with Stick Knight and Shrub Dragon locked in their endless battle.

After handing the plates to Mama, Emma wandered over to the bed and traded her nightgown for the blue dress Nan had surprised her with. It fit much better than her old one, stopping a little above the knee, and didn't have a single rip. As soon as the soft material slid over her body, a feeling of calm settled her nerves. Her grandmother hadn't mentioned anything about magic, but she had to have put some in the dress. The garment possessed a comforting energy stronger than what should have come from simply knowing Nan made it. She tied a lighter blue strip of cloth around her waist as a belt, missing the weight of Nan's dagger... but with Da taking her, she didn't need a weapon.

She padded to the front door, waiting as he donned his boots, brigandine armor, belt, broadsword, and satchel. As always, Mama gave him a small bundle. Despite his non-belief in magic, he still accepted her potions, though Emma wondered if he'd ever used them or just took them along to humor her. Then again, he had fed her one when he found her with the Banderwigh... so maybe Da really did believe, but didn't like to talk about it?

Her parents exchanged a kiss, and he walked outside.

Mama winked at her and nodded toward the door. "Best go before he changes his mind."

Emma smiled. She hurried out to where he waited in the middle of the dirt path and took his hand.

"If you're to be going into the woods, we'll need to see about getting you some proper boots."

Emma looked down and flexed her toes. "I don't need them. I'm a druid."

He chuckled. "Be that as it may, sharp rocks don't care who steps on them."

Emma tilted her head. "Elfs don't wear boots."

"Elves… and of course they do."

"Nan says they don't wear clothes either."

Da coughed. "There are different kinds of elves. The ones your grandmother is thinking of don't usually leave their forests. Civilized elves like the Ilmari and the Astari aren't so different from us."

"Oh." She swung her left arm while happily walking at his side toward the edge of Widowswood. The interior looked dark, but held none of the fear she'd come to associate with it. "The forest is happy today."

"Is it now?" He smiled.

As they approached the tree line, Emma closed her eyes. *Linganthas, guide my step.*

A faint tingle spread over her. She smiled. Mama taught her how to ask the spirit of trees and vines for protection. For a while, even the sharpest thorns or thickest brambles wouldn't harm her. She decided not to waste her breath trying to convince Da she could step on anything natural and not cut herself. He would only say she made it up.

Sunlight weakened soon after entering the trees, making the air cool. Damp ground squished with each step, lofting the fragrance of moss and dew. Emma took a deep breath of it, savoring the majesty of nature, and had nary a care toward enormous green spiders in her mind. They followed a trail of rich brown pine needles and soft earth for some time. She couldn't stop grinning at him. Da had *believed* her. He went with her. Having him at her side filled her with confidence.

Snapping and crackling accompanied her father's march, and he wound up letting go of her hand to keep his balance as they crossed a thick patch of undergrowth. Emma kept going for six steps before she noticed he'd fallen behind. She glanced back to find him staring at her in shock.

Da raised an eyebrow. "Do you even know where you're going?"

Emma looked down; the weeds came up to her thighs, yet nothing had snagged on her dress or her skin thanks to her magic. She grinned. "I was going to walk into the woods until I found a spider and ask it where to go."

He chuckled and forced his way past the bramble, again taking her hand. As they continued, he seemed to notice how the foliage flowed around her while his armor snagged and tore at the growth, staring as if entranced at the plants moving.

"Stryxian, please grant me the Wildkin Whisper," said Emma, holding her arms out and desiring the ability to speak to animals.

Da started to say something, but clamped his mouth shut at the appearance of four tiny nimbuses of spectral white light at her fingertips. The glowing spheres whirled around her arms and careened into her chest, bursting in a shower of delicate, but faint sparkles. His astonishment faded to a prideful smile. He patted her head and stroked her hair.

Emma grinned up at him and spotted a sparrow.

"Excuse me," she yelled, directing her voice at the bird.

Da blinked at her and suppressed a chuckle.

"What?" The sparrow ruffled its feathers and glided to a nearer branch. "Did you just speak?"

"Yes." She waved at it. "I'm looking for the spiders. The big green ones. I need to talk to them. Do you know which way they are from here?"

"Dangerous for you," said the bird. "They will eat your kind."

Emma nodded. "I know they used to, but I've made an agreement. They won't hurt me." A tremble ran down her back. *I hope.*

"This way then, silly child." The bird glided across their path to another tree.

"You're whistling," said Da.

"The magic lets me talk to the sparrow." Emma gestured at it. "He's going to show us where the spiders are."

She headed toward the bird, following as it moved in a series of gliding hops from tree to tree so she could keep up. Eyes skyward, she barely noticed the passing of terrain save for a patch of cold mud and a soft bed of pine needles.

"Emma, don't go so far ahead," called Da from a frightful distance behind her.

"I'm sorry," yelled Emma. She spun to look back at her father forcing his way past a snarl of bushes up to his waist.

The bird shifted on the branch. "He makes as much noise as ten bears."

Emma giggled into her hands.

He reached her in a few minutes and took her by the wrist, a hold that said she wasn't to run off again. The sparrow led them past a moss-covered boulder half the height of the outhouse and curved on one side.

Carved symbols marked the flattest face, partially hidden beneath the thick carpet of green.

"What's that?" Emma pointed.

"An old runestone. There's a few of them here and there in the forest. Most of the townspeople think they mark burial sites, but it's wizard's work."

She stared at it, wide-eyed. "Is it dangerous?"

"It's a rock." He chuckled. "If there's any power in it to do anything at all, only a wizard could use it."

"How do you know it's a wizard and not a druid, like Nan?" She brushed her fingers over the markings as they passed it.

Da watched the bird for a few seconds. "Astounding how that critter seems to be waiting for us."

"He *is* waiting for us." She poked him in the side with her free hand.

"Druids don't often write things down. Usually if there's markings, it's a wizard... or worse." He cringed as soon as he'd said it.

"Worse?" She glanced down at sudden loud crackling along the ground and sent grateful thoughts to Linganthas at the sight of a dried-out vine with three-inch thorns receding from her path. "Are wizards bad?"

The sparrow took a long gliding swoop, following a tunnel formed by dozens of trees lined up in neat rows.

Emma pointed. "That way."

"Being a wizard doesn't make someone bad any more than carrying a sword makes a man bad. By worse, I mean necromancers... or sorcerers. One traffics with the dead, the other with demons. You're too little to worry about them yet."

"Yes, Da." Emma shifted her attention back to the sparrow. Since he didn't want her to know about such things, she figured they were quite bad indeed, and she did *not* want anything else to give her bad dreams.

He gave her a look of surprise. "That's it? You're not going to beg to know?"

She shrugged. "I've got enough nightmares."

He chuckled. "And yet here we are, walking right to your worst one."

Emma trembled. "Yes, I know. But you're with me, so I'm not scared." She took two more steps. "Much."

The sparrow tweeted at her. That she could no longer understand him implied they'd been walking for over a half hour or more. She concentrated on the spell again and beseeched Strixian for the Wildkin Whisper.

"Sorry. The magic faded. What did you say?"

Da chuckled at her. Emma smiled; to him, she sounded like Mama whistling at the trees.

"The creatures you seek are that way. Be careful, little one."

"Thank you." She curtsied at the bird.

Da glanced around. "We've gone quite a ways into the forest. I hadn't expected you'd drag us this far in."

Emma pointed at a section of woods darker than the rest. With all the trees tilted this way and that, she couldn't quite say for sure if she'd been here before. Of course, running in terror from the Banderwigh hadn't left her any time to take in the scenery. Another minute of walking led them to a modest stream where a narrow log lay across. Most of the bark along the top had flaked away, exposing yellowed wood dotted with patches of green algae. Thick cattail weeds sprouted from the water, which looked too deep for swimming.

"I'm sorry, Da. I don't remember where I was. I couldn't see much in the dark and I was scared."

He took a knee and hung his hand on her shoulder. "Are you sure you want to come back here so soon?"

"I promised." She pointed ahead at traces of white amid the branches. "Look, there are webs in the trees." His hand at her shoulder squeezed.

She winced, but kept quiet. Sure enough, large swaths of spidersilk hung in the boughs far off the ground, higher than the roof of their home. Several cocoon pods implied birds, squirrels, and other small creatures had met their doom. Da stood and grasped her wrist again. Emma swallowed hard, but forced herself to walk forward.

At the stream, she stepped up onto a fallen tree, which formed a natural bridge. Da kept hold of her arm as she walked heel-to-toe over the narrow span. The wood bent lower with each step, dipping her to the ankles in icy water at the midpoint. Da trudged across, knee-deep, sloshing and splashing as loud as an army of boar. She jumped to the bank on the far side, skipping the last several feet of wood covered in beetles.

Her toes sank in gooey webbing along the forest floor not ten paces later, though the patch had lost much of its stickiness to age and weather. She kept on, despite the rising torrent of worry twisting her breakfast about. The flavor of melon and cheese burbled at the back of her throat. Da grasped the hilt of his broadsword.

"Da, no." She stopped and looked up at him. "Don't make them think we're here to hurt them."

"I don't like this." He narrowed his eyes at the trees. "It's too quiet. No birds. Nothing's moving. Feels like we're walking into an ambush."

Emma peeled her foot away from the sticky mass and stepped on clear dirt. "I-its f-fine."

He let go of her arm and pulled her into a hug. "You're trembling, child. That's it, we're going home."

She clung to him, staring past his armored gut at the forest. A large mound near a tiny creek caught her eye. Amid dozens of head-sized rocks embedded in the dirt, a huge patch of spidersilk surrounded a cave opening. She pointed. "There! I remember that cave."

He pivoted to look.

"That's where I came out."

"If we're right on top of their damn nest, there should be hundreds of them coming after us."

"Maybe they sleep in the day?" Emma blinked. She leaned back and held her arm up for him to grab. "We're here. I have to try."

He grasped her hand and set her back on her feet.

She pulled him over to the cave, which required crossing another shin-deep creek. The frigid water had her teeth chattering in seconds. Emma stopped at the cave mouth, terrified by the silk-covered walls. The last time she passed this opening, she'd been so scared she'd thrown up. That same fear churned a warning deep in her gut. She held her stomach and took a few deep breaths.

"I'll be right back."

He tightened his grip on her shoulder. "You're not going in there alone."

She curled her toes in the dirt and bit her lip. "She might be angry."

"Angry spiders be damned. I am *not* sending my daughter into a spider nest alone. In fact, I'm about to pick you off your feet and march straight back home. I have no idea why I even agreed to this."

"You trust Mama." Emma held her breath until she couldn't tolerate another second of it, and let it out in a long gust. "Okay."

She stepped toward the cave opening, cringing in on herself at a brush of spidersilk on her arm. Her father peeled it down without ceremony and had to stoop to fit in the tunnel.

"This does not bode well. Not enough room in here to round a sword."

Da hesitated for a few seconds, muttering something she couldn't make out. "You're sure about this, Em?"

"Y-yes, Da." She brushed webbing from her face and fluttered her eyes. "They won't hurt us."

Da shook his head, frowning, but he chuckled. "May Belloch grant the rest of the Watch your courage."

Skittering and scratching echoed off the passage walls, and for a second, a faint sour smell crossed her nose. Emma stared at her feet, barely able to breathe through the fear of stepping on something venomous, hairy, or just plain disgusting.

The cave curved to the right, permitting only about a fifteen-foot view ahead. Each step deeper thickened the amount of sticky white gauze clinging to the walls. With the exit a mere spot of light at her back, the dirt underfoot gave way to a complete carpeting of silk. Only a hint of its former glue remained. An unsettling peeling sensation tugged at her soles with every step.

A massive dark green bundle of hair appeared out of nowhere, a rearing, hissing spider as tall as Da. Emma fell back into him, too petrified to scream. Droplets of venom as big as her fists glistened at the tips of wicked black fangs longer than Nan's dagger. Da emitted a startled gurgle and pulled her back.

"Oh... Apologiesss, little egg-layer," said the spider. It lowered its chelicerae into a more humble pose. "Forgive my sssudden appearanccce. It isss my duty to protect our home."

No longer rearing, the spider stood eye-level with Da's chin.

Emma wanted to scream, cry, curl up into a ball, and suck her thumb —but fear paralyzed her.

"By Belloch's beard..." Da cleared his throat. "I've never seen a spider that large... It's the size of a bloody wagon."

"Come, little one." The spider backed up. "The queen awaits."

"Em?" Da shook her. "Em?"

She looked up at him, mouth agape. It took her a second to comprehend the shape in front of her was a person, and another to recognize her father. She clamped on to him, trembling.

"I think we should take that luck and get out of here." He pulled her up to her feet. "I don't know why that thing just hissed and scurried away, but we—"

"Da... It's okay." She closed her eyes, cheeks hot as her heart pounded. "It scared me when it jumped out. It's like you... a guard. It didn't know who we were until it saw me." She wanted so badly to let him carry her home, but anyone the spiders killed would be her fault. "The queen's waiting."

"Oh, I'm sure she is." He scowled.

She found her nerve again and tugged at his arm. He shook his head, but followed. Emma crept ahead. The curve straightened after about twenty paces allowing her to see the massive sentry spider's backside. Hundreds of smaller emerald creepers, some as small as Da's hand, swarmed around the walls and ceiling. Tiny whispering voices chittered her name over and over, most sounding shocked she'd returned.

"Uhh," said Da. "There's gotta be thousands of them."

"If you w-want to w-wait h-here..." Emma couldn't stop shaking. "Y-you c-can. I-I'll be r-right in t-there."

His fingers dug into her shoulder, a little too hard.

She whined. "Ow. Da..."

"If you're going in there, I'm going in there. The only reason I'm not dragging you out of here now is how they seem to be almost... welcoming you. Spiders shouldn't be acting like this."

Wincing, Emma reached up and pulled his hand from her shoulder to her forearm. She gave him a grateful smile despite her worry of how the queen would react to having an armed man with her, even Da.

She focused on the creepers. "This is my Da. He won't hurt any of you."

The collection of whispery voices silenced. All the spiders stopped moving, rotating to face them.

"What are they doing?" asked Da.

"I just told them you were my father and you're not here to hurt any of them."

Emma stepped forward—two inches—and froze. After a breath, she forced herself to take another step, also about half the length of her foot. Little by little, she navigated the cave. The last span of tunnel before the opening, a corridor as long as her house, contained dozens of spidersilk pods. Some held the silhouettes of goblins. One had a deer leg protruding at the bottom. Many likely wrapped rabbits or similar-sized creatures. Dinner-plate-sized spiders on the walls and ceiling shifted to keep watching them, though none said another word. The darkness above glimmered with several thousand spots of red glowing light, in clusters of eight.

Da muttered prayers to Belloch, the patron of warriors, his favorite among the gods, asking for courage.

That her father, the master swordsman, seemed every bit as worried about spiders as she did triggered a nervous giggle she couldn't stop, but it made walking easier.

"What's funny?"

"You are." She reached across her chest and gave his hand a squeeze. "You're scared of them too."

"In a tight cave, with sharp fangs at every turn, critters all over every surface… I'm on edge."

She smiled up at him.

The sentry spider squeezed itself past the end of the tunnel. His enormous body compressed more than she expected possible, fluffing back out to full size once he'd entered the central chamber. "My queen, the human hatchling isss here."

Emma swallowed and attempted a smile, though she felt certain the expression on her face looked more of a grimace than happy. The feeling of walking on squidgy, sticky, padding reminded her of being trapped like a fly not too long ago.

Easily ten times the number of spiders as lurked in the cave occupied the giant room. Emerald creepers of all sizes, from babies no larger than a woman's hand all the way up to the wagon-sized sentry, milled about attending to various spidery tasks. Some toted prey into storage areas, others tended to egg sacs, and a continuous flow of spiders entered and left from a network of tunnels closer to the surface. Curved walls stretched upward as high as a four-story building, teeming with an uncountable number of darting green furry creatures. Hazy sunlight leaked in shafts down through a tangle of roots and webbing near the top, where several dead birds dangled.

In the center of it all stood the largest spider in Widowswood; at least, she had to be. The Spider Queen made the sentry look like a puppy. Some peasant hovels would be small if placed next to her. Several creepers as big as her brother crawled around the giant spider's abdomen, picking among spear-like hairs and clearing away scraps of roots and old web.

A tunnel behind and to the queen's right stuck out in her memory. That passage led to the trap chamber where she'd fallen. Emma looked away from it.

"What is thisss?" The Spider Queen loomed forward, waving her two foremost legs in the direction of her father. "You bring a merccccenary into my nessst?"

"I am sorry." Emma dropped in a deep curtsey. "He's my Da. He means no harm. You know I am only a child… umm hatchling. I would not have been allowed to return if he did not come with me."

The queen shifted her weight side to side, mouthparts moving in a flurry. Emma gulped; spider eyes betrayed no emotion or intent a human mind could read. Was she angry? Thinking?

Lightheaded, Emma tried to slow her breathing. She looked down, hoping the Queen would take it as a sign of respect. "I promised I would return to honor our agreement."

"I did not expect to sssee you again." The queen took a step closer. A leg the size of a small tree appeared at Emma's side. "You sssuprissse me." Da leaned back when the gargantuan arachnid moved yet closer, as if sniffing him. "Thisss one hasss not claimed the blood of any of my children." She grumbled. "I did not ssspecccify you were to return alone."

Emma's stomach bubbled. She let a relieved sigh out her nose. "The man who trades in silk has agreed to only accept the silk I bring him. He will not pay others for silk they collect from hunting."

The Spider Queen backed up a few paces, rotating side to side. She waved her forelegs about. "You are a hatchling… and an egg-layer. Humansss do not obey their egg layersss. You have been decccceived. I knew you would not be lissstened to."

"What?" Emma forgot her fear and approached. "What do you mean?"

"Humansss are prowling around to the north and wessst. I sense their ssstepsss. They ssseek to harm my children for sssilk." The queen lowered her body, her mouthparts less than an arm's length from Emma, but her form still towered over her. "Thisss, I do not think isss your fault, ssso I ssshall not resssscind my decccision to allow you to live."

Emma gulped. "Thank you, queen. I don't know why they're hunting spiders again." She stomped. "Marsten said he wouldn't."

"What's wrong, Em?" whispered Da. "I must say it is most unsettling to hear you hissing and clicking like that."

The queen made a series of contemptuous noises and chattered at other spiders too fast for the Wildkin Whisper to translate.

Emma twisted about to look at her father. "She says there's men trying to kill spiders again. Marsten said he'd make up a story about the spiders being too dangerous and he doesn't want to risk people going into the woods anymore."

Eight or so spiders scurried around by the outer walls, collecting wads of discarded silk and bundling them together.

Da rubbed his short beard in a few seconds of thought. "It might not have anything to do with Marsten. Giant spider silk is a valuable commodity in the arcane circles. Wizards can make all sorts of things out of it... a bundle like what you showed up with before is worth more than our home to the right people. If Marsten stopped paying trappers, they might try to go around him and sell the silk directly in Calebrin. I could try to convince Braddon that counts as poaching. The Watch could look into who's prowling around."

Emma sighed. "I told Marsten I couldn't get any more silk if anyone hurt the spiders."

"What isss your soldier sssaying?"

She drew a breath to correct the queen, but held it. *She sees us as soldiers and egg-layers. Maybe there is no way to explain it?* "Da said the humans who are snooping around might be from far away and don't know about me. He's like your sentry. He guards our nest. They are going to look for the other humans and make them go away so they don't hurt your babies."

The Spider Queen stared in silence at Emma for a frightening minute before rising to her normal height.

"I promise." Emma balled her hands into fists at her side. "I wasn't lying to get away."

One spider, easily large enough for Emma to ride, darted over and dropped a mass of silk beside her. The spherical wad had to be three feet across. Da gawked at it.

The Spider Queen prodded the bundle toward her with one leg. "Take it. I ssshall trussst you for the time being. Sssee that you keep your word, human egg-layer hatchling. But know thisss—we are watching."

"Thank you." She curtsied again before hugging the ball. Emma adhered to it on contact. She grunted, unable to get her arms free or peel it off her chest. "Da... I'm stuck."

"Well I suppose you won't drop it, then."

The enormous spider shifted to regard Da for a few seconds before rotating away and crawling off up the wall to a hollowed-out nest space. Once inside, she settled in and gazed down on them from two stories up.

Emma grumbled, pulling at her hands. Memory of being caught in the web got her heart beating fast. "This isn't old silk.'

Da bowed at the Spider Queen, put a hand atop Emma's head, and guided her toward the cave. "Let's go home before this encounter becomes any stranger."

Too annoyed at being glued to a ball of silk to remember to be afraid of spiders, she plodded along behind him until a tiny voice cried out from the floor.

"Eek! Watch where you're putting thossse giant feet!"

Emma stopped short. An eight-inch emerald creeper flailed four of its legs at her and poked her in the ankle twice.

"Sorry! I can't see with this thing." Emma waited for the little one to dart off before continuing. "Da?"

"I'm right here, Em."

She followed the sound of his voice, struggling to peek at the floor and scooting her feet across the ground to avoid stepping on any unwary spiders. After several arduous minutes, she emerged from the cave into a fresh breeze and sunlight.

Fear fluttered in her belly, but rather than throw up, the surge of relief at walking out of the spiders' nest alive for the second time drained all the strength from her limbs.

"Da, can we rest? I'm tired."

He grasped her right hand and gingerly peeled her arm free, spinning her away from the gummy wad. She rubbed her hands over arms to chase away the icky feeling while he hefted the bundle.

"We shouldn't stand around with this much silk. Half the thieves in Calebrin would kill someone to take it."

Emma froze. Her gaze shifted from distant trees to her Da's belt buckle, then climbed inch by inch to meet his. "K-kill?"

"Yes, Em. This is worth a foolish amount of kingscoin to the right people. Fortunately, those people are in Calebrin... and not out here in the woods. And not one of them would believe a girl your age could possibly collect it."

She exhaled with relief.

3

RATS IN THE WEB

*W*ith the giant ball of silk stuck to her back, Emma clutched her hair at her chest to keep it from getting caught. The wad didn't weigh too much, less than Tam clinging to her. What Da said about thieves made her want to carry it in case he had to fight. He wouldn't be able to protect her if his arms became caught up in a gummy mess. That, and the magic that let her navigate the underbrush without snagging extended to the ungainly package as well.

He kept a hand on her shoulder and his eyes on the woods. She combed her hands down her hair in a rhythmic nervous gesture as they walked. Da didn't seem worried; rather, he wore a bewildered smile. His confidence chipped away at her fear, both because he didn't act as though he expected danger and knew the way home.

For a time, Emma amused herself by looking down and smiling whenever a branch or root shifted out of her way. All of what Nan told her about the spirits and how living, mystical energy existed in everything had to be real. Each time she should have snagged on brush or stepped on something painful—and didn't, the feeling she'd become *part* of the energy grew. She no longer lived as most humans do, on top of or outside the world. Emma had joined it, and Widowswood welcomed her.

Free of her terror, she grinned at the trees and squinted at the sunlight leaking past the branches above. Da still looked confused, so she quirked her eyebrow at him.

He shook his head with a halfhearted chuckle. "I'm still not sure what to make of you standing there clicking and hissing at a spider large enough to carry *me* off... Or that none of them tried to attack."

She stopped kneading her hair and merely held it to her chest. "The magic lets me talk to animals, but people hear noises. The first time Nan showed me how use that spell, I tried to talk to her to say it worked and I wound up squeaking at her. I'd been talking to a mouse."

"It seems I have myself a family full of surprises. I never imagined you'd want to be anywhere near one of those creatures when it was alive. The dead ones scare you seven shades of white. I'm very proud of you for overcoming your fear, Em."

"I'm still afraid of them." She stopped walking and shivered.

"Aye." He patted her shoulder and sighed. "I thought you'd gotten lucky last time."

"I fell through a hole running away from the Banderwigh and got stuck in a giant web. The Spider Queen started wrapping me up." She leaned against him, trembling.

Da clasped the back of her head, holding her close. "You're safe now, Em. You don't have to go back there again."

"I do," she whined. After a couple of deep breaths, she stood tall. "They were going to eat me because humans have killed her babies for a long time."

He resumed walking, tugging her along by the shoulder. "Those spiders have been a danger to people long before anyone realized their silk was of use to mages. I'm sure it said..." He laughed for a moment. "It said. Now you've got me thinking of those things as intelligent."

"They are." Emma smirked. She paid attention to the ground long enough to navigate a tiny stream by stepping rock to rock. "She might have said that to be mean. I begged her not to hurt me because I was just a child. She told me about people killing spiders. I said I could make them stop."

Da jumped over a trench where the stream curved back on itself and cut a furrow into the earth. Once across, he reached out to catch her. "That's frightening."

Emma jumped across into his arms. "What is?"

"That the spider had the ability to reason that a chance to protect its brood outweighed whatever satisfaction it might've gotten from harming you." He took a knee and embraced her. "I couldn't imagine how I'd react if anyone hurt you."

She clung to him for a moment or two, sniffling. Da rarely ever cried, and seeing him almost to that point filled her with guilt.

Once his upwelling of emotion subsided, he leaned back to smile at her. "Come on, Em. The sooner you get that stuff out of sight, the better."

She nodded, wiping at her eyes.

After a few more minutes of walking, he glanced down at her. "How much silk did you agree to bring Marsten?"

"Once a month," said Emma.

"For how long?"

"Umm." She looked up with an 'oops' face. "I just said once a month… Guess I'll not be afraid of spiders after a time."

He exhaled. "Well, I can't imagine things will continue forever. When people kill one of the hunter spiders, they get a lump of silk about the size of a fist." He held his up for emphasis. "It's valuable because it's dangerous to get any, and the quantities are small." Da poked a finger into the bundle on her back. "If you keep bringing them giant bundles, it won't be as valuable after a while."

"That's good, right? Means people won't want to hunt the spiders."

He smiled, though his expression remained worried. "That's one possible outcome, yes. I can't say I'm well versed on the spidersilk trade, as it's quite limited to those who dabble with the arcane. Anything that valuable always has men chasing after it, seeking to control the money." He stopped and took a knee, grasping her by both shoulders. "I need you to promise me you won't talk about your arrangement with the spiders to people you don't know."

Emma stared at him dumbfounded. His sudden worry left her speechless.

"Em?"

"Yes, Da." She resumed running her hands down the length of hair in front of her. "I promise."

"Good then." He smiled, stood, and took her hand.

The remainder of the walk out of Widowswood passed without conversation. A little before noon, they emerged from the trees and followed the dirt path down the hill toward their home. The building appeared dark and empty.

"Your mother's probably off on her errands with Tam and Kimber in tow."

Emma nodded.

He walked her the quarter mile or so to the town proper, along the dirt path past seven other farmsteads. Soon, earth gave way to cobblestones. Da hurried her down a street and took a left at a corner by a distillery. Another length of road brought them past a series of homes, small and scrunched together like too many people trying to fit into the same room. The second street ended at a T, facing a leatherworker's shop. Da turned to the right, down the street leading to the middle of town. Here, the air frolicked with the fragrance of apples and cinnamon, fruit, and baking meats.

Emma took a deep breath, already hungry. She peered around him at a bakery shop; though it smelled beautiful, she dared not ask to go inside. Both older men who owned the place disliked children, assuming them all thieves trying to steal sweets. The one time she'd gone in, Mister Carrow hovered at her side, and no matter how polite she'd been, he'd given her such a sour look she decided not to spend the coin Mama had given her there. Another bakery, deeper in town, had a much friendlier man, even if his treats didn't smell quite as wonderful.

Ahead, the town square looked busier than usual, teeming with many unfamiliar faces. Da guided her by the hand into the fray, walking at a brisk stride to the southeast corner. Few paid her any attention, as most of the travelers gathered around merchant carts circling the fountain. Da hurried her along a short length of street away from the square to the steps of Marsten's apothecary.

As usual, the two rocking chairs on the huge porch sat empty. A wooden wedge held the left of the two double doors open, the square panel glass coated in a fine layer of yellow-green pollen.

"I need to attend to the Watch. We've got too much to do with all these people." He grumbled, eyeing the square for a few seconds before looking back to her. "When you are finished here, either find your mother or go straight home."

"Yes, Da."

He ruffled her hair, gave her a kiss atop the head, and hurried back to the square. Emma slouched, exhaling in a relieved huff. All the fear and worry from being *that* close to so many spiders left her shaking for a few seconds. She forced herself to think about how polite the sentry had been. *They're not monsters. They're just hairy. They're not monsters. They're just hairy.* Eyes open, she hovered in the doorway and watched people walking by for a little while as she tried to calm down. The idea of not being terrified of spiders seemed almost possible. At least, possible when she didn't have hundreds of them nearby.

Emma shivered out the last of her fear, yawned, and walked into the shop.

A few steps in, an assault of fragrance made her cough. Herbs of all types, medicinal, magical, and ordinary, warred over her sense of smell. She headed down the closest passage between two tall shelves crammed full of bins, each packed to overflowing with flowers, mushrooms, roots, and leaves of every color. She sneezed three times along the way, and emerged from the other end with a runny nose and watering eyes.

Two older women stood in the open space in front of the counter, waiting for the absent Marsten, who rummaged around out of sight in the back. Emma crept up behind them, still clutching her hair to her chest, and waited patiently in line. After a few seconds, an uneasy feeling stirred in her stomach. A quick glance around revealed no obvious dangers. She fidgeted. The second time she sniffled back the effects of the pungent air, the women turned and glanced at her.

"Oh, Emma." The shorter one who still had some brown in her hair smiled. "Hello, sweetie."

"Aren't you adorable," said the other. She stood a head taller than Mama, with hair whiter than snow.

Both wore blue-green dresses and soft leather shoes.

"Good day, Mrs. Harrow." She curtsied to the shorter, heavyset woman. "And to you Mrs. Dunay."

"My, what a curious pack you've got." Mrs. Dunay leaned over. "What is that?"

Emma hesitated. *Da said people I don't know...* "It's silk for Marsten."

"Oh." Mrs. Harrow fanned herself. Her utter lack of reaction said she hadn't the first clue of the value.

"Right, there we are!" Marsten burst out of the maroon curtain separating the back room from the store. "Found some." He held up a small burlap bundle, spotted Emma, and promptly fainted.

The women exchanged a glance.

Mrs. Dunay went around the counter and stooped out of sight. A moment later, Marsten groaned and sat up. A meaty hand slapped atop the wood, and he pulled himself to his knees. His face, bright red and wide-eyed, hovered half-hidden, eyes over the countertop staring at her.

Emma fidgeted, feeling uneasy. "I-is something wrong, Mr. Marsten?"

"No!" He lurched to his feet and broke out in a sweat. While no one could call the man fat, he had a bit of weight to him. Generous cheeks pulled up in a warm smile at the elders. "Here you are, ladies. Eight coppers if you please."

The women each picked out four coins and paid. Both paused by Emma on the way out to pat her on the cheeks.

"So glad to see you home safe, child." Mrs. Dunay, tall, thin, and dour, had always frightened her from a distance, but the concern in her eyes looked too real to be fake.

"Thank you, Mrs. Dunay."

"A credit to your mother." Mrs. Harrow patted both her cheeks at once.

Emma wobbled from the exuberant show of affection, and exhaled with relief as the two elders shuffled past her on their way out. She walked up to the counter. "I've brought the silk for the month."

Marsten ran a hand over his chestnut-brown hair. "By the gods, girl…" He wheezed, looking as out of sorts as she must have at the spider's nest. "Did you clean out the whole nest?"

"No. The queen gave me this bundle, but she's not happy."

He hustled around the side of the counter to her. "What's that then? Not happy?"

"People are snooping around the woods. If they kill any spiders, I won't be able to get more silk." She turned her back to him.

"Right. I remember that much."

A tug preceded Marsten hoisting her into the air. Emma dangled by her dress, stuck to the wad of spidersilk.

"Careful!" She clamped her arms tight to avoid sliding out of her garment. "Please don't tear the dress Nan made me."

Marsten set her down. "Aye, that stuff's quite fresh." He put a hand on her shoulder and eased the bundle away inch by inch. Once it popped free, he hefted it on one hand. "Weighs almost nothin', too. And look how it's faintly glowing."

She faced him, tugging her dress back into place. "Are you still paying people for silk?"

"No, luv." He patted the wad. "You made the particulars of the arrangement quite clear last time. One moment."

Emma fluffed her hair over her shoulders while Marsten ducked into the back room again. The silk caught the curtain and tore it down, sending wooden rings bouncing across the shop. He stumbled over the metal rod as it clattered to the floor amid a bevy of indecipherable mutterings. A heavy *crash* rocked the boards under her feet, followed by a louder series of grumbles, and a muted growl of pain.

"Mister Marsten, are you hurt?" yelled Emma.

"Fine. Fine. Just got tripped up in this damnable curtain. I'll be just a moment."

She nodded, despite no one being there to see, and clasped her hands in front of herself while eyeing bins of Azurevine, Faeberry, and Creeproot to her left. They sat on a shelf in the corner where she'd cowered away from the dead emerald creeper the trapper had dropped on the floor. She smirked at herself for being terrified of it after seeing much larger—and live—ones up close.

"Well, that was silly of me," she muttered. "Being scared of a dead spider."

The floorboard under her right heel shifted.

She twisted around to glance back at a thin man in a dark grey cloak, his face shadowed by a short, poorly tended beard of dark brown. He looked younger than Da, though something in the way he regarded her made her wary. He offered a pleasant smile, a curt nod of greeting, and continued picking around a bin of Dreamroot, examining pieces resembling long dehydrated yams.

Emma returned a smile of politeness, but little sincerity. She edged away from the shelves to the counter, keeping the man in view out of the corner of her eye. He selected a robust length of Dreamroot before gliding around the interior end of the shelves into another row and searching over the herbs there.

Marsten returned a few minutes later, rubbing his hands together as if trying to start a fire. "I've yet to see a batch so sticky. Now what's this about problems?"

Emma kept her voice low. "The queen told me there's people snooping around. She thinks they're hunting spiders. Please do something to help."

"Of course, girl." He puffed his cheeks with a great exhale. "If you're to bring a bundle like that each month, only a fool would risk losing out on that. I'll see about it. Don't you worry at all."

"Thank you." She peered back at an empty shelf row between her and the door. "Good day, Mister Marsten. I need to go home."

He raised a hand. "Em, would you be a dear and do me a small favor?"

She bit her lip and looked back up at him. "Hmm?"

Marsten gestured at the doorway to the back. "I need a new curtain. Would you run a note across the way to Norrington's?"

Her instincts wanted her to race off out the door and sprint home, but she couldn't be rude to Marsten. "Yes, Mister Marsten."

"Capital." He smiled. "Give me a moment to jot down the measurements then."

She nodded before staring down at her toes. Marsten took a bit of paper from below the counter and set to scribbling upon it.

The cloaked man glided out from the rightmost shelf and walked up to stand beside her at the counter. Emma shifted her eyes toward him without moving her head, watching him set a few items on the counter. Two large daggers hung at his left hip, beneath the fold of a loose black shirt. His belt held a handful of pouches, some swollen as if packed full of sand, others slack like coin purses bearing a pittance of copper. Well-worn leather boots also held a dagger apiece in sheaths strapped to the sides, and a small crossbow slung across his back peeked out from under his cloak. Once again, he smiled down at Emma.

"Good day, child."

Emma rendered the most minimal of curtseys. "Mafindwel, sir."

The man chuckled and patted her on the head. "May the day find thee well, also."

Must everyone touch me? She resisted the urge to pull away, not wanting to be impolite.

Marsten looked up. "Good day, sir. Ahh, trouble sleepin'?" He handed a small paper to Emma. "Thank you, luv."

She snatched it from betwixt his fingers. "Welcome."

"Indeed. Lot on the mind as of late. A bit of dreamroot tea with mint should do the trick." The man flashed an easy smile at Marsten while tugging a coin pouch from his belt.

Emma darted for the door, paper crinkling in her grasp. She halted at the top of the stairway connecting Marsten's porch to the cobblestones. Norrington's tailor shop waited a short distance down the street to the left, along the eastern edge of the town square. She'd have to go past it anyway to get home, so the errand wouldn't take too long.

A glance over her shoulder found the cloaked man watching her while waiting for Marsten to count copper coins.

Her heart pounded in her ears. Something felt wrong.

Quite wrong.

4

MOUSE

G athering her dress in two fists, Emma rushed down the stairs and took off at a run toward the left. After passing six or seven buildings, the street ended at the southeast corner of the town square. She turned right as soon as she entered, running north along the row of shops at the eastern edge. People packed every inch of the center of Widowswood proper: workers building things for the feast, people from nearby villages, curious children, visiting merchants, and the usual assortment of locals.

She ducked and swerved among the crowd, trying to move as fast as she could. Unable to run with so many people around her, she let go of her dress and raised her hands to help navigate the ocean of bodies. Something told her that man walked behind her, but it seemed impossible for anyone to be able to follow a child among so many people.

Two women parted enough to let her slip by, straight into the oncoming backside of a rather rotund man in a bright green tunic. She managed a yelp of surprise before he bumped her off her feet and she tumbled to the ground. He, and another man, dragged a large wooden framework, perhaps a portion of stage or some such thing.

"Oh, dear." He set his end of the wood down and swung himself around to offer her a hand. "My apologies, child."

Emma reached up, and he pulled her standing. "I'm sorry. I couldn't see where I was going."

"Is something amiss, my dear?" He raised a huge, bushy eyebrow. Generous cheeks and a broad jaw made his head as round as a carved pumpkin set atop a man's shoulders. "You look the fright."

"I'm…" Up on tiptoe, she looked around, but couldn't find any sign of the cloaked man among the people. A breath of relief melted out of her. "Fine, sir."

"Very well." He smiled before retaking his grip on the burdensome bit of carpentry behind him.

Emma scurried ahead a little farther to the shop she disliked so much. At least with Nan giving her a new dress, Da hadn't insisted she wear the one he'd bought here. Still, she decided to don it once a week anyway. He *had* paid money for it, and done so out of concern for her. Smooth varnished wood met her steps across the porch. A heavy door bore a handle thicker around than her broom, engraved with a diamond pattern. She grasped it in both hands and hauled backward, grunting from the effort as her bare feet slid on the slick surface as much as let her pull.

Eventually, she spun around the edge, pushed the door wider, and ducked inside.

The stale smell of fabric and some unknown spice hung in the air. Walls of dark wood and red velvet surrounded nine or ten people examining skeins of material on shelves around a central raised dais where Mister Norrington worked. He took the measurements of a greying older man in a dark suit that made him look like one of those barristers Da had such distaste for. On the far left, a woman examined items on a table full of children's clothes, while a pair of boys Tam's age seemed asleep on their feet nearby, waiting for her.

She looked outside at the crowd. *I'm acting like a baby again. Nothing to be scared of.*

"Mister Norrington?" Emma approached the dais.

The tailor, a thin man with tall cheekbones and a long face, turned to peer down at her. The shape of his nose conjured the image of a heron-like bird that had taken the form of a person. Light blond hair stuck out from under a small top hat of dark shiny green. When he raised an eyebrow at her, his monocle fell away and dangled on a cord.

"Yes, child? Can you not see I'm busy at the moment?"

"I've a message, an order, from Mister Marsten. He's in need of a curtain." She held up the paper.

Norrington's irritated smirk faded. "Ahh. Very well. Thank you." He took the paper, tucked it in his coat pocket, and continued attending to his customer.

The besuited man offered Emma a polite nod with a smile.

She bowed at him and ran out, eager to go home.

A shadow caught her eye in the gap between buildings. Emma froze, the toes of her right foot barely touching the cobblestones two doors south of the tailor's shop. The grey-cloaked man leaned against the wall, acting as though he hadn't noticed her. A tremor ran through her body.

Da... She wanted to scream it, but nothing came out of her mouth.

Emma walked northwest, heading for the trail out of town that would bring her home. *I'm still scared from the Banderwigh.* She tried to calm down, but her heart raced anyway. After ten steps, she looked behind her. The grey cloak had vanished. She backed up for a few paces, scanning the crowd for him, but couldn't find him anywhere at all. Guard Arnir strolled among the crowd to her right, though they already thought her skittish and she didn't want them to regard her as one of those girls who screamed at her own shadow. If she went to the guard, it had to be for a good reason, not a 'bad feeling.' Since she didn't see the grey cloak anymore, she decided against seeming the worried little child yet again. Of course, the last time she'd told Guard Kavan it felt like someone chased her, it turned out to be a Banderwigh.

For a moment, she didn't move, tapping her big toe on the ground and trying to think of what to do. She'd already run to the Watch once in a fright when nothing was there. If she made a habit of that, they'd think her nutters, or the sort of child who liked to make up stories for attention. The man had seemed pleasant at Marsten's, though she couldn't explain the uncomfortable feeling she got from him. It could've been leftover fear from the spiders, but Nan and Mama both told her to always trust her instincts.

She headed due north, around the fountain, acting as though she'd come to sightsee the merchant carts. With the Feast of Zaravex approaching, people from all the tiny villages in the plains east of town had started arriving to join in the festivities. According to Da, some traveled for over a week. Nan had even teased the kids with stories of real satyrs coming out of Widowswood in the night to dance around the fire.

The street leading north out of the square went to the part of town where most of the shopkeepers lived, a wealthier area with fewer people. She searched around for a guard, wanting to keep one in sight, but not a single one caught her eye. *They're all in the square watching the visitors.*

Out of nowhere, a feeling of imminent danger, the same as she'd experienced in the seconds before the Banderwigh grabbed her, came on. With a gasp, she spun around, drawing a breath to scream. The grey-cloaked man hovered at the entrance to North Market Street, a good four or five houses behind her.

He's following me. Tears gathered in the corners of her eyes. She wanted to shout for Da, but couldn't manage it. Head down, she scurried north as fast as possible without breaking into a run. The man had to know she'd seen him. She risked a peek back and caught him slipping into an alley about three buildings distant.

Oh, no. A quick panic-stricken glance around locked her attention on a pink-painted cake sign. The nice baker. She sprinted about twenty yards ahead to the bakery on the other side of the street and burst in the door.

Where Marsten's shop offered her senses an unpleasant greeting, the confectioner's shop instead met her like a hug from Nan. The scents of fruits and chocolate filled her nose; various pastry sweets lay arranged on a rectangular table in the middle of the room, under glass domes. One rack on the left wall held breads and muffins, while the shelving on the right contained bags of flour and sugar, and bins of other ingredients.

The middle-aged man behind the counter looked up from whatever he'd been reading. A bit of silver streaked his black hair over both ears. "Be mindful, dear. If ye touch anything, you've bought it."

She nodded at him and backed away from the table, clasping her hands behind her. A sunlit patch by the left bay window warmed her feet while she hovered at the glass, observing the street outside. Emma stared into the shadowed alcoves between expensive homes on the opposite side, though none held a grey-cloaked man.

Her breath fogged the glass. As wonderful as it smelled in here, the room felt little different from the Banderwigh's cage, only fear rather than bars kept her inside. She gathered her hands at her chin, and kept watching for that man.

Minutes later, the clomp of hard shoes approached behind her. Emma glanced back over her shoulder at the baker, who wore a spotless apron. He moved to her side, head tilted to his right.

"Is something the matter, girl?"

Emma swallowed. "I think a man is following me. He's wearing a grey cloak and has a lot of knives."

The baker leaned close to the window and looked to either side. "There doesn't seem to be anyone there. Have you seen this man before?"

"No, sir." Emma shook her head. "Not before today."

He frowned and stepped out onto the street, again checking in both directions. Emma crept out behind him, also searching anywhere someone might hide.

"Well, I don't mind you waiting here for a guard to walk by if you care to. Mind your fingers." He smiled.

Emma looked to the west, at the dark green swath of Widowswood above the buildings in that direction. She contemplated sending a bird in search of Mama, but couldn't spot so much as a horse in this part of town. Her gut tightened from how bad she wanted to go home, but she didn't trust walking alone down a long empty street to open meadow.

"Thank you. I don't see him anymore."

The baker nodded at her.

She left the shop and ran south, heading once more for the crowd in the center of town, glancing back every few steps. The grey-cloaked man reappeared out of an alley four houses away from the square. That time, she let off a weak scream and sprinted with tears flying from her eyes.

Patches of color from people's clothing flashed by. She didn't pay attention to faces, or even if they were men or women. She grabbed the corners of carts to fling herself around obstacles, pushed off bodies left and right, and tripped over something into a somersault. Somehow, she bounced straight back into a run. Her toes throbbed, but she kept going.

Random darting brought her out the other side of a crowd at the base of Eoghn's Inn. Mama stopped in here all the time to bring seasonings she'd put together. Most of the herbs she combined could be found in any kitchen, but after learning the truth about her family, it made much more sense how everyone praised the man's cooking. Mama's spices had to use a little magic.

Emma raced up the stairs, bounded across the porch, and tried to stop on a throw rug made from the hide of a bear, which slid with her for a few feet. She waved her arms to keep balance, gulping down warm air laden with the fragrance of roasting turkey and flame-seared beef. The room, all thirty some-odd tables of it, looked as full as she'd ever seen it, with visitors crammed in for the mid-day meal. Two families even sprawled on the floor by the fireplace.

A hint of apple pie came and went, drowned in a wave of garlic and potato.

Near the bar, a gasp drew her attention to a tall, pudgy boy with a head of red curls. Rydh Cooper. The thirteen-year-old had her by at least six inches in height and probably three times in weight, yet he stared at her with an expression of clear worry. Seeing him brought her back to the day she'd caught him stomping Stick Knight's horse into splinters and making Tam cry.

All the fear and helplessness she felt at being chased through town by a grown man covered in daggers somehow became Rydh's fault, adding to her disgust at a boy who laughed while tormenting her little brother. She glared at him.

Eoghn, and his huge curved moustache, shook with laughter at the sight of the chunky boy backing away from tiny little Emma. "Aye, lad. She may be fifty pounds wet, but that family's none ta be trifled with."

Rydh let off an uneasy whine from his nose, and stomp-ran into the kitchen, likely heading for the back door.

"Oy, lass. What'd ya do to the poor lad?"

"I thumped him." Emma folded her arms. "He was being mean to my brother." Her glare softened. "Is my Mama here?"

Eoghn shook his head. "Sorry, Em, she popped in a while ago, well a'fore noon."

Emma slouched. She scurried to the right, hiding by a narrow strip of window beside the door. The grimy glass reduced most of the outside to blurs of color, useless for spotting anyone trying to do something bad to her. *What did I do?* She closed her eyes and tried to calm down. Being terrified wouldn't help. She had to think. She had to be smart.

Voices behind her discussed the upcoming feast. Women chatted about which satyr they hoped fancied them. Some male voices spoke fondly of chasing fawns, while others bragged about the ales they'd brought for the contest, new recipes they hoped would win a prize. Emma glanced back at them, wondering what young deer had to do with a festival about people falling in love. She shrugged and skirted to her left, ducking behind heavy white curtains to stand by the cleaner window.

She looked back and forth among the people out in the square. Every so often, she spotted a familiar face, someone who lived here, but the vast majority appeared to be travelers she'd never seen before. Emma shivered, feeling like a little mouse hiding in a box from an angry, nasty cat. She wanted so much to run home, but going outside at all felt dangerous. She'd hide here until Da or Mama came searching the town for her.

As time passed, a few people finished their meals and left, others came in and sat.

Adeline, who waited tables, pulled back the curtain. "Oy, Em. You playin' wif your friends? Hidin'?" The maybe seventeen-year-old winked. "Care for some water or anything? You've been standin' there a while. S'not a great hidin' spot ya know. See your shadow on the cloth plain as day."

Emma peered up at the girl, who wore a crushed red velvet bodice over a plain, white, long-sleeved dress. It took only a second of eye contact for the barmaid's playful grin to melt away to concern.

"What's the matter, child?" Adeline stooped.

"Someone's following me," whispered Emma.

"What? Why?"

Emma's thoughts stopped on the only possible reason: one of Old Man Drinn's thief friends from the big city had found out he'd been killed. They'd come for revenge. But... why not hurt her while they'd been alone on the street by the baker? Her throat tightened. *They wanna take me.* She glanced at the crowd again. *Why?* Her eyes widened. *They gotta know Mama killed him! They want to hurt me so Mama suffers.* She blinked. *Dreamroot. That wasn't for him; it's for me!*

She burst into quiet tears.

Adeline cuddled her. "Oh, Em, what's wrong?"

"I wanna go home." She sniffled and got herself under control. "I..." Her voice quivered. "Have you seen my—"

A patch of golden brown moved above the crowd outside. Guard Kavan, head and shoulders taller than most people, strode with ease across the square. Emma grinned.

"Mafindwel, Adeline." She pointed at Kavan. "I'll be okay."

The young woman stood and held the curtain back for her. "You run right on home, Em. Your mother's to be worried out of her mind soon."

Emma sprinted out the door, bounded down three steps and took off on a beeline for Kavan. She caught up to him on the western edge of the square, where he'd stopped to chat with a beautiful dark-skinned girl about the same age as Adeline, selling necklaces and rings from a tiny stand. Her grasp of the common tongue was weak, seeming limited to "I'm from Drajmir," "Yes," "No," or stating prices.

"Kavan!" Emma ran straight into his left leg and wrapped her arms around him.

"Another spook in the woods?" asked Kavan.

Emma managed not to cry when she made eye contact. "There's a man in a grey cloak following me. He's got a lot of knives on him and pouches and he bought some Dreamroot. I think he's trying to grab me."

Kavan straightened his posture and turned his gaze over the crowd. After a few seconds, he picked her up and perched her on his hip. At almost eye-level with him, she had a clear view over the heads of everyone else. After a few seconds of searching, she spotted the man lurking behind the awning of a cart selling scented oils. The merchant looked like he might've been this Drajmiri girl's father.

"There." She pointed. "By the blue cart."

Kavan shifted his weight, but almost as soon as he seemed to spot him, the grey-cloaked man darted out of sight. "Seems your forest phantom's a little more of the mundane this time 'round. Now why'd someone like that be followin' you?"

Emma sniffled. She couldn't outright tell Kavan that Mama had poisoned Old Man Drinn. As much as the mean old wretch deserved it, Mama shouldn't have done that. She whined. "I don't know."

Kavan brushed at her hair. "No right reason for a man like that to stalk a wee thing like you. P'raps some fools think they can send a message to Captain Dalen."

Emma dug her fingers into his tunic. Her toes curled with worry. She hadn't even thought of that. *How many bad people has Da put in jail?* "Please, will you take me home?"

"Certainly, luv." He took a few slow steps to the west in a rotating stride that let him survey the area.

Seeming confident the man had run off, Guard Kavan carried her out of town along the path home.

5

MAGIC

*E*mma stared over the guardsman's shoulder as they walked away from Widowswood proper. She waved and called 'hello' back to people sweeping porches without looking at them. No one emerged from the town to follow them. About fifteen minutes after they left the square, he set her down in front of her home.

"Thank you, Kavan." Emma stood on tiptoe to hug him around the neck.

The towering guardsman bowed at her. "My pleasure."

Emma darted across her porch and rushed inside, slamming the door behind her.

Mama, over by the kitchen window, jumped and dropped a knife on the counter. "Goodness, Emma, what's gotten into you?"

Bumps and bangs in the rear left of the house, Nan's room, brought comfort. Her grandmother had returned. Emma leaned against the door, hands flat upon the wood, and breathed. Mama hurried over, put a hand on Emma's forehead, then pressed one over her heart.

"Emma..."

She leapt forward into a hug. "Mama... a man was following me. He bought Dreamroot from Marsten's, and kept looking at me. He had a lot of knives and a big grey cloak. Guard Kavan walked me home."

A squeal of glee from Kimber echoed out back. Tam shouted after her, sounding playful.

"Slow down, Em." Mama guided them backward to the table, sat, and pulled Emma into her lap. "What happened?"

Emma recounted her chase around town. "I think it's Old Man Drinn's thief friends... they wanna hurt me to get revenge."

"Oh, Em." Mama held her close, rocking her side to side. "If that lousy excuse for a man had any friends, they'd have no way to know you threw apples at him." She winked.

Emma smiled despite her worry, but it didn't last long. "Not the apples they'd be mad about."

Mama stroked her hair. "Don't worry yourself over a man havin' too much wine."

"He..." Emma lifted her gaze. The look in Mama's eyes said she knew what Emma meant, and the matter was settled. "He shouldn't have 'ad so much wine." She lowered her head onto Mama's shoulder.

Killing the man was wrong. The law wouldn't have done that... at least not unless he'd hit Kimber a little too hard one day and she didn't get up anymore. *That* thought brought more tears, and Emma curled up in Mama's lap. Could it be right what her mother did? The man had been little use to anyone. When he didn't force her to beg for money, he treated Kimber like an unwanted stray dog, and he'd hit Emma. Not one person in the town of Widowswood seemed to miss him. He could've killed Kimber at any time in a drunken fit. Who knows what he'd have done to Emma if Nan hadn't shown up and squawked at him. Nan knew what Mama did, and hadn't scolded her for it.

Emma sighed. Maybe she wasn't old enough to understand such things.

Nan trundled in muttering. The way she held her arms made her look like an upset swan. She opened her mouth, saw the look on Emma's face, and seemed to forget whatever had put her in a bad mood.

"She's had a fright, Mother."

Nan looked from Mama to Em. "What's got your blood hiding again?"

Emma rubbed her cheeks, trying to get some color back in them. "A man followed me in town." She told the story again.

"Well, there's more than one way to handle snoops." Nan ruffled her hair and winked.

"I'm glad you're home." Emma leaned over to hug her grandmother.

Nan patted her on the back. "I may not be young like your mother anymore, but I've not quite yet got one foot in the grave."

Emma let out a guilty giggle.

"Well, at least *one* of that man's kin wants me to stick around." Nan winked at Mama.

"Liam's from a different world, Mother. And even they don't want you to pass on…"

Nan set her knuckles on her hips. "Oh, they'd just as soon I stop existing altogether. You too, for that matter."

Mama sighed.

Emma looked between them. She knew she had another set of grandparents, but couldn't remember ever meeting them. "What? Da's parents don't like us?"

"Oh, I'm sure they'd adore you and Tam." Nan headed for the cooking cabinets and readied some pots and pans. "So long as they don't know you're a forest witch."

Emma stuck her tongue out.

"Speaking of… it's getting about time to teach you more." Nan smiled.

Mama plucked a cloth from the table and handed it to Emma. "Go and fetch some cherries from the tree."

"Yes, Mama." Emma slid out of Mama's lap. "Are they for magic?"

"Yes. Powerful magic." Mama winked. "They're for Nan's pie. Hurry back."

"Oh, you…" Nan chuckled.

Emma went out the back door and caught a pang of guilt at the sight of the laundry already down from the line. While she'd been hiding, someone else had to do her chore. Kimber raced past from right to left, waving Stick Knight over her head.

"Give it back," shouted Tam, chasing behind her.

"The knight is going to marry the princess!" Kimber giggled and waved at Emma.

"No!" Tam howled. "He's gotta fight the dragon."

Her siblings, and their laughter, disappeared around the left corner of the house. Emma squinted at the woods on the far side of the meadow. Whatever the man in the grey cloak wanted of her, she would not let him hurt her family. She'd become a druid now… well, almost. Still, the spirits of Ylithir, Uruleth, and Linganthas had allowed her to call upon them.

"What do you think, Mother?" asked Mama in a hushed tone.

Emma froze, and backed up to the door so she could listen in.

"Isn't it obvious, Beth?" Pans clattered. "Where'd she first see him?"

"Marsten's."

"Right, and what was she doing there?" Nan grumbled.

Soft thuds on the floorboards announced Mama heading for the window. "She's in over her head again. Perhaps my friends have seen these thieves."

Emma hurried off the porch, a hand over her mouth to keep from gasping out loud, lest she be caught eavesdropping. *The silk!* A bundle of emerald creeper silk so big Marsten fainted at the sight of it. *He didn't want to hurt me... He wanted to find where I'd gotten it from!* She ran across the meadow, heading for the cherry tree a good hundred yards from the porch or more. Grass whipped by in a rich green blur dotted by yellow and white wildflowers. Behind her, Kimber let off a loud shriek.

Her heart in her throat, Emma whirled, expecting the man in grey— but found Tam rolling around the grass on top of her trying to get Stick Knight back. The redhead wriggled away from him and kissed the bit of wood before hugging it.

"Knights don't marry princesses!" shouted Tam. He pounced.

Kimber ducked again, but held out the toy for him to take.

They both collapsed with laughter.

Emma grinned and resumed her trek to the great tree. Nan had planted it long before Emma was born, in a rounded clearing flooded with sunlight. By its size, she never would have believed it to be a young tree if not for her family's connection to the spirits. Her grandmother had to have used magic to make it grow large and fertile. The trunk split off in multiple directions at about the level of her head, sending long branches upward in a cone, all studded with pink-white flowers and great clusters of cherries. It seemed odd for the tree to have flowers and cherries at the same time, but she doubted any other cherry tree had fruit all year round, or produced as much as Nan's tree.

It's magic.

She stopped in its shade, one hand against the bark. Amid the stillness of the forest, she tried to listen to the tree's spirit. Tam and Kimber continued to laugh and squeal in the background, though in the distance, they didn't break her focus.

"Thank you for giving us cherries to eat."

The mood in the clearing changed with an almost imperceptible shift toward contentment. Perhaps she imagined it, or perhaps a spirit *did* inhabit the tree. She patted the bark before pulling herself up into the branches. One of the larger boughs lay at a shallow enough angle to allow her to walk up the coarse bark, holding her arms out for balance. When she'd climbed within reach of the cherry bundles, she straddled the branch and set to filling the cloth.

Every few handfuls, she glanced back at the house from her elevated perch. Though height should have given her a better view, all the flowers made it harder to see. Continued sounds of play from Tam and Kimber kept her smiling as she worked, filling the towel until the corners barely met.

She gathered her bundle on the bobbing branch, wondering how she'd manage to get down while carrying it. After a few futile efforts to get her feet under her, she decided it better to pick cherries up than break a leg and let the bundle drop to the ground. An explosion of little red dots covered the grass below.

Snap.

Emma froze. Four breaths later, she shifted her gaze toward the woods where the sound came from.

Muted crunching moved among the underbrush.

She grasped the branch in front of her, straining to listen for signs of who'd snuck up on her. The tree didn't sit so far away from home that a good scream couldn't reach her family. Emma drew in a breath. If the man in grey found her, she'd let off a cry that'd wake up the whole town. The tree felt safe, high enough up that he couldn't reach her without climbing, and that would give her plenty of time to call for help. It almost scared her to think of what Mama would do to a man who wanted to do worse to her than slap her around in a drunken fit.

Snap. Thud, thud, thud.

She whipped around, gazing to the right, the sharp motion of her head making the limb bob up and down. Nothing stood out in the woods. The motion sounded like an animal, a boar or deer, but she imagined thieves would act like animals to hide.

She leaned forward, putting all her weight on her hands, and drew her feet up onto the branch. Cherry blossoms fluttered into the wind, making her cringe. *Oh, no. If that man is watching me, he's going to see me bouncing.*

Kimber let off a long, squealing giggle. She didn't have to look to figure Tam had jumped on and tickled her. The urge to protect her siblings swept her fear aside. Emma leaned her weight back onto her feet. She gripped the branch hand over hand as she walked backward toward the trunk, and stopped with her foot braced in the spot where all the boughs met at the top. No longer on a bouncy perch, she rose to her full height and stared into the woods.

A large doe lifted its head, pointing its huge black eyes at her.

Emma exhaled. *I'm being a baby again.* "Strixian, please grant me the Wildkin Whisper."

The doe twitched at the dancing lights orbiting Emma's arms.

"Hello," said Emma.

"Oh." The animal's nervousness evaporated. "Hello, human."

"Are there any other people near us?"

"There are not." The doe nibbled on something out of sight.

Emma crawled back up the branch and grabbed another sprig of cherries. "Have you seen anyone in the woods around here?"

"Only you." The doe approached.

She walked down the branch to the trunk, squatted, and leapt to the ground. The doe nuzzled up to her and accepted the bundle of fruit. Emma patted the doe's flank for a little while before moving to collect the scattering of cherries she'd dropped back into the towel.

"Please warn me if you see someone creeping around."

"If I am able."

"Thank you." Emma smiled and gathered the towel closed into a bulbous pouch. *This is too much for a pie.* "Oh well, I guess we'll have to eat some fresh."

As soon as she reached the top of the small hill nearest the woods, Tam and Kimber came running over.

"Cherries!" yelled Tam.

"Nan's making a pie." Emma held the bundle over his head. "And it's almost time for dinner."

"Aww." He pouted. "C'we have just a couple?"

Kimber gave her the same look she'd used when selling apples, but didn't say a word.

Emma fished out a handful for him, and another for her sister. They fell in step behind her on the way to the house, munching. She peered at the house, and upon not seeing Mama or Nan watching from the window, helped herself to a few as well.

6

A SPRIG OF NYMPH'S BREATH

*N*ot long after the sun sank into the west and Mama lit two candles, Emma climbed into bed. She propped herself up against the pillow in the corner by the wall. Tam and Kimber finished changing into their nightclothes and scrambled up to join her. With the promise of Nan's story time, Tam didn't complain, nor did he run about to delay.

He sat on her right, clutching his wooden sword while resting his head on her shoulder. Kimber crawled up on her left and Emma put her arms around them both. Their bellies full from dinner and pie, sleep nearly took them before Nan ambled out from the back hallway carrying a small and rather old leather-bound book. She pulled a chair from the table over to the bed, sat, and opened it.

Emma stared at it, knowing the story didn't lurk in the pages of any book, but in her grandmother's head. The last time she'd read them a story, she'd clutched Da's logbook. Emma leaned up to get a peek. She'd never seen this book before. Scrawled handwriting inside didn't look at all like anything her father would've put on paper. She furrowed her brow and settled back down, wondering if it might be magic, like a wizard's book.

Nan cleared her throat. "Where were we?"

"Sir Aemon was gonna fight the dragon," Tam yelled, wooden sword thrust high.

"No he a'not." Kimber shook her head. "He'a stuck inna ice. Isabelle getting help from'a faeries."

Tam grumbled. "He's gotta help her."

"Shh, Tam." Emma squeezed him. "Let Nan tell the story."

Nan smiled and turned a page. "The faeries did offer to give Princess Isabelle a way to break the spell that trapped Sir Aemon in ice, but to get the Hearthfire potion, she had to help them. An evil necromancer had come too close to the faeries' home, and brought death and darkness to the forest."

"A neck-a-monster?" asked Tam.

Kimber shivered. Emma bit her lip.

"A necromancer is a kind of wizard, but one who uses magic powered by the netherworld, where the souls of the dead go."

Tam pulled his knees up to his chin. Kimber's eyebrows drew together.

"What is it, child?" Nan tilted her head. "What's put that look on your face?"

"If'a bad wizard was hurtin'a faeries, wouldn' a knight help? Faerie's donnae give 'er the potion so's they kin both help?"

"Faeries didn't trust her to help them if she got what she wanted right away," muttered Emma.

Nan nodded. "Indeed. Humans aren't known for their trustworthiness, and even faeries know that."

"Donnae faeries steal babies?" asked Kimber.

"Not that I've seen." Nan clucked her tongue. "Balderdash from 'civilized' folk who fear the natural ways." She shook out her sleeves and turned a page. "Now then..."

"Isabel's imacent," said Tam. "They kin trust her."

"The Spider Queen didn't trust me." Emma shifted to let her dinner settle. "And I'm littler than her."

"But—"

Kimber put her hand over Tam's mouth.

"The necromancer wanted something at the bottom of a long forgotten tomb," said Nan, "and he used the darkest of dark magic to bring the dead back to serve him."

Emma shivered.

"For days, skeletons attacked the stones and the earth, burrowing deeper. Though he probably didn't know the faeries lived so close, the stain of his magic seeped into the forest. They feared for certain that the darkness would drain the very life from their home, and so they asked Princess Isabelle for help."

Nan turned a page.

"It took her two days, walking through a forest too thick to ride in, but she happened upon the necromancer's camp in the middle of the night. Now, being a princess, she'd wanted to try diplomacy first." Nan paused at the bewildered looks on Tam and Kimber's faces. "Diplomacy. She wanted to try talking to him, to convince him to leave the forest."

Tam scoffed. "Wizards who make the dead get up and walk won't listen to a girl."

"Princess Isabelle saw the glow of unnatural fire, sickly and white, and marched ahead. A rattling hiss startled her. She jumped back with a hand on her sword as a skeleton charged out of the trees, its blade high over its head." Nan mimicked a raspy hiss.

Kimber and Tam squeezed themselves into Emma. She found herself holding onto them for much the same reason. Before she believed in things like Banderwighs, Nan's stories weren't so scary. Maybe... just maybe... such a creature as a walking stack of bones could be real.

"Isabelle, despite being a princess, remained a fifteen-year-old girl. She screamed in fright and leapt to the side as the rusty longsword bit into a tree. At that moment, she understood this man would not give in to a simple request." Nan pantomimed a skeleton struggling to get its sword unstuck. "The fiend wrenched its blade from the wood and swung again, *whoosh!*" The kids ducked. "Isabelle jumped to the side and rolled, pulling her weapon from its sheath."

Tam held up the wooden sword. Nan play fought with him.

"Around and around they went, trading swings and parries. The bones moved faster than any opponent Isabelle had seen before, forcing her to keep backing up, learning how it moved."

"Was she a'scared?" whispered Kimber.

"Oh yes." Nan nodded. "So much so that she stopped thinking. Her arms moved as if on their own, the way Sir Aemon had taught her, but the skeleton moved too fast. It stabbed her in the leg"—Nan poked Tam in the left thigh—"and Isabelle fell to the ground."

Kimber and Emma gasped.

"The skeleton drew back its blade, and a flash of lightning lit the sky behind it." Nan's eyebrows wiggled. "Isabelle thought of her father, dying at home on his bed. She thought of Sir Aemon, who'd be frozen forever without her help, and she conquered her fear."

"What hap—?"

Kimber covered Tam's mouth.

"The skeleton held its longsword high, ready to take Isabelle's head, but she hurled herself at it, and the two of them crashed to the ground. She rolled to the side, wrapping her body around its sword arm, and kicked it in the jaw over and over until the skull popped off."

The kids stared in rapt silence.

"She'a *touched* it?" Kimber scrunched up her face and shivered.

"Isabelle relaxed, but as soon as she let go, the headless thing sat up!" Nan flung her arms high; the sudden motion made all three of them scream. "She grabbed it by the arm and kicked it as hard as she could in the chest. The skeleton's shoulder broke with a loud *crack!* Bones went spilling down the hill, bouncing off rocks and tree stumps, flying to pieces."

Emma sighed with relief, as did her siblings.

"Perhaps the faeries had helped, or perhaps the spirits watched out for her. Isabelle crawled into the bushes to hide, but nothing else came after her. She bandaged her leg, but couldn't stand on it. Inch by inch, she crawled toward the deathly white firelight. There, in the glow of four ghostly torches, stood the necromancer."

Kimber whimpered and squeezed Emma.

Nan turned a page. "He waved his arms in a wild display, chanting words of dark power. Specters and spirits whirled around. Before Isabelle's very eyes, a great column of bone rose out of the ground behind him and split apart. Inside, a swirling black portal to the netherworld itself!"

"No!" yelled Tam, waving the wooden sword. "She can't let him do that!"

Emma stared at Nan, clutching Kimber and Tam to her sides like giant dolls for protection.

Nan grasped handfuls of air as though dragging herself over the ground. "Princess Isabelle now understood why the faeries had been so worried. The man hadn't been after some buried treasure. This portal he'd opened would surely doom their kingdom. She crawled as close as the forest allowed. She couldn't bear the pain of putting any weight on her wounded leg, so she couldn't use her sword. Instead, she readied her shortbow. The necromancer's voice thundered in the air, as if the clouds themselves spoke for him. Ghostly faces spun about in a cyclone around him, some staring at Isabelle with hatred in their hollow eyes."

Tam lowered his sword and sniffled.

At his trembling, Emma cuddled him and gave Nan a 'stop it you're scaring him' look. She shivered as well, perhaps wearing an expression even more frightened than her brother's. She'd seen the stare Nan described, that empty-eyed glare, upon the face of the Banderwigh.

"Princess Isabelle knew she didn't have much chance if she missed. If she tried to stop the dark magic and failed, she may well give her life for nothing."

Kimber sniveled. Tam got quiet and still, his hands balled in fists, the sword abandoned on the mattress at his side.

"She couldn't give up on Sir Aemon, nor could she walk away and let all the faeries suffer. The energy in the nether gate glowed violet. Something on the other side drew close. Princess Isabelle loaded an arrow and aimed at the necromancer's heart. The second she loosed, he raised his spellbook, intending to hold it up to the sky."

"No," whispered Tam.

Nan clutched her book to her chest and slapped it. "The arrow struck the book and pierced through to his chest, but only a little." Emma shrank in on herself, fearing for Isabelle's life. "His chant cut out with a mangled word. It took him a second to realize he'd been struck with an arrow. When he did, he plucked his book away from himself." Nan jerked the book forward from her chest. "His blood stained the pages, and he looked straight at her."

Kimber hid her face against Emma's chest, sniveling. Tam covered his eyes.

Nan leaned back. "But the spell had been broken."

The kids looked up.

"Isabelle's arrow made him say a word wrong. The blood on the pages turned black and caught fire, burning bright violet. With a screeching wail, the nethergate shattered. Dark, swirling energy lashed out in all directions. Princess Isabelle threw herself flat to the ground and covered her face. A great and terrible *boom* echoed over the woods, and the faint screams of the necromancer faded away to nothing."

Kimber clutched two fistfuls of Emma's nightdress, staring at Nan. Tam sat with his mouth open. Emma stopped breathing, hanging on Nan's next word.

"When Princess Isabelle sat up, the necromancer, the gate, the skeletons, the torches… everything had disappeared. She lay on the ground for some time, trying to think of a way to travel two days' worth of walking without being able to stand. She slipped in and out of sleep for a while. One time when she opened her eyes, she found three faeries hovering over her chest."

"Yay!" cheered Tam.

Kimber clapped.

Emma started breathing again.

Nan turned a page.

"They used their magic to mend her wound. The faeries kept their promise. Two of them brought her the Hearthfire Potion." Nan lowered her voice to a whisper. "It took two of them to carry it, as they're only about this big." She held her hands six inches apart. "The bottle warmed Isabelle's hands like a heat stone. The faeries told her if she gave it to Sir Aemon, it would break the curse trapping him in ice. She hurried back to the faerie's home where she'd left her horse, and spent the next three days riding to her knight's side. He remained as she had left him, a statue of blue ice, frozen in a lover's pose."

Kimber grumbled. "Tha's a mean trick, wha' the ice demon did. Should'nae use love like'at."

"You're right." Nan smiled. "But Aemon did not love her. Her magic tricked him."

Da, in a chair by the fireplace, mumbled something to Mama that made her thump him on the arm. He grinned, and she leaned in to kiss him.

Emma looked away.

"Does the Heartfire Potion brea—?"

Kimber put her hand over Tam's mouth.

He pulled her arm down. "Stop doing that."

"Donnae askin' when Nan's tellin'." She poked him in the side.

"Well…" Nan turned a page.

Mama walked up behind Nan. "Time to sleep."

All three children whined "aww" at the same time.

Nan closed her book. "Don't worry. You've plenty of nights left for stories."

"She's still gotta get the Nymph's Breath to make the potion to save the king," said Tam.

Emma lifted Kimber to the side before scooting forward so she could lay flat. "Nan? Are there really potions made from Nymph's Breath?"

"Oh yes. Some of the more potent healing elixirs use it."

"Wha's et look like?" asked Kimber

Nan's eyes sparkled. Emma grinned. Talking herbs and potions wound her up like Tam and knights, an easy way to delay bedtime by a few minutes.

"It's a pale blue flower that grows on trees. Nymph's Breath isn't part of the tree, but they live together." She knitted her fingers. "The flowers are tiny, and sprout from long thread-like runners that dangle from high up. They're very delicate, so whenever the wind blows, the whole group of them moves like smoke."

"Could Mama make a potion to fix Sir Aemon?" Emma yawned. After the day she'd had, her body called out for sleep, but she fought to stay awake to hear the answer.

"I imagine she might be able to find a way. Your mother always did have a knack for potions. The magic we weave is quite different from that of wizards. Remember how you invoked Uruleth over the herbs?"

Emma nodded.

"When a wizard creates a potion, they cast a spell into the crucible to lend magic to the effect. The results are often quite different from what we do."

Da cleared his throat.

"Good night, Em." Nan stooped over to kiss her on the head. "Good night, Kimber." The girl giggled at Nan's kiss. "Good night, Tam." She gave him a peck on the cheek, picked up his wooden sword, and put it on the wall peg.

Mama made the rounds of goodnight kisses next, followed by a head pat apiece from Da. Emma snuggled under the blanket and closed her eyes.

7

IN THE ACT

*E*mma dreamed of fighting skeletons to protect her brother. She pictured herself older, using Mama's staff, with Uruleth's magic giving her strength. Bones flew, skulls bounced, and a legion of undead returned to the earth.

She awoke to a gentle shaking and looked over her shoulder at Kimber.

"You'as havin' a bad dream?"

Da's snoring filled the darkness. Quiet moonlight drew spots of pale blue on the floor.

Emma wiped her eyes. "No. Why?"

"Keep hittin' me wif yer elbow, an' kickin' the wall," whispered Kimber.

"Sorry." Emma rolled flat. "I was breaking skeletons."

"Oh." Kimber's head fell on Emma's shoulder.

THE SUN ON HER FACE DRAGGED EMMA OUT OF SLEEP. KIMBER STOOD AT the foot of the bed, wriggling into her day dress. From the yelling and laughing out back, Mama chased Tam around trying to get him in his tunic. Nan set the table for morning meal.

Emma scooted to the side of the bed facing the house and let her feet dangle. "Nan, where's Da?"

"Out already with this upcoming festival." She clucked her tongue.

"Oh." Emma yawned, stood, stretched, and wobbled.

The temptation to fall over backward and sleep more almost won, but she forced herself to trudge out to the privy. By the time she returned, Tam and Kimber sat at the table waiting. Mama hovered at the window over the counter, whistling at birds. Emma glided to the shelf by the bed and traded her nightdress for the one Nan made her.

Mama portioned out pieces of hard, flat bread sprinkled in scallions. Everyone took from a large bowl of sliced carrots, tomatoes, and melon in the middle of the table. Emma ate, staring at her mother the whole time with an expectant look. She didn't seem worried or concerned. Perhaps Mama didn't want to remind her of the scare she'd gotten yesterday.

Emma nibbled on one of the bread squares, not quite caring for the overpowering onion flavor, but it was what Mama provided. Tam made a 'bleh' noise and dropped it. Kimber stuffed everything in her mouth at once, pausing only long enough to offer Tam a trade of melon for the bread he didn't like.

"C'we go inta town?" asked Tam. "I wanna watch them set up the tables."

"That's boring," said Emma.

"The acrobats are practicing today, and some of the visitors are already selling treats." Nan winked.

"Akabats?" Kimber bounced in her seat.

"Some performers this year. One or two from Calebrin, so I hear." Nan examined a piece of bread before eating it.

"Don't they celebrate the feast there as well?" asked Mama.

"Oh yes." Nan munched a bit of the hard bread. "But quite a few people think it's more proper to do it near the woods. Satyrs aren't terribly fond of large cities."

"I've got quite a few potions to deliver today, and Anna's with child. Any day now, they'll be ready." Mama smiled over a hunk of melon at Tam before breaking into a chuckle at the look Kimber gave her.

"I can take them," said Emma. Princess Isabelle got over her fear to help others. So could she.

"I'll walk you to town. You can play in the square, but I don't want you putting even one toe outside it until I'm with you." Mama gestured at her plate. "Finish your meal first."

Emma smiled. Relief brought her appetite back in a flood, and she devoured the pungent bread without hesitation. Soon, she and Kimber took the plates out back to the water pump to rinse. The younger girl couldn't stand still. Excitement at getting to see the performers and all the setup for the feast kept her bouncing in place. Emma couldn't help but smile at how happy Kimber was with a real family.

After they'd finished washing the plates, the girls carried them inside and set them on the counter. Mama waited by the door with her traveling cloak on and staff in hand. A large satchel laden with potions on her left hip clinked each time she moved. Emma rushed to her mother's side, smiling.

"Alright then." Mama looked at Nan. "Off we go."

"Oh, have fun." Nan waved at them.

Emma took Tam and Kimber's hands, then followed Mama across the porch to the dirt trail leading to the town proper.

Even so far from the village center, the echo of many voices made the town seem alive with people. Mama stopped at the second house on the right, a good two-minute walk away from home, and knocked. Emma waited behind her, Tam and Kimber tugging at her in hopes of getting a better look into town.

Mrs. Holstead, Anna's mother, answered. She looked younger than Nan, though Emma had heard here and there that Nan had been a little old when she'd had Mama. The woman invited them in to a plain, but cozy room with several soft chairs arranged around a fireplace.

"Sit here and be patient." Mama squeezed Emma on the shoulder. "I'll just be a moment."

Emma pulled Tam and Kimber around to the front of the sofa. "Yes, Mama."

Mama and Mrs. Holstead went into the back of the house, discussing Anna's 'condition.'

Emma sat for a few minutes swinging her feet while Tam made sputtering noises of boredom. Eventually, Mama reappeared, looking content. She waved Emma to follow and paused at the door while Mrs. Holstead opened it.

"Give her a spoonful in some tea when she wakes and right before she retires for the night," said Mama.

"Thank you, Beth." Mrs. Holstead held the door for them and eased it closed once they walked outside.

"Is'a baby healthy?" asked Kimber.

"Yes. Anna's doing well." Mama smiled.

Tam kicked a pebble out of the dirt road.

"Why were you worried?" whispered Emma.

Mama brushed a hand over Emma's hair, patted her head, and seemed to think over the question for a few paces. "Anna's a slight girl. She's not too tall, and she's too thin."

Emma looked her mother up and down.

Mama laughed. "Yes, like me... only short."

They made one more stop, on the left, within sight of the beginning of cobblestones. At Mr. Farrow's house, Mama only handed him a small bottle in trade for a little sack of coins. They exchanged pleasantries, and continued into town.

A narrow street, a left turn, another street, and a right turn brought them to the end of a wide avenue leading to the town square. All manner of tables had been set up here and there around the fountain under colored streamers. Pushcarts brought in from outlying villages gathered in clusters, likely several merchants from the same place keeping close. Some had wares already set out despite the feast not officially starting until tomorrow.

Mama took a small pouch from her satchel and handed it to Emma. "Have a little fun, but keep your wits."

Emma took the coin purse and tied it to her cloth belt. "Thank you, Mama."

The banging of hammers and a few random flute notes filtered through the din of a hundred people talking at once. Her mother looked around, and seemed satisfied at something. She smiled at the children and walked ahead into the square. No sooner had they reached the point where the crowd thickened, did Guard Kavan and Filner wander over to say hello.

"Mafindwel, lady." Guard Filner bowed at Mama.

She smiled. "And to you."

"Mrs. Dalen." Kavan rendered a bow as well.

Mama nodded to him.

Emma slid forward, losing the battle to hold her brother and sister back.

"Go on, Emma. Remember, stay in the square until I get back."

"Yes, Mama." Emma didn't want to let go to wave at the guards, fearing either sibling would zoom away. "Hello!"

Tam pulled harder than his size seemed to allow, and dragged her forward. Emma caught a glimpse over her shoulder of the guards nodding, probably her mother asking them to keep an eye on them. She let him pull her along at a jog, Kimber laughing already from the energy in the air. A short distance later, Tam swerved left without warning, making her fall as her stumbling stride slammed her ankles together. She lost her grip on both children and fell to a hobbling limp for a few seconds.

"Ow. Tam, wait!" She sucked in air between her teeth at how much such a little thing hurt.

Tam raced up to where a man threw and caught five small swords, staring at him in sheer awe. Kimber slowed a little, looking back with a hesitant expression. Once the pain faded, Emma stormed over, took Kimber's hand, and stomped up behind Tam. She seized his hand, but her anger fell short of yelling at him. He hadn't meant it, as much as the spectacle of a sword juggler had mesmerized him.

"Be careful, Tam."

He looked at her for a second before staring up at the juggler again. "I'm not too close."

The man, average in height and slight of frame, whipped shortswords into the air and caught them by the handles. Silver blades twirled and spun, catching the sunlight in a dazzling display. A crowd of between twenty and thirty oohed and gasped each time he added a trick spin or tossed one high and seemed to forget it, until snatching it from the air a split second before it would've stabbed him.

Having held Da's shortsword, Emma thought they looked a bit thin and not at all sharp. Still, they created a beautiful display while in motion. The man continued throwing and catching them for a few minutes before tossing them all, one after the next, into a hay bale behind him without looking. Every one speared into the hay in an almost-straight line.

People clapped.

"Come back tomorrow, good villagers," said the performer. "When I shall do this and even more with *sharp* blades. Perhaps even light them aflame."

A few adults tossed coppers in a hat at his feet.

He proceeded to bow and thank them.

Kimber pulled Emma to the left, which in turn dragged Tam across an open path where the crowd separated, to a spot where a young woman and two boys about Emma's age balanced on brightly painted wooden balls. All wore tight silk costumes covered in a red and white diamond pattern. She figured them for brothers and sister, the boys twins. Over the next few minutes, the boys walked backward on the spheres, going in circles around each other while jumping over their upside-down older sister. Eventually, they dismounted from the spheres and performed a series of bends, flips, and aerial tosses. The older girl threw one boy into the air, but didn't let go of him. For seconds, he did a handstand on top of her upraised arms, then plummeted downward only to slide like a thread through the needle of her legs instead of striking the ground. She hauled him airborne again and threw him into a midair somersault. He landed on his feet and struck a pose with his arms raised.

Everyone watching them gasped.

The family proceeded to perform a series of contortions and stacking displays involving several more near-miss falls with last-second catches.

Emma's bones ached from watching them bend in ways bodies weren't supposed to move.

Kimber stood on one foot and tried to pull her other leg up behind her head. She came within a few inches of her heel touching hair before she lost her balance and Emma caught her.

Emma blinked at her. "Didn't that hurt?"

Kimber shrugged.

Once the acrobats stopped to rest, Emma walked her brother and sister along, following the path in the crowd. Left of the central fountain, a large stage (the source of the hammering) appeared half-built. The round man who'd knocked her flat the other day dripped with sweat while hauling boards into place.

Tam found some amusement in watching them work, but as Emma predicted, he soon grew bored.

"Ooo!" yelled Tam. He started to zoom off, but stopped himself. "Look!"

She peered after his pointing finger at a small table full of sweet breads covered in icing. Kimber's eyes lit up as well. Emma bit her lip, a momentary feeling of guilt at the cinnamon roll she'd never managed to bring Kimber.

"Okay," said Emma.

A kindly older man behind the table perked up as they approached. Tam's nose reached the top of the table, though he stood on his toes to see the assortment of blue, yellow, red, and green treats. Some resembled small loaves of bread with icing, others swirls of dough with a dollop of jelly in the middle.

"W'as 'at?" Kimber pointed at one of the swirls with a red middle.

"Strawberry," said the man. "Anything you fancy, little miss? Every one's a bit."

"An 'aat?" She pointed at a dark-centered one.

"Blueberry."

Kimber nodded and looked at Emma. "Kin I 'ave 'at one?"

Tam moved back and forth, studying the bounty for a full minute before settling on one of the small loaves covered in green icing. He pointed at it. Emma fished in the pouch Mama had given her and found ten copper coins. She plucked out three and handed them up to the man.

Her brother took his sweet bread. Kimber held out her hands as the man offered the blueberry jam tart. Emma pointed at a flatter, squarer bun with an X of white icing across the top. Everywhere about the treat proved sticky; it smelled of honey and offered no place to touch without getting her fingers all gooey.

With two smiling children in tow, Emma headed to the fountain and perched on the rim with her back to the water. Kimber sat on her right, while Tam flopped cross-legged on the ground in front of her.

After two bites, Emma discovered apple pie type filling inside her bun. Kimber caught a whiff of apple and looked away, though the downturn in her mood faded away almost as fast as it appeared. The redhead took great care to nibble off the sugarcoated pastry around the jam-covered center before tossing the middle part in her mouth in one bite.

"I can't wait for t'morrow," said Tam, past a mouthful of sweet roll. "I'm gonna eat a whole chicken!"

"I'as gonnae find the most firefruit!" Kimber flashed a blueberry-stained grin.

Emma recalled the Harvest Hunt from last year, running around Hadrath's fields searching for buried, painted fruits. She couldn't remember Kimber there, quite likely because Old Man Drinn hadn't allowed her to go. "You sure will." She patted her back.

Kimber licked sugar from her fingers, bouncing with glee.

Another two years or so, and Emma would be too old for the Harvest Hunt. The child who found the most firefruit got to play the baby in the parade, between the man dressed up as Zaravex, and whoever among the unmarried women won the game with the flowers. Past twelve, the kids didn't bother with searching for fruit, and as a girl, she had another four years to wait before she could collect flowers. Sixteen was the youngest a girl could participate. Mama had told her she'd played once… by the time she'd turned seventeen, she'd been married to Da.

She didn't care too much about the Hunt. The past two years, she'd spent more time stopping Rydh and his friends from stealing Tam's fruit than hunting on her own. Julianna would be too old this year, so the blacksmith's daughter couldn't win again.

Emma smiled. She'd go to watch Tam and Kimber have fun, maybe pick up a fruit or two herself if she could find any, but she didn't care who won. Her family didn't need the little prize money, and she had no interest in pretending to be someone else's baby.

Content with her immediate future insofar as holidays went, she looked around. A boy of about fourteen teetered by on stilts, following a man who resembled him enough to be his father. The elder moved on the stilts as though they'd been part of his legs from birth. The son looked more like a foal a minute after birth.

A great, rotund woman in a bright red velvet dress swept by, pausing long enough to hand Emma and Kimber each a small white flower and wish them a merry feast. Tam gawked at her. As soon as she hurried off in search of other girls lacking flowers in their hair, he looked up at Emma.

"Is there gonna be 'nuff food?"

"Tam!" Emma swatted at him. "Don't be mean. Mrs. Greenbriar was nice to us."

Kimber covered her face in her hands, laughing.

Emma sighed and stuck the flower in her hair over her left ear, then helped Kimber with hers. "Now what—"

She froze, staring off to the southeast, down the street that led to Marsten's Apothecary. The place appeared empty, the front doors shut, curtains down, and no light on inside. *It shouldn't be closed this early. It's not even noon yet.*

"Something's wrong," she whispered.

"Hmm?" Kimber looked over, still snickering.

Emma stood. "I'm worried about a friend."

Kimber followed her gaze to the apothecary. "At's outta tha square. Mama said we donn'ae go outta the square."

She held her stomach to quell the unease brewing. Sugar, honey, and apples crept up the back of her throat. "If someone's hurt, it would be more wrong not to do anything because we were told not to than to help."

"You'a gonna get inna trouble." Kimber shook her head.

"Wait here. I'll be right back."

"No." Tam grabbed her hand. "Mama said we're s'posed ta stay wif you. I don' wanna get inna trouble."

Emma sighed. "Okay, but you need to stay quiet. This is serious."

He nodded.

She took Kimber's hand as well and hurried to the southeast corner. Not quite out of the square yet, she peered around in search of anything dangerous. As before, the street looked deserted, save for flickering lanterns in some of the homes. The closed doors and lack of light at Marsten's stood out.

Emma took a deep breath, held it, and let it out.

"You'as sure?" whispered Kimber.

"Yes. Watch behind us. If you see anyone following, tell me."

Kimber nodded hard, throwing her long, thick hair into a frazzle.

Emma fast-walked to Marsten's porch and padded up to the door without making a noise. She released Kimber's hand, trusting her ever so slightly more than Tam not to run away on her own, and grasped the handle. It rattled, locked.

Something heavy thudded to the floor inside.

Kimber held her left hand flat, poking two fingers from her right into the palm before pointing at the window.

Emma blinked. "What?"

"I'as hear two men inside," whispered Kimber.

"Get the guards?" whispered Tam.

"Could just be Marsten moving stuff around." Emma crept to the far left end of the porch and slipped under the banister to the ground.

Tam and Kimber jumped down after. Again taking their hands, she crept along the narrow space between Marsten's and the neighboring candle maker's shop. At the back end of the building, a gate hung open.

Emma squeezed past the opening, her body small enough to fit without having to touch fence or gate. Kimber followed and stifled a gasp. Emma whirled. The redhead pointed at a small glass bottle balanced on the inside handle. An adult couldn't have fit into the backyard without pushing the gate open wider, which would've made it fall and break on the cobbles.

Kimber put her hand over Tam's mouth and gave him a fearful stare. He seemed confused about why a bottle frightened his sisters, but nodded.

Emma got down on all fours and crawled around the back porch to the stairway.

"Where is it?" whisper-yelled a man.

"If I knew, why would I tell you to *look* for it? Idiot."

In the corner by the stairs, Emma rocked back on the balls of her feet and stood only enough to peer over the porch surface.

The wide-open back door offered a view into a storeroom. Marsten lay flat on his front, a trickle of blood running down from above his left eye. Three men in cloaks, two grey, one black, rifled the drawers and cabinets. Noises from deeper inside suggested additional men were making a mess of the store.

Emma dropped to her knees and pointed at the gate.

Kimber nodded, as did Tam.

She got to her feet, crouching so no one inside the shop could see her, and hurried to the fence. Her siblings crawled behind her, quiet and close. Once clear of view, she darted out of the yard without touching the gate. Kimber pushed Tam through and followed him after hesitating for a second.

Emma took their hands and raced back to the town square, the length of five or six houses away.

Guards Haim and Kavan hovered at the edge of the crowd. The way they looked at Emma suggested the men had been about to come after her. She bee-lined right to them.

"Kavan! Haim!" She skidded to a halt, breathless, and pointed back. "Men are robbing Marsten. They knocked him out! He's bleeding."

Haim stuck his fingers in his mouth and let off a whistle that made Emma clamp her hands over her ears. Arnir and three other men from the Watch perked up out of the crowd and came running when Kavan waved to them.

"There's…" Emma gasped for air. "There's a bottle on the gate. It'll break if you—"

Kimber tapped her on the arm and held up the bottle. "I'as broked their 'larm."

Emma grinned. "Hurry! Between the candle shop, the gate."

"You three stay right here." Kavan pointed at Emma.

"Yes, sir." Emma wrapped her arms around Tam and Kimber, pulling them tight.

The guardsmen ran off and filed into the space between Marsten's and the candle maker's shop, one after the next. Kavan diverted to the right and crept up onto the porch.

Tam pantomimed pulling a sword from his belt. "Halt, knaves! In the name of Sir Tam, throw down your weapons."

Emma squeezed him. He strained to lean forward, trying to get a view. She held him back, grabbing a fistful of his tunic. She'd already disobeyed Mama once. As it turned out, she had been right. Disobeying the guards was foolish. Three children would only get in the way.

Muted shouting came from the apothecary. Kavan drew a broadsword and took on a ready stance. Something crashed inside. The door flew open and the black-cloaked man came running out—straight into Kavan's left hand.

The seven-foot guardsman caught the little man off his feet with a hand to the chest, and slammed him down on the porch, flat on his back.

"Yeah!" screamed Tam.

Emma cringed.

The cloaked figure wheezed, making no attempt to move.

Another figure in a brown cloak came out the door in a tumbling roll. Clinks of blades crossing echoed from inside. The tumbler sprang to his feet with a dagger, but Kavan whipped his broadsword around so fast it looked like a toy. Weapons crossed. With a *clank*, the dagger went flying into a window across the street, shattering it. A man's startled shout from inside followed. The thief stumbled to the side favoring his wrist, ducking the guard's swing.

A third man rushed Kavan with a shortsword in his left hand. He pulled it back in a striking motion, but spun the other way, flinging his weaponless right hand upward at Kavan's face. The broadsword whiffed at empty air where no shortsword attack came.

The giant guardsman stumbled to one side, hand over his face, blood streaming between his fingers.

Guard Filner stomped out onto the porch, the tip of his sword stained red. The man with the hurt wrist and the one who'd thrown something in Kavan's face took off running to the east, away from the town square, down a street leading to the plains.

Arnir wandered out behind the other three guards, a knife sticking out of his right shoulder. He stepped on the wheezing man Kavan had slammed into the porch. The rest of the guardsmen hurried off after the thieves.

Emma dragged Tam and Kimber along as she rushed toward Arnir and Kavan. The older guardsman, a little grey in his sideburns, glared at her.

"You were told to stay back," yelled Arnir.

"Kavan's hurt. I can help!"

"My eyes," muttered Kavan.

Arnir pulled the knife from his shoulder as though it merely annoyed him. He tossed it aside and rolled the stunned man over on his chest, searching him for weapons. "Get back, Emma. You're not to see what's inside."

She cringed. "Is Marsten okay?"

"Aye, lass. Bump on the head." He grabbed Kavan's arm and pulled him to the stairs. "Go with 'er out of here. Emma, go back to the square."

"Yes, sir."

Emma grabbed Kavan's huge wrist in both hands and led him down the street to the southeast corner of the square. After guiding him to sit on a hay bale, she climbed up next to him and knelt. Kimber and Tam crowded at his knees.

The man's face sparkled with a dusting of what appeared to be tiny ice flakes. His eyes had gone puffy and closed.

She held her hands an inch from his face and concentrated on her desire to heal. "Great Uruleth, please grant me the gift of life." Green glowing energy coalesced between her hands. Emma willed it to flow into Kavan.

His bleeding lessened and the swelling around his eyelids reduced, but didn't fade entirely.

"That feels… better." He reached up to test the area, cringing when his fingertip brushed his eyelid.

"Whoa," whispered Tam.

"Mama!" shouted Kimber.

Emma looked up. Mama sprinted through the crowd, cloak flowing behind her. For a second, Emma thought an aura of faint light surrounded her, as if a great ghostly panther followed close at her heels. People whirled about as Mama passed them, evidently startled by her speed. She rushed to a halt beside Kavan and looked him over.

"Em, fetch water."

"Yes, Mama." She hopped down from the hay bale and ran to the fountain. Not thinking to ask, she grabbed an empty bowl from the ground by a merchant cart on the way and plunged it into the water.

The woman to whom it belonged gave her a confused and angry look.

Emma hurried by, trying not to spill much. "Sorry. I'll bring it right back."

Mama had Kavan lying flat, head bent back over the edge of the hay bale. She took the bowl from Emma and poured it over his face and eyes.

"Open your eyes, Kavan. The water needs to get in."

He moaned.

"Don't step in any of that," said Mama. "It's crushed glass."

Emma backed up two steps and curled her toes.

Once the bowl ran out, Mama rested her hand on Kavan's face. She bowed her head, eyes closed, and held her other fist against her chest. "Lady Mythandriel, spirit of all that is alive and verdant, I call upon thee to bear forth the waters of life. Grant your gift of renewal." A faint breeze stirred up in a whorl around her, tinted with the fragrance of mint and rain. Pale green light radiated out from her left hand, flowing like ethereal smoke into Kavan, who ceased moaning and lay still.

Mama lifted her hand from his face, which showed little sign of a wound other than a few traces of blood. Emma ran the bowl back to its owner, curtseyed, and rushed to stand by Mama once more.

He blinked and looked around. His smile soon turned to an angry glower. "Damn fiend. I've had a sword all the way through my arm before and even that hurt nothing like this. You have my thanks, Beth."

Mama smiled. "Emma helped. Her magic kept you from grinding up your eyes so much even I couldn't save them."

He started to grumble about the thieves, but smiled and patted Emma on the head.

Another guard and Da ran by, heading for Marsten's.

"Mama. Marsten's hurt, too. And Arnir had a knife in his arm." Emma looked down. "I'm sorry for going out of the square."

"We'll talk about what happened soon." Mama gathered the children and sat them next to Kavan. "Wait with him."

"Yes, Mama," said three voices at the same time.

With that, she jogged to the apothecary and followed Da inside.

Kimber looked over at Emma. "You'as think we's inna trouble?"

"I dunno, but it's okay if I am." She put an arm around them both.

CRICKET SONG FILLED THE DISTANT DARKNESS OF WIDOWSWOOD. A FEW scattered fireflies left brief glowing trails over the meadow, winking in and out. From the northeast, a steady, cool wind swept over the house.

Emma sat at the edge of the porch, feet together, hands clasping the wood by her knees, head bowed. Mama sat behind her, working a brush through her hair in gentle, continuous strokes. She gripped the earth with her toes as the heaviness of guilt in her gut grew. That Mama had delayed her bedtime worried her.

Mama hadn't said another word about her leaving the town square since they'd returned home. Aside from a long, silent hug, Da hadn't either. Nan had skipped reading them a story, though in the chaos of getting home late, rushing a meal, and putting the children to bed, maybe she'd forgotten. Emma picked at the porch edge. If the lack of story was her punishment, she'd accept it... but they should've at least told her.

The brush pulled over her scalp, a soft scratch that left her in complete understanding of why cats adore being pet. Mama took great care with the process, never snagging hard enough to hurt. Even after she'd disobeyed, her mother didn't even want to pull a hair or two.

Emma sniffled.

Mama set the brush down and wrapped her arms around from behind. "There, there, Em."

She raised her hands, clasping Mama's arms where they crossed her chest. A few tears slid down her cheek.

"Do you understand why I asked you not to leave the town square?" Mama's breath puffed at the back of her hair.

"Yes, Mama," whispered Emma. "You don't want us to get hurt."

"I'd just left the Donnegals' place when Guard Fauen came to tell me you'd wandered off out of the square." Mama's arms tightened. "How do you think I felt?"

Emma sniffled. The stone in her belly got heavier. "Worried?"

"At first, I was disappointed that you'd disobey me, Em. Especially when I knew you understood the reason for what I told you not to do."

"I'm sorry." Emma took a few breaths to keep from surrendering to tears.

Mama rested her chin atop Emma's head and rocked her side to side. "All I want is for you to be safe. As much as I want to, I know I can't be there *all* the time to protect you. Some things you'll have to make your own decisions on."

Emma snuggled back against her mother.

"Why did you decide to go against what I told you?"

Her mother's soft tone made her feel guiltier. She didn't even seem angry. It took Emma a moment to swallow the lump in her throat to let words out. "Marsten's door was closed. It's never closed. All those people in town, why would a shopkeeper close? That man in the grey cloak started following me from Marsten's... I was afraid something happened to him."

Mama sniffled and hugged her too tight to allow breathing, but only for a second.

"I peeked inside the back door and saw Mister Marsten on the floor. We ran to get the guards."

"You're such a brave girl, Em." Mama kissed the back of her head. "It's possible you saved Marsten's life, but who knows what those men would have done if they saw you. I can't be angry with you because you acted out of compassion, but you scared me to death. Until we know why that man was following you, *please* be more careful."

"I'm sorry. I should've asked one of the guards to check instead of leaving the square, but I was..."

"Worked up and too eager to help someone you are fond of." Mama sighed and let go. "Someone's up past their bedtime."

Emma stood and turned around. "Am I to be punished?"

Mama wiped the tears from Emma's cheeks with her dress. "I think perhaps you've punished yourself already. What you did was noble, but dangerous."

"Like a knight," whispered Tam from the doorway.

Emma cracked a grin.

"Tam!" Mama pointed. "Bed. Now."

Emma climbed the two steps to the porch, her muscles heavy from worry, relief, and the need to sleep.

"You too, Em." Mama got up.

Head down, Emma plodded over to the bed, changed into her nightdress, and crawled in next to Kimber who'd already passed out. Tam grinned at her, but closed his eyes as soon as Mama approached to tuck them in.

8

THE FEAST OF ZARAVEX

$\mathcal{E}$mma sat cross-legged on the back porch, holding a bright red firefruit in her left hand while dabbing berry-dye with a brush to make eyes. The rubbery rind of the turnip-sized fruit soaked up the dye, drying in seconds. She finished off eyelashes and set to work painting a crown of flowers around the top. Even unpeeled, it gave off a powerful fragrance similar to cherry and cinnamon.

Kimber covered her fruit with random patches of color and shapes, singing to herself in a barely-audible whisper. She'd never before gotten to paint fruits for the Harvest Hunt. The town elders gave out three to each child not yet twelve. Up until a few weeks ago, Emma had assumed they came from a faraway land... but two days ago, Nan let her watch the magic that sprouted them from seeds in a matter of minutes.

Emma had pushed two of her fruits to Kimber so she could paint them. She looked back at her work-in-progress and frowned, trying to guess what that awful man had done with the ones Kimber had received in years past... or even if the town had bothered with him.

Tam being quiet made her look up. He sat to her left in his skivvies, more paint on him than the fruits in front of him. Much to his delight, Mama had insisted he *not* wear a tunic, since the colors couldn't be washed out of cloth. He'd discovered the berry dye tasted sweet like juice, and his entire face vanished behind the bowl of black as he drank from it.

"Tam!" Emma grabbed his arm. "Don't drink that."

He stuck out an inky tongue. "It's yummy!"

"We're not done with it... and be careful. Mama puts magic in it. It'll turn your wee black."

Wide-eyed with eagerness, Tam tried to drink more, but Emma held the bowl down.

She gave him a stern look. "Tam, no."

He reluctantly set the bowl down, grabbed a brush, and resumed painting fruit. From the look of it, he decorated it to be Stick Knight's helm.

Emma drew a nose in the form of two black dots. Her 'Princess Isabelle' firefruit finished, she set it down in front of herself and watched Kimber work.

The past four days had gone by too fast. Well, two at least. On the first day of the Feast of Zaravex, Mama and Nan accompanied them into town, wary after what happened at Marsten's. The shop remained closed, but Da had assured her Marsten hadn't suffered any serious injuries and would be fine.

By the second day, Da's mood improved. None of the Watch had found any trace of thieves, scary men in grey cloaks, or anything that made them concerned. Though Nan and Mama had remained with the children throughout the night of watching performers, actors, musicians, and dancers, the revelry gradually took their minds off what had happened.

Nan went so far as to claim that even thieves were afraid of the gods, and would probably not want to disrupt a feast. Da thought her foolish, but Nan fixed him with that one wiggling eyebrow. She'd said something about how some gods meddle in the affairs of mortals more often than others, and Zaravex was one of the more frequent visitors.

The third and fourth days had more feasting. Morning and afternoon passed with chores, though aside from some bread and cheese for breakfast, the entire town ate in the square, a communal celebration lasting five days. Everyone cooked and contributed, even the people from outlying villages.

Today, the fifth day of the Feast of Zaravex, would be the last, on which the Harvest Hunt, the Flower Ceremony, and the parade took place. Nan and a few of the town elders would collect everyone's painted firefruits, take them to Hadrath's farm, and hide them.

Mama emerged from the house, collected Tam, and brought him inside for a quick bath. Kimber sprawled on the porch, chin on her crossed arms, and smiled at her artwork. After a little while enjoying the late morning breeze, Emma gathered the fruits in a sack, which she set inside the front door. Theirs would be the first batch Nan collected on her rounds.

Hours later, after sweeping, tidying, and clothes washing, Mama grouped the children by the bed. Kimber squealed with delight when Mama presented her with a new dress, a long burgundy velvet one with puffy shoulders and tight sleeves. After putting on a circlet of white wildflowers with a pink trailing ribbon, the little redhead danced about the room.

Emma had the dress Nan made half on before she realized Mama had also bought her something fancy for the festival. She put her beloved garment back on the shelf and accepted a dress similar to Kimber's, only in dark blue. The soft material felt as though she wore a blanket. She tugged at it here and there, not used to a garment so clingy about the chest. Mama set a circlet of flowers on Emma's head as well and smiled at her.

When Mama reached for another bundle, Tam's eyes widened in horror.

"I don't wanna dress!"

The house rang with laughter, except for Tam's. He looked about ready to cry.

Mama unwrapped a green velvet tunic and brown leggings. The boy relaxed, took the leggings, but paused.

"No flowers in my hair."

"No flowers." Mama patted him on the head.

Emma smoothed her hands down her dress, feeling a little guilty at liking something Nan didn't make. Mama changed into a larger version of a similar dress, hers in dark emerald green. Unlike the girls' garments, her neckline plunged a little. She donned a crown of white wildflowers interlaced with blue silk ribbons that hung all the way down her back. Emma "oohed" and fussed with them until they sat just right.

With everyone done up in their festival best, Mama led the way outside and down the path to the town proper. Distant music grew louder as they approached, accompanied by the din of many conversations, merchants hawking wares, and actors reciting lines. The smells of baking ham, turkey, pies, and beef saturated everything, with the occasional whiff of oil-soaked torches.

As luck would have it, Da stood post near where they entered the square at the northwest. At the sight of Mama, he stared as if unable to remember how to speak.

Emma looked everywhere but at her parents as they hovered close and kissed. Kimber edged up to her and cringed. Emma nodded at her with a 'yeah, I know' expression. Tam bounced up and down, pointing at a flash of silver and bright orange.

True to his word, the sword juggler hurled real weapons into the air, each lit aflame. Several men all in black, wearing faux wooden horns, navigated the crowd handing out long-stem flowers to young women. Far to the right, a tall satyr wandered around. Grey from head to toe, and clad in tattered pants, he moved in a gait more of a dance than a walk. Thick horns emerged from black ringlets of hair studded with flowers, the points curved past a chin bearing a pointed goatee. Emma had to blink a few times before recognizing the costume as a costume. Peter, the son of Eoghn the inkeep, had won Mayor Braddon's pick to represent Zaravex.

Tam hid behind her as Peter approached. Kimber squeezed her hand.

Emma didn't bother ruining it for them.

The 'satyr' clomped over and bowed at Emma's parents. Despite Mama hanging on Da's arm, Peter gave her a flower.

"No fairer beauty doth grace mine eyes this eve."

Mama's face reddened.

Peter grinned at Da. "I shall have to steal your magic, for to lure such a creature away from the affections of the gods is no small feat."

Mama threw her head back and laughed, before plunging into another kiss with Da.

Emma looked away.

Peter crouched as much as the faun legs allowed. He smiled at Emma and Kimber. "Hmm. What's this then?" He appraised her for a moment, rubbing his pointy beard. "Not ready for flowers... but." Two pink hard candies appeared in his hand.

Kimber, wide-eyed and mute with awe, took one. Emma glanced up at Da. He smiled, so she accepted the treat.

"Thank you," said Emma.

"'Fank yas," whispered Kimber.

Peter strode off into the crowd.

Emma looked around for Tam. Worry started to build, but collapsed at the sight of his toes sticking out from under Mama's cloak. *He really believed Peter was Zaravex.* She giggled.

Tam peered out a moment later, and not seeing the satyr, emerged from his hiding place.

Mama patted Emma on the head. "It's okay to explore a bit. Stay where I can see you and *don't* leave the square. I'll be along in a few minutes." She leaned against Da.

"Yes, Mama." Emma looked down.

She took her siblings' hands and walked along a path defined by tables and carts. Her guilty doldrums faded a moment later at the sight of Tam's face alight with wonder at the sword juggler. While her brother and Kimber stared at dancing fire swords, Emma watched the shadows.

After a while, the man stopped to rest, doing the same behind-the-back toss that resulted in five swords speared into a hay bale. Since it didn't catch fire, she assumed it had been soaked in water.

They walked to the right, deeper into the square, trading greetings and smiles with the random townsperson who recognized them. People from the outer villages smiled at them or disregarded them entirely.

Kimber's head perked up at the sharp notes of a mandolin string piercing the noise. Her mouth hung open a little and she stood tall, searching for the source. An eerie flute joined in, somehow strong enough to make itself known over the ruckus without being painful to the ear. The music carried the kind of energy that seemed to go with the idea of dancing around an enormous fire, as Peter would be doing later that night, along with whichever woman won the flower game.

Emma followed it, rounding curving pathways of open ground between merchant stalls and tables full of food for anyone to take. Tam helped himself to a chicken leg, Kimber a small bread. A rattling tambourine-like accompaniment joined the song. She pulled her siblings around another bend in the path toward the center of the square. A large crowd gathered around two obvious outsiders, a man and a woman.

The woman sat on the edge of the fountain, and the sight of her knocked Emma's mouth wide open. Two catlike ears perched atop a thick mane of chocolate-brown hair. Ice-blue eyes with vertical-slit pupils practically glowed in the waning afternoon sun. Her skin had two colors: pale beige for the most part, with dark brown 'boots' and 'gloves' the same shade as her hair that crept midway up her arms and legs. Another dark spot covered the middle of her face, and a musical shaker dangled from the tip of a long, feline tail. It couldn't be fake like Peter's horns, for its movements were too fluid and fast. Her loose-fitting white top bared her shoulders and stomach, and her black gypsy skirt left most of her right leg out in the open. Bells around her ankle jingled as she tapped her foot in time with the music. Sharp claws plucked crisp notes from mandolin strings, and her smile revealed fangs.

The man seemed far more normal at first, though too perfect to be real. He resembled a statue brought to life, without a single flaw in his chiseled features. The flute player stood a touch shorter than Da, but had a slender body like Mama. Straight white hair fell in a fluid mass to the length of his belt, capped by a silver headband with three green leaf emeralds. He spun about and danced while playing a flute made of glass, and after the fourth spin, pointed ears caught Emma's eye.

An elf? And a.... Emma gawked at the woman with the mandolin.

A big floppy, feathered hat collected coppers, bronze coins, and even a few silvers at the woman's feet

Tam tilted his head far to the right, then back the other way.

Kimber leaned up to whisper in Emma's ear. "Is 'at n'elf?"

People from the distant corners of the square crowded in to watch them. Emma furrowed her eyebrows. Something wasn't quite normal here. They *felt* strange... magical. She stared at the furry tail snapping with sharp, rhythmic motions to rattle the shaker. *She's not wearing a costume.*

Emma studied the crowd. No one appeared to be acting odd. The music didn't sound bad, so perhaps their magic only made it louder. After a while, she found herself staring at the elven man and thinking perhaps it might not be so bad a thing to be a princess.

Mama's hand on her shoulder snapped her out of her daydream of visiting the elven court. She smiled up at her. Her mother regarded the skalds with a measure of curiosity, but didn't give them much more than a moment's glance.

"It's almost time for the hunt," said Mama.

Kimber cheered.

Tam bounced in place.

Mama walked with them to the north edge of the square. They stopped at a table to have a proper meal of turkey and potatoes, seated among locals and visitors alike. Not long after they ate, Mayor Braddon called out over the crowd to announce the hunt. Children swarmed down the street, the villagers obvious in their rougher tunics or dresses. Emma felt overdressed for a little while, until she caught sight of a few girls from town whose fathers owned shops in the square. They had elaborate, frilly things Emma couldn't imagine being able to breathe in, and worst of all *shoes*.

Soon, the procession left the town proper, headed north to Hadrath's farm. Men with lanterns surrounded the post-harvest field, still with clumps of corn stalks or discarded leaves littered here and there among buckets, barrels, and sacks. A few of the wealthy girls chattered at each other about 'running around in the dirt.' One seemed horrified at the thought, but the other two couldn't wait.

Julianna hung on her father's arm, watching. At thirteen, she couldn't participate again, but despite being caught in the boring part between too old for Harvest Hunt and too young for the Satyr's flowers, she appeared to be having fun.

Mayor Braddon waddled to the gate in the fence surrounding the field, wearing a long tunic the color of raspberries and sky blue tights. Emma led Kimber and Tam over to the crowd of children forming up around him, with parents, grandparents, and older siblings behind them.

"Welcome, everyone!" called Braddon. "It is my pleasure to open the Harvest Hunt this year. There are over a hundred decorated firefruit hidden in the field behind me." He patted a wooden bin full of burlap sacks. "Whoever finds the most by the time the sun goes down is the winner. Alright then. Everyone collect a bag and line up at the gate."

The mayor stepped aside. Emma followed the crowd of children in a circular path past the pile of bags. Tam eyed the gate, ready to race off the instant it opened. Kimber bounced on her toes. Emma looked between them, unsure who she should follow if they went in different directions.

Before she made up her mind, Braddon yelled, "Go!"

Two of Hadrath's farmhands pulled the gate open, and a stampede of five to twelve-year-olds charged, cheering and screaming with glee. Emma wound up following her brother, constantly looking back and forth between him and Kimber.

Emma found her first firefruit by stepping in a gopher hole. The rind cracked, but she didn't weigh enough to crush it. She tossed it in her bag and hurried to catch up to Tam. He crawled around, sifting through bundles of discarded cornstalks, and sure enough found three fruits in a matter of minutes.

Kimber cried out in victory a short distance away. She squatted in the dirt, holding a fruit over her head in both hands. From the grime on her fingers, she'd dug it up.

Eventually, Emma felt confident none of the older boys would bother

Tam. She allowed herself to slip from 'little mother' into 'little girl,' losing herself in the thrill of searching. She spotted a pair of seed bags on top of an overturned wooden bucket and decided to move them. Two fruits hid under the bucket.

As she dropped them into her bag, a growling little blonde girl of about five raced by. Her simple flaxen tunic suggested she lived in one of the smaller villages. The tiny waif dove headfirst into a pile of mulch, digging and clawing at it like a hound after a bone. She unearthed a fruit, bagged it, and scrambled off so fast she fell twice.

Emma laughed at the little one's energy.

Tam's battle cry filled her with the sort of dread she often felt whenever he did something stupid. She spun around and caught the tail end of the splash he made going into a giant puddle at the far northwest corner of the field. Two townsmen with lanterns converged on the corner, raising their lights. One shooed him out of the water and back into the field.

"G'won, boy. No fruits in the water."

The hesitant, wealthy girl in the lemon-yellow ball gown tiptoed around. She hadn't found a single fruit, but she didn't look to be trying. As much as Emma loathed the thought of Da dragging her off to Calebrin someday, this girl appeared to have the same radiant distaste for the Hunt. She glanced at Emma with a look of mild curiosity, evidently approving of her fine blue dress, but seemed aghast when she looked down enough to notice her lack of shoes. Emma grinned and hurried off.

A patch of yellow caught her eye under a dense pile of browning vegetation along the rearmost fence around the farm, a spot that did not appear well-tended. The firefruit she'd painted to be Isabelle sat inside a hollow, surrounded by fury, black bees as big as hen's eggs—mouseaters. Though the fruit would've been easy to spot, no child had gone near it. The presence of their nest likely explained why none of the farm workers came near this spot.

Will it work? Emma crept closer. "Strixian, please grant me the Wildkin Whisper."

Soft lights swirled around her for a second or two before sinking into her chest.

She took another step closer and focused on a bee. "Hello?"

The plump insect stopped to a hover and rotated to look at her. Fading sunlight glinted from eyes like rubies. "Danger."

"I won't hurt you."

It glided closer and settled on the back of her hand. "Why talk?"

She studied the fuzzy, winged insect. The hair around its midsection gave it the appearance of wearing a fur vest. Wings longer than her hands had the same dark red coloration as its eyes. At the back end, a jet-black stinger the size of one of Mama's sewing needles pulsated. For no reason she could think of, it didn't scare her at all.

"I'd like to pick up that fruit, but someone put it in your home. I'm not attacking your nest. Can I please take the fruit?"

The mouseater rotated to face the nest. Others paused to look at her. The spell caught bits and pieces of whispering, enough to guess they discussed whether to allow her closer or sting to protect their queen. Its wings buzzed to life, and it floated up to her nose. "Take fruit thing. Go away fast. Do not touch hive."

"Thank you. I won't touch your home."

A few kids close by yelled at her to watch out for mouseaters. One girl screamed when Emma got down on her knees and reached into the hole. Dozens of the giant bees circled around her; a few landed on her back and arms, said "hello," and flew off. Their presence surrounded her in a buzzing chilly wind. Somewhere behind her, a girl's scream rang out. The wealthy daughter must've seen her covered in giant bees and shrieked like she'd watched a person killed.

An older boy ran up to within two steps behind Emma. "Hey kid, get away from that... it's a mouseater's nest. You're gonna get killed!"

"They won't hurt me."

Emma grasped the Princess Isabelle firefruit and pulled it out with great care not to touch the sides of the hive. As soon as she could, she rolled back onto her feet and retreated from the swarm. Mouseaters took wing, leaping off her back, shoulders, and arms as she walked away from their home. Once none of the insects remained in contact with her, the older boy grabbed her by the armpits and lifted her, hauling her another few paces before putting her down.

He gawked at her. "What are you doing? Those things could'a kilt you!"

"Finding a fruit." Emma faced him, showing off her prize.

One of the townsmen jumped the fence and ran to her. "You stung, girl? Bah. What fool put a fruit in there?"

Emma traced a thumb over her paint. "I think I know."

The man gave her a cursory look-over for bee stings. Finding none, he cautioned her to avoid the nest and returned to his post by the fence. She thanked the older boy for his concern and hurried around the pile of decaying plant matter to rejoin Tam. By now, most of the fruits had been located, though everyone kept searching in hopes of finding one more. As minutes passed, the light weakened.

Braddon clapped a few times. "Alright, children. The Harvest Hunt is over. Everyone please come out from the field and line up with your treasures."

Emma blinked at how dark it had gotten. She pulled Tam over to Kimber and followed the crowd out the gate. All the children lined up in a single file horseshoe, facing the mayor.

"Three," said Braddon, checking the bag of the first boy.

The wealthy girl in the yellow dress and a few other children who found one or two (or zero) fruit left the line and returned to their parents.

"Three." Braddon nodded at the next kid in line.

"Four," said Braddon, patting the head of a village girl with black hair.

The first two boys let off 'awws,' and trudged to their families. Five other kids with three fruits grumbled and walked off.

Emma peered into her bag. She'd found four as well. She eyed Tam's bag, whispering, "How many did you find?"

He looked. "Six."

Emma grinned with pride and ruffled his hair.

Kimber sniffled. "I'as got five."

"It's okay." Emma put an arm around her. "You had fun, right?"

"Yeah." Kimber brightened in an instant. "I'as had lotta fun!"

"Five," called Braddon.

Everyone looked at a scrawny brown-haired boy about Tam's age. He grinned, showing off a lack of front teeth.

A handful of kids wandered back to their families.

Emma left the line, but hovered in front, facing Tam.

Braddon gave her a curious glance.

"I've only got four." Emma held up her bag. "Staying with my brother."

He nodded at her and peeked into Tam's sack. "Six!"

The grinning boy with five kicked at the dirt, but seemed to get over it in mere seconds, and ran back to his mother. Kimber and the rest of the children left the line, except for the little blonde girl who'd almost run Emma over. She held the burlap over her shoulder like some sort of sprite-goblin creature forced to work in the deep mines.

Tam frowned. "I bet she's got more. That girl was runnin' back and forth so fast."

Braddon waddled over to the tiny one. At first, she didn't want to let him near the bag, but after a second or two's coaxing, she held it out. He blinked and reached in to count. "Well, more than six. Closer to fourteen." He patted her on the head. "We have our baby!"

Everyone cheered, though Tam's clap was half-hearted.

Mama and Da emerged from the crowd. Kimber and Tam ran to them, but an odd presence fell over Emma from behind. Flickering firelight framed a shadow of a figure stretching forward past Emma's feet. Someone moved up close enough for her to hear them breathing. She stiffened, staring at her parents. Neither of them looked in her direction, occupied with her over-energetic siblings.

Fear hit a peak, and Emma whirled around.

9

LOST GIRL FOUND

The figure belonged to a young woman with light brown hair to her waist, pulled back in a neat ponytail under a bonnet rimmed with cloth roses in pastel pink and yellow. She had a haunted look in her eyes, made more eerie by her gaunt frame. Her somber expression made her look as if she'd come to announce a death in the family.

Emma put a hand to her heart, gasping with relief. The girl didn't seem threatening, more wounded. "Oh, you scared me."

The older girl looked down for a second.

"What's wrong?"

She clasped her hands and fixed Emma with an unblinking stare as if trying to see into her thoughts.

"I'm Emma. What's your name?"

The girl didn't react.

Emma squinted at her, her brain tugging on a thin strand of familiarity. Something about this girl... She imagined her hair long enough to touch the ground, loaded with forest debris, and no clothing but for a scattering of leaves. "Hannah?"

The girl nodded.

"Oh..." Emma bit her lip. "I'm sorry it took you."

Hannah's distant stare continued.

"The Banderwigh is gone."

Hannah bowed her head.

Emma reached out and held the older girl's hand. "Really gone." She softened her voice to a whisper. "Dead."

The girl lowered herself in place and sat on the grass. Emma glanced back at her parents, hugging each other with the occasional kiss. Kimber and Tam also sat on the ground, each helping themselves to a firefruit, both kids' faces smeared with bright red juice. Many of the kids who'd participated in the hunt had similar thoughts, and the air grew heavy with the smell of cinnamon.

Emma sat facing Hannah. "It made me see awful things, but none of it was real. Did it show you lies, too?"

The teen's forlorn stare moved from Emma to the ground. She grasped a twig and fidgeted it at the dirt.

"I'm so sorry..." Emma squeezed her hand. The creature had only kept her for a day or two... Hannah had lost ten years. No words came to her; what could she say? The cage didn't look like it would've grown. At sixteen, Hannah couldn't have been able to move much at all inside it. How terrifying would that have been? Emma swallowed hard, imagining being trapped in a cage only a little bigger than her. She thought about the vacant look in the girl's eyes when she'd appeared on the trail.

Maybe it hadn't been scary at all... Hannah had stopped caring.

"He used to be a man. A banderwigh got his son, and he went out to find him. They killed the monster, but the axe had a curse. When he touched it, he became a banderwigh too."

Hannah looked up at her with the same sorrowful face. After a moment, she reached out and touched the back of her hand to Emma's cheek. The older girl's lower lip quivered.

Emma grumbled inside. The girl seemed sad for *her* somehow. "I don't blame you for it taking me. It's not your fault. It made you so sad inside it couldn't steal your strength anymore. Banderwighs do what banderwighs do. My Nan told me about them, so I knew it wanted me to be sad and scared." She glanced over her shoulder at Tam and continued in a whisper. "If I was alone, I... might still be gone. It took my little brother too, and I had to protect him."

The girl's frown receded to a neutral expression.

"Please don't feel guilty." Emma smiled at her. "I'm really sorry it took you away from your family for so long, but it's gone now. It can't hurt anyone else."

"Hannah?" asked a heavyset woman with a shock of white in her chestnut hair. "It's getting late, child. Come on home."

A skinny man beside her, somewhat older than Da, kept his arm around the woman. He appeared weary in every sense of the word, but his presence radiated warmth. "Aye, lass, heed your mother."

Hannah twisted the stick into the ground. Minutes passed as she gouged a little hole deeper and deeper.

Emma offered an apologetic look at the man and woman. Watching the girl ignore her parents made her uncomfortable and almost as guilty as if Emma had done something wrong.

"Hannah, your parents are calling."

The teen continued twisting the stick back and forth. She looked up at Emma for a second and returned her gaze to the ground.

Emma put a hand on the girl's shoulder. "What's wrong?"

"He took you, too," whispered Hannah.

Mrs. Abbot gasped and clutched her chest. "Hannah!"

Mr. Abbot grunted, reddening in the face as he supported his wife's weight, lest she collapse.

Emma looked at them, confused, while Hannah continued twirling the stick into the ground.

Mama and Da hurried over at the woman's outburst.

"Are you all right, Ma'am?" asked Da.

"Hannah's not spoken a word since she'd returned," wheezed Mr. Abbot.

Mrs. Abbot fanned herself. "Oh, baby, please say something more. Please come back to us."

"It's dead." Emma leaned forward and to the side, trying to make eye contact with the hunched-over girl hiding behind long, brown hair. "It's really gone forever."

Hannah sat up straight and almost smiled. "I felt it when he died. My dreams are not so full of shadows anymore."

The girl's mother wrapped herself about her husband and sobbed out of joy. He wheezed from the effort needed to hold her upright.

Hannah stood, leaving the stick poking up out of the hole she'd made. "I need to go home now, Emma. It was nice talking to you."

Emma smiled and waved. "Happy dreams."

Mrs. Abbot grasped her daughter in a tight embrace, sobbing into her shoulder. Fathers exchanged grateful, knowing looks, and the Abbots made their way off toward home. Distant cheering signaled the start of the parade. Emma stood on tiptoe and reached up for Da to carry her. He chuckled at her unusual display of childishness, but obliged her.

Smiling, Emma rested her head on Da's shoulder as he carried her back to town, Mama at his side, Tam and Kimber holding her hands.

10

TRAVELERS

*a*n hour or so after morning meal, Emma pushed a broom around while Mama worked at *the cabinet*. Puffs of strong mint, fruit, and a smell like wet moss came and went on the breeze. Kimber wanted to try making cookies again and knelt on a chair by the table mixing dough with Nan's guidance. Stick Knight and Shrub Dragon had it out for the hundred-and-whateverth time on the floor by the fireplace, Tam providing roars and battle cries.

As much as Emma had liked the fancy dress, she felt 'right' again wearing her blue one and hummed happily to herself while stepping around the pile of dirt she'd gathered. She stooped and worked the broom under the kitchen table, catching a moment of mirth at teasing Kimber's toes with the bristles. The redhead tried to move out of the way of sweeping, but as soon as she realized the broom chased her feet, she shot Emma a 'stop it' look. Two seconds later, they both erupted in giggles.

A knock rattled the front door and brought the entire house to a standstill. Being closest, Emma padded over, leaned the broom against the wall, and turned the knob.

Rydh Cooper squirmed under her gaze, scratching at the lopsided curly red mop of hair atop his head, trying to act casual. "Hullo, Emma."

She glared. "What do *you* want?"

Tam scrambled to his feet, clutching Stick Knight and Shrub Dragon to his belly, and zoomed into the side hall to hide in Nan's room.

Rydh raised his hands in surrender. "Pa sent me ta talk with yer momma."

Mama walked up behind Emma and rested a hand on her shoulder. "I'm here."

"Sorry to bother you, ma'am." Rydh couldn't seem to figure out what he wanted to do with his hands. After remembering his pants lacked pockets, he clasped them behind his back. "Me Pa sent me ta ask ya fer help. One'o the cows is with calf an' he's 'fraid they's both gonna die. Not lookin' good."

Emma relaxed. Since he hadn't shown up to antagonize her little brother, she gave him an 'okay, I'll tolerate you' look.

"Of course," said Mama. "Let me gather some things and I'll be along as soon as I can."

"Thank ya, ma'am." Rydh bowed, and ran off.

Emma got back to her chore, working the broom around by the bed.

Mama returned to the crucible full of mixed ingredients and asked Uruleth for endurance. A momentary yellow-green light flooded the rear corner of the room. After transferring the completed potion into a bottle, she put everything back in the cabinet and closed it. Emma paused in her sweeping to quirk an eyebrow at Mama not turning the lock.

Her mother gathered a few items into her satchel and waved Emma over.

She leaned the broom against the shelves holding the family's folded clothes and hurried to Mama's side.

"Em, would you pick up a few things while I'm out?" Mama handed over a pouch of coins. "Apples, grapes, some cheese... also see if the baker has a pumpernickel round. Your father's had a bit of a craving."

"I could use some air," said Nan. "I'll take the walk with them."

"Mother... don't tax yourself."

Nan put her fists on her hips, smirking. "You're as bad as Em. Rushing me into the ground. G'won and tend to those cows." She winked.

Mama walked over to Nan, muttering, but not low enough for Emma to miss it. "Emma needs to know I still trust her."

Emma smiled at the floor. She resumed sweeping as Mama and Nan mumbled back and forth for a little while. Once her mother left, she looked over at Nan. "Why did you put the firefruit in the mouseaters' nest?"

"Oh, found that, did you?" Nan helped Kimber break the cookie dough into portions on a baking iron. "I suspect you asked them not to sting you?"

"Mouseaters are more like bees, not wasps. They only sting when they feel threatened or they're hunting food. I told them I wasn't going to hurt them."

"Do'as 'ey really 'eat mice?" Kimber chewed on her fingers, somehow managing to get a shade paler.

Emma nodded. "Yeah. They can carry mice all the way from the field to their nest."

"Eep," whispered Kimber. "Ia's don' wanna git stung."

"They won't sting people unless they think you're going to attack their nest." Emma gave Nan a playful accusatory look. "*Someone* put my Isabelle firefruit in there."

Nan chuckled. "So you *did* talk to them."

"Was that wrong?" Emma bit her lip.

"No... no..." Nan shooed Kimber off to wash up and carried the iron platter to the oven. "Insects are a little different. Not everyone can speak to them. Your mother can't."

"Oh. Is that bad?" Emma guided the clump of swept dirt to the front door.

"It's more than likely a sign that Ylithir likes you... or perhaps you've gotten Iskarun's attention."

"What's a wolf have to do with bugs?" Emma shoved the dirt onto the porch and shut the door.

Nan added a log to the oven's fire and eased the hatch closed. "Ylithir is known to be cunning. That's like saying 'sneaky,' but without it sounding like a bad thing." She winked. "Clever, too. Some druids think of insects as being beneath animals, lesser things not worthy of attention. Ylithir sees opportunity everywhere."

"Oh."

Nan turned about, smiling and wiping her hands on a cloth. "Well then Em, shall we go or would you prefer to brave town on your own?"

Emma stood on one leg, rubbing her right foot up and down her calf. "Umm. I'm still a little frightened, but if Mama thinks it's safe..."

"I wanna go!" Tam ran in from Nan's room.

"We're going out?" Kimber came in from the back door, hands wet, dress soaked.

Nan laughed. "Did you fall in a lake, girl? I send you to wash your hands and you come back drenched."

"I'as sorry." Kimber flashed a cheesy smile. "Da pump burped."

"Why don't we all go then," said Nan.

A weight fled from Emma's shoulders, and she smiled.

Once Nan collected a black shawl and a walking stick, she led the way down the dirt trail to town. Most of the villagers had left town earlier that morning, headed back to their homes in the outlying fields. Emma wondered if Mama could turn into a bird like Nan, if she'd be tending to all of the villages too instead of only the town. Maybe that's what Nan did whenever she disappeared? She held her grandmother's hand, gazing up at the clouds and trying to picture what it felt like to fly.

"Nan, can you teach me how to turn into a raven?"

The old one chuckled. "I can tell you that Ralthir, the Raven Spirit, is the one who gave me his power. Whether or not he decides to share it with you is not for me to decide."

"Is Mama ever going to learn how to change into something?"

"I wanna be a dragon!" yelled Tam.

Kimber leaned far to the right, took a step, then leaned far to the left. "I'as a mouse. Nae one a'sees mouses."

"It's possible." Nan scratched at her chin. "Beth… Your mother hasn't seemed drawn to any particular spirit yet."

"She always talks to birds," said Tam. "She a bird?"

They reached cobblestones and turned left. The first street lined with houses seemed silent as a tomb and deserted compared to the revelry of the past week.

"When she feels the time is right, if she ever does, she'll learn to take on the aspects of an animal spirit." Nan smiled.

Emma nodded.

They chatted with people along the way, exchanging pleasantries. A few men gave Nan a wide berth, refusing to make eye contact with her and offering deferential bows as they scurried away. Emma shot a questioning glance up at her grandmother, which drew the simple answer of "superstitious fools."

Emma bought a cheese round at the market square, the sharp orange type Da liked best. Two tables over, she selected a number of apples. Her next stop secured a huge bundle of dark purple grapes, each as big as Tam's fist.

Her brother grumbled at how quickly all the performers had vanished. He wanted to watch the man with the glass spheres again; even Mama couldn't explain how he'd made them seem to hang in midair while he moved his hands around them. Tam provided the obvious answer: magic, though he didn't radiate any strange energy like those two musicians had.

They spent a little while wandering around watching the carpenters disassemble the stage. Emma couldn't remember much about the Zaravex play. According to Kimber, she'd spent most of the last two hours asleep on her feet, leaning against Da with her mouth hanging open.

"That's about it then?" asked Nan.

Emma grasped the pouch. The crinkle of paper reminded her of the herbs. "Mama needs herbs."

She thought of Marsten with worry as well as eagerness to make sure he was okay. Emma had to fight not to run to the southeast. The apothecary came into view once she'd gone far enough to the south of the square to see down the street leading from the corner. Her heart leapt with joy at the sight of the door propped open, but her brain stopped when she saw who sat in the two chairs on either side of it.

The skalds.

Emma slowed, but kept going forward. As they passed the candle maker's shop, the feline girl glanced at them and her eyebrows perked up. She wore the same outfit, though she'd removed the shaker from her tail and the bells from her ankle. The mandolin rested on the wall behind her seat. A new accessory, a thin rapier in a scabbard on her belt, made Emma grasp Nan's hand tighter.

Nan seemed fascinated by the elven man, and made the same face Mama often gave Da whenever he had his shirt off.

"Hello," said the woman, tail swishing.

"Well met." The elf stood and bowed.

Emma peered in the door, at a quite healthy-looking Marsten behind the counter, chatting with a younger man in metal armor composed of chainmail and plates.

"Hello," said Emma.

Tam gawked at the woman for a moment. "What are you?"

Kimber covered her mouth in shock and blushed.

Nan stifled a chuckle, and rapped him on the head with one knuckle. "Be polite."

"Oh, it's alright. I am asked that a lot." The woman flowed out of her chair. She didn't look much bigger than Hannah, though she carried herself with the poise of a grown woman. The cat-eared skald glided down the steps and squatted to eye level with Tam, her tail coiling around her feet. "My name is Naluri, and my people are called Simari in your language." She gestured behind her. "This is Feldurin, my traveling companion and friend."

The elf bowed again.

Tam regarded her for a moment, then reached out, petting her head.

Emma's cheeks warmed with embarrassment. She grabbed him. "Sorry."

Naluri laughed. "He's adorable."

"Are you a people or a cat?" asked Tam.

"Both." Naluri stood, a touch shorter than Nan. "Many, many lifetimes ago, the goddess Naraja visited the realm of mortals. She had many suitors, and gave birth to the Simari, among others."

"Are you'as claws sharp?" asked Kimber.

"Do you believe in magic?" Naluri grinned, showing fangs.

Kimber nodded.

"A little of the goddess' magic exists within my kind." She held out one hand. In a brief flash of golden light, her pointy black fingernails more than tripled in length, becoming talons. Kimber leaned back with a gasp. "It's okay, sweetie. I won't hurt you."

Kimber extended a hand and gingerly touched one claw.

At Nan's calm, Emma decided to trust the young woman as well and touched a claw.

"Now it's my turn to ask a question." Naluri winked, and retracted her claws. "My friend and I travel far and wide seeking knowledge and fanciful tales. In Calebrin, we heard tell of a horrible creature defeated by a brave little girl."

Emma bit her lip. "Why do you want to know about that?"

Naluri grinned. "How many stories do you know where a little girl kills a monster? It's usually a big, strong knight or a mysterious wizard with more secrets than spells."

"Or princesses," muttered Tam.

"Did you do magic on the people last night?" asked Emma.

Feldurin descended the stairs with such grace he appeared to be levitating. "Our music carried a minor enchantment, sufficient only to suppress the noise and allow all those in attendance to hear us playing."

Nan smiled at him.

Tam picked his nose. "How old are you?"

"Nineteen," said Naluri. "Oh... you meant him."

Feldurin offered a beleaguered smile. "How old do you think I am, boy?"

"Uhh." Tam wobbled his head side to side. "You're probably real old, like Da. Thirty?"

"If I were thirty, I wouldn't quite be walking yet, and would be smaller than you." Feldurin pursed his lips in thought. "As a human, I'd be about twenty."

"As an elf?" asked Emma.

He tilted his hand side to side. "Close to four hundred."

Naluri held the back of her hand to her mouth as if to hide her words from him. "He's 394. Don't mind him, the Astari are sensitive about their ages."

He overacted a gasp of offense.

Emma giggled. "I'm the girl you heard about. A banderwigh took me an' my brother in the night."

Naluri crouched to get a better look at her. "I thought so. Such rich blue eyes and so pale... not too common a trait. Will you tell me your story?"

Emma looked up to Nan.

"It's your story to tell." Nan smiled. "But remember, a lot of people may hear it. These two are skalds. They make their living telling stories far and wide."

Don't mention spiders. Emma nodded.

She sat on the steps with the musicians, whiling away an hour or so while telling the tale of the Banderwigh. Feldurin produced a vellum and took notes with a quill, while Naluri listened. Every so often, her left ear twitched back to face the doorway. Emma started from when she spotted Hannah emerging from the woods and ended with her breaking the curse. After a short hesitation, she added her well-meaning Da accidentally killing the man, followed by what Nan told her about him being doomed anyway.

"The man would've endured an ordeal most arduous," said Nan. "It was a true kindness to spare him that, even if her father had no idea."

"Mama will be worried," said Emma. "We've been gone quite a time."

"She knows." Nan winked and whistled like a bird.

Naluri tolerated Emma and Kimber feeling her tail fur, and asking numerous questions about Simari. The goddess Naraja had created several different tribes, collectively known as Ailuren. Some embodied traits of tigers, some resembled Emma with dark hair and pale skin, and others had more feline faces, like lions walking on two legs. Naluri preferred meat, but could tolerate vegetables and other foods if she had to.

Feldurin laughed. "Don't let that one have bread... She's trying to trick you." He cringed, waving a hand past his nose. "Empty an entire inn."

Naluri made a playful growl, a sound no human throat could reproduce, and stared at him with narrowed eyes. The beige portions of her face pinked with blush.

"An apothecary is an odd place to find a pair of skalds," said Nan.

"The good shopkeeper has hired us on for a short time. It seems he has an issue with the local filches, and requires some assistance." Feldurin patted a slender elven longsword at his hip. "Playing to fill the hat may allow us to eat, but the man offered quite the wage."

"Oh, those filches aren't local." Nan wagged her walking stick at nothing in particular. "And if they know what's best for them, they'll stay out of Widowswood."

"I hope they do." Naluri curled back up on her chair, pulling her feet under her. "Getting paid to sit around is the best job."

"Hmph." Nan chuckled. "You should run for mayor."

Feldurin chuckled.

Emma waved at the skalds and headed inside. "Mister Marsten!" She ran down an aisle between two shelves full of bins, and leapt up onto the counter, kneeling. "You're okay!"

The herbalist grunted as he got up from his stool. "Aye. Bit sore, but thanks to your mother, nothing I won't forget in a few days." He gave her a brief hug and a back pat. "I'm told I've you to thank as well."

She wiped a happy tear. "I'm glad you're okay. Sorry those men hurt you."

"Not your fault, lass. They're not after you. They came for what ya brought. Shouldn't be an issue now." Marsten gestured at the armored man, and pulled aside his new curtain to reveal a second swordsman in the back. "The Watch are good men, but they can't spend all their time here. Hired on some guards of my own."

She nodded, fished out Mama's note, and handed it to him.

Nan tapped her on the shoulder. When Emma climbed down off the counter, her grandmother pushed Tam and Kimber into her. "Watch them a moment, Em. Looking for a few herbs myself."

Marsten glanced at the note while Nan roamed the shelves. "Hmm. I'm afraid I can't much help you with this list."

"What?" Emma blinked.

"Chives, ginger, saffron, savory, and thyme are not the sort of herbs I deal in." He winked.

Emma hung her head, feeling dumb. "Right. I… didn't ask."

Nan shuffled over with an armload of blue leaves, long yellow mushrooms, and a stringy mass that resembled brown hair. "I've been looking for Dragonsbeard for ages… Where did you find it?"

"That Feldurin chap had some." Marsten chuckled. "Came in here looking to sell it for some extra coin. I wound up hiring them on for a little while 'til things quiet down."

The armored man smiled at Emma, but he didn't unsettle her the way the grey-cloaked man had. Tam hadn't stopped staring at him since they'd come inside. His silvery metal armor looked more expensive than the brigandine worn by the town watch. Between it and his broadsword, the boy likely thought him a knight.

Sensing no malice, she smiled back at him, and waited for Nan to count out coins.

11

SPIRIT OF LIFE

*a*fter dinner, Nan brought Emma outside and sat in the meadow about half way between the house and the edge of Widowswood. Kimber tagged along, curious to hear what the old one would say about spirits and magic, but Tam preferred to spend the time before bed in Da's lap, hearing tales of knights and dragons.

Emma dropped cross-legged at Nan's right, while Kimber knelt at her left.

Nan shook out her sleeves, twisted her hand over, palm up, and cradled a small orb of pale green light. A darker green shape in the middle suggested a feminine outline. The little orb glowed stronger than a campfire, bathing them in sharp shadow.

"This is a gift from Mythandriel, the Spirit of Life."

Emma tilted her head. "Isn't that Uruleth?"

Nan drew a deep breath. "To a point. Uruleth, the bear spirit, embodies life in the sense of being healthy and strong. Druids seek his guidance to gain strength, to mend small wounds, and to endure things they could not endure otherwise.

"Mythandriel is the one who breathed the very light of life into our world. Men like your father think her one of their 'gods,' but that is a simplification for those who are content not to seek deeper understanding."

"Mythandriel is a spirit like Uruleth?" asked Emma. "Not a goddess?"

"Well." Nan chuckled, twirling her hand around the light orb. Wisps of energy trailed her fingertips, coiling and wrapping like glowing smoke. "Linganthas, hear me." Green leafy plant matter welled up out of the ground beneath her outstretched hand. She reached into the center of the growing mass and plucked an unnaturally large carrot. "I will tell your father this is a vegetable. He will say no, it is a carrot."

Emma smiled. "I understand."

Kimber nodded.

"It is both, though such is not the case for all spirits. Gods per se, have a more humanlike temperament, wants, and desires." Nan snapped the front third off the carrot and handed it to Kimber. "Among their kind exist greater gods and lessers." She snapped another piece off, which she gave to Emma. "Lesser deities' power ebbs and flows like the tides. The more followers who exalt their names, the more influence they have." She munched on the remaining third.

Emma ate some of the carrot, nodding.

"I'as knows that." Kimber gnawed on her portion.

"Mythandriel is both a druidic spirit as well as a greater goddess. Their influence does not concern itself with the opinions of mortals. As much as your father's family may disagree with the notion, the natural world and the realm of the gods are not enemies or truly separate."

"Uruleth is a spirit, but not a god?" Emma furrowed her eyebrows. "Because he doesn't have priests?"

"He is an aspect of life, an embodiment of a quality of the natural world. Strength, toughness, physical power." Nan smiled, clutching her fists to her chest.

"And Ylithir is loyalty to his pack and... cunning." Emma nodded. "And he's also not a god."

"Correct. Nor is Ralithir."

"Wha's 'e do?" asked Kimber.

Nan pursed her lips and wagged the carrot at her. "It depends on who you ask. The Raven Spirit is the harbinger of omens. He also represents tenacity."

Kimber tilted her head.

"He's stubborn," said Emma, in a flat tone.

Nan poked her. "*Some* people may tell you he represents trickery and deceit."

Emma flicked her toe at a blade of grass. "Like Da's parents?"

A wheezy chuckle escaped Nan's lips. "Aye. They still think I ensorcelled him to marry my daughter." She raised a hand. "She did that all on her own."

Emma gasped.

"No... you misunderstand me, child. The only magic your mother used on him was what she'd been born with."

"Oh."

"They fell in love." Nan winked. "As natural as the woods around us. Now then, Emma. You've gotten Strixian to lend you the whisper. Uruleth has granted you a small ability to heal. It's time you try something new."

"Linganthas allowed me the Dryad's Step." Emma beamed.

Nan raised both eyebrows. "Really now? Mind telling an old woman how that happened?"

Emma grinned. "Mama told me about it. I tried asking when I went out with Da to get the silk, and he listened."

"I suppose you don't need me to teach you more then." Nan huffed playfully, crossing her arms. As soon as Emma looked worried, she winked. "You are too easy to tease."

"Nan..." Emma frowned.

"Alright." Nan closed her eyes for a second, and waved her hand through the light orb, dispelling it.

Emma blinked at the complete darkness. "Did you make it dark? Why can't I see the stars?"

"You just had a very bright light near your face. It will take your eyes a moment to get used to the change. Don't worry. Now, *you* try and ask Mythandriel for light."

"Mama asked her to heal Kavan." Emma held her hands out in the darkness, picturing the light orb reappearing.

"Channeling the power of a spirit as great as Mythandriel is quite taxing, Emma. Her healing magic is far stronger than that of Uruleth, but you are not ready to call upon that. If she decided to answer you, the strain would be too great for your little body. You would most assuredly fall asleep where you stand."

"Yes, Nan." Emma closed her eyes. "Great Mythandriel, I have not called to you before. I am Emma Dalen. Please grant me a little of your light so that I may not sit in the dark."

She pictured the orb again. *Wanted* to be heard. Wanted to see.

Cool tingles spread up her back and sides, as though a damp breeze had gotten under her dress. The sensation coiled down her arms and over her fingers. An air of mint filled her senses, followed by a gossamer caress across her cheek, the hand of a ghost. Emma concentrated on directing the odd energy flowing around her into the space between her hands and turning it into Mythandriel's light.

Seconds later, a green orb appeared with a faint *pop* and a sputter of green vapor.

"You'as did it!" yelled Kimber.

Nan bowed her head to Emma. "Well done, child."

The peach-sized orb glided around like a curious faerie. Where Nan's had hung unmoving between them, this one zipped about at random. Before long, it settled in a slow orbit around Kimber's head. The redhead gazed in wonder at it. She tried to catch it, but the light passed through her hand.

"Is a faerie?" Kimber chased it with her hand, smiling.

"Not exactly," said Nan. "It is a tiny piece of Mythandriel's light, an elemental spirit of life."

"It's alive?" Emma gawked.

Nan patted her back. "No. It *is* life."

"It likes her." Emma looked up at Nan. "Can Kimber learn magic, too?"

"Perhaps. Our family are far from the only people who can. It depends on if the spirits choose you." She winked. "Could be, Mythandriel likes her."

Kimber held out her hands. "M'thandril, p'ease lemme 'ave a li'l light spirit."

After a few minutes, and no second light orb appearing, Kimber's lip quivered.

"It's okay…" Emma offered a sympathetic look, followed by a mischievous smile. "Maybe she can't understand you."

Kimber narrowed her eyes, crawled around Nan, and thumped Emma on the shoulder. "I'as speakin' roight."

Emma grabbed her in a hug, and they broke into giggles.

Kimber repositioned herself at Emma's side, the orb still hovering nearby.

"You are still a few years younger than Emma. She's only ten and even that's early. I wouldn't worry yet." Nan winked. "Now if you're my age, and it's still not working… maybe Mythandriel didn't listen."

The girls laughed.

Emma paused. She thought about wanting the light to float around in front of them, and it obeyed. At her desire, it moved toward Nan and back. Whenever she stopped thinking about wanting it to go anywhere specific, it resumed meandering.

Nan smiled. "You has the knowing."

Emma growled. "Don't speak goblin." She shuddered. "I don't like those things."

Nan cackled. "No, I imagine you wouldn't."

"Nan? Can I ask something?"

"Of course, Em."

"Mama didn't lock *the cabinet* today. She used to yell at us for even getting too close to it." Emma plucked a small wildflower and stuck it in Kimber's hair. "Why?"

"You already know what's in there." Nan shook her head. "No point now."

Emma thought back to all the odd things she'd seen as a little girl. How Mama whistled at birds, how Nan always seemed to have a raven feather or two in her clothes or room, the potions Mama always gave Da, and how Nan sometimes moved like a much younger woman without the need for a cane. "You were hiding it from me. You both were. I said it was all made up nonsense, and you both let me keep thinking that."

"You are correct." Nan bit the last piece of her carrot with a loud *snap*.

"Did you hide it from Da too?"

"No... the man sees what he wants to see. Though, he's seen too much to keep his head in the dirt. The Banderwigh made sure of that."

Emma blushed. For years, her mother and grandmother had teased her, letting her think she'd been right. She felt like a fool, jester's cap and everything. Her breath shortened, announcing an imminent explosion of tears. "Why did you hide it from me so long instead of showing me it was real?"

Nan rubbed her back. "There, there, Em. Calm yourself. You needed to find it on your own, and come to believe from inside."

Emma blinked, her emotional storm quieted, but her face still glowed with warmth.

"We did not want you accepting things simply because *we* told you this is the way of the world. You are such a good, dutiful child, you would've have accepted it without understanding it. You found it on your own, Em —earlier than either your mother or I thought possible. It's alright if you decide to be upset with us for making you play the fool, but you are stronger for it."

In some way, it did make sense. She thought of the first time trying to speak to the mouse, how difficult it had been to cross that chasm of believing such a thing possible even *after* seeing the Banderwigh. How impossible would that have been if Mama or Nan had merely told her 'go ahead, talk to the mouse?'

"I think I understand."

"Good." Nan ruffled her hair. "Now close your eyes and open yourself to the spirits. Feel the moon, the stars, and the wind on your face. Feel the grass at your feet. We are part of this world, as well as their world."

Emma leaned back, hands on her knees, much as she'd done when she'd first beckoned Greyfang to visit her. She didn't call to anything specific. As Nan instructed, she bared her essence to the spirits as if to say 'I am among you.'

Mythandriel's orb glided by, emanating more warmth than it had moments before. The radiance touched her with physical heat, and stirred a feeling that reminded her of Mama looking upon her with pride.

Out in the endless dark, a yellow-amber glow appeared, a light she did not see with her eyes, for they remained closed. Without opening them, she stared at it. The apparition drew closer and took on the shape of a spectral wolf. A scent like wet fur embraced her.

Ylithir.

She thought the word and it thundered across her mind, so loud she imagined the whole town hearing it. The wolf-spirit's name repeated in a series of echoes, each quieter than the last, until silence returned.

She hadn't called to anyone, yet the Ylithir had shown himself. Emma bowed, feeling grateful and humbled.

After a slight nod of acknowledgement, he strode away into the nothingness.

"Emma," whispered Nan.

She opened her eyes to the sight of her crossed legs and grass.

Nan patted her back. "The spirits do not seek our worship, only our respect."

Emma nodded.

"Come, Em." Nan stood with little effort and reached out to either side. "Kimber."

The girls each took a hand.

"Now you two must commune with the spirit of sleep."

Emma smirked.

FAERIE LIGHTS

O ver the course of several days, the town of Widowswood
continued on as it always had. Emma gradually ceased staring
over her shoulder at every fleeting shadow, as no trace of the grey-
cloaked man had reappeared. The children had returned once to the
stream, and Kimber had only hesitated for a minute or two before joining
them in the water, though she still only went in far enough to sit on the
same rock. While they played in the meadow, Tam brought over a 'cat'
he'd found. Emma had realized with no small amount of horror that her
little brother had detained a skunk. It doused them liberally before Emma
could invoke the Wildkin Whisper, and rendered a polite apology after
the fact, not realizing none of them had meant him harm. The remainder
of that day's light had been spent sitting in the washbasin outside the
house, laughing while Nan repeatedly poured a mixture of herbs over
their heads to get the smell out of their hair.

A week and a day after the Feast of Zaravex, Emma had more or less
forgotten all about the men in Marsten's shop, or that she'd have to visit
the spiders again in two weeks' time.

Emma crawled over the bed to the head-side corner. Flat on her
stomach, she reached down between the mattress and the wall, and pulled
the sheets up. She scampered to the foot end and repeated the process.
With the wall-side free, she scooted to the open edge and hopped to her
feet, gathering the bed linens into a pile.

Out back, the pump squeaked as Kimber washed plates. Tam ran circles around the room, making Shrub Dragon fly and breathe fire on little towns built on the arms of chairs or empty spaces on shelves. Emma carried the bundled linens to the wooden basket set aside for dirty things. After stuffing them in, she headed to the closet in the hall opposite Nan's room to fetch a clean set.

Her grandmother had flown off right after morning meal in search of some rare plant Feldurin had asked about. The Astari claimed he could return in some weeks' time with more Dragonsbeard in trade, and Nan had jumped at the chance.

Emma hugged the fresh linens to her chest and hurried back to the bed, threw them onto the mattress, and proceeded to get into a fight with the giant pillows. They didn't care to be put into pillowcases.

Mama caught Tam, preventing the fiery destruction of yet another imaginary village, and carried him to the front door. "Em, I'm taking your brother to the tailor's. He needs a few tunics since he keeps destroying them."

Tam offered an innocent shrug.

The boy played *hard*.

"You'll be okay for a little while?"

Emma fluffed a sheet out over the mattress and climbed up over the billowing linen. "Yes, Mama. I'll tend to the porch once I've got Nan's bed done."

Mama padded over, kissed Emma on the top of the head, and patted her shoulder. "Good girl."

She beamed.

Tam hung from Mama's arm like a trapped housecat. She set him on his feet by the door, took his hand, and slipped out. Emma crawled around the bed, fitting the sheet to the mattress. That done, she tossed the top sheet and blanket in place.

Kimber walked in with an armload of dripping dishes. "Done! C'we play out inna meadow?"

"I have to change Nan's linens first. Stay on the porch."

"'Kay."

A trail of red hair zoomed out the back door.

Emma jogged to Nan's room. Dozens of talismans, carvings, and feathers on the walls charged the air with energy she'd only acknowledged recently. Before she'd learned of druids, she always thought the feeling came from fear of getting in trouble for going in there. Any one of the items on the wall could have magic in it, and she wondered how long it would be before Nan taught her any of this stuff.

Nan's bed didn't touch the wall, so changing the sheets required less crawling around. She'd just about gotten the clean sheets on when Kimber shouted from the back door.

"Em! Em! C'mere. You'as gotta see!"

"Almost done," called Emma. Grumbling, she picked up the mass of dirty linens and carried them to the basket.

Kimber hung in through the back door, waving at her. "Em!"

"Just a minute." She dropped the dirty sheets in the bin, dusted off her hands, and marched around to the little hallway. "What?"

"I'as saw a faerie!" Kimber jumped up and down.

"Probably a firefly." Emma walked over.

"Nuh uh!" Kimber backed onto the porch, spun, and pointed. "Out by 'a creek."

Emma followed her to the steps, searching Widowswood. "The creek's in the forest. We shouldn't go that far away from the house 'less Mama or Nan are home."

"It nae firefly." She stomped. "M'thandril maybe likes me, an' send a faerie friend like youa's wolf."

Emma bounced down the three steps to the rock trail leading to the privy, but veered left onto the grass. The woods appeared sunny and calm, but nothing came close to glowing or flickering. "I don't see anything. Maybe. Perhaps it's gone."

"Aww." Kimber ran up and took her hand. "C'we please look?"

"Not 'til Mama's back. We shouldn't go into the woods alone."

Kimber smiled. "Not inta woods." She pulled on Emma's arm.

Emma sighed, but allowed Kimber to drag her out across the meadow, about to the spot Nan chose for the lesson last week. With a good fifty yards of grass on all sides, Emma felt fairly safe she could see anything bad coming. Her sister stopped and looked around.

"Ia's saw it there." Kimber pointed at the woods.

Emma stood at her side, arm around her back. *There's nothing there.* "I don't see it."

"Faerie?" asked Kimber.

Something crackled in the distance, like a thin branch snapping under a boot.

"Nothing." Emma squinted at the woods. "We should go in—"

"'Ere 'tis!" Kimber bounced and pointed again.

Emma shifted her gaze about a house width to the right, where a shimmery silver-white light flickered among the trees. "Wha?" An almost musical tone accompanied the glow, a steady peal similar to a bell, changing pitch in time with the glimmer brightening or dimming. "I... what is that?"

"A faerie!" Kimber squealed with glee.

Emma took her hand and walked closer, circling to the right so a large tree trunk blocking the source slid out of the way. After a few paces, a gold and bronze lantern came into view, hanging from a branch. She prepared to sigh in disappointment, until the shape of the brilliant glow inside the beveled glass moved.

A tiny woman stood inside the chamber, banging her fists on the walls.

"Oh, no!" Emma bit her knuckle. "That's horrible! Who would do that?"

Kimber clung to her side and whispered, "I'as said 'ey real."

"Is someone there?" yelled Emma.

They listened only to the whisper of wind in the trees and the quiet pulsing bell-tones for a moment.

"She's trapped." Emma walked to the tree line and peered up at the faerie lantern perhaps another thirty paces in.

The faerie, for it could be nothing else, radiated misery. She resembled a tiny Astari elf with wood-brown skin and silver-white hair, but the size of a small doll. Her metallic silver butterfly wings appeared mashed up like someone had stuffed silk napkins in a glass bottle. Despite not having wings, Emma cringed at the sight with sympathetic pain.

Overwhelmed with pity, she ran up to the base of the tree. The lantern hung from a knot of rope affixed to a branch a good ways up. If Da were here, she could stand on his head and still not reach it.

The light dimmed as the faerie stared at Emma, her miniature mouth opening and closing as if she screamed, but only melodic tones made it out of the lantern. She waved and pointed at the girls, pounded on the glass, and pointed again.

"She's in pain," said Emma.

"Ia's not wanna be in ae bottle." Kimber shook her head. "Frow a rock an' break it?"

"That could hurt her." Emma approached the tree, sizing it up for a proper handhold. "Wait here, I'm gonna climb."

"Mmm!" yelled Kimber, muffled.

Emma glanced back at the strange sound. A man in a cloak had grabbed Kimber from behind, covering her mouth with a cloth.

Before she could scream, black-clad arms grasped Emma from behind and mashed a gooey-damp rag over her face. Nauseating strong mint and herbal essence smashed into her throat. She gagged as the world swam into a spinning mess.

"Mmm!" yelled Emma before coughing from the overpowering substance on the cloth. She squirmed and kicked, but with each second, her arms became slower, her vision blurrier. "Mmm…"

The cold touch of leaves met her cheek. For a second, her vision cleared enough to perceive Kimber unconscious on the forest floor a few feet away. She tried to reach for her, but her arm refused to move.

Everything swirled into a blur and faded to darkness.

MORE FRIGHTFUL THINGS

a foul herbal taste lingered in Emma's mouth. Her head hung like a stone from her neck, wobbling about on its own. She found it difficult to breathe. Each intake of air caused tightness to press in on her chest. Her eyes peeled open. Pale blurs sharpened to her legs, a dark spot becoming a mass of coarse rope tied about her ankles.

Fear killed her grogginess in an instant.

She lifted her head, gazing around at earthen walls and wooden shelves. Roots laced across a dirt ceiling overhead, gathering in clusters around wooden braces. Across the room, a stairway led up to a dark wooden door flat in the ceiling. Daylight seeped in from gaps surrounding the frame. Cold dirt under her bum had soaked her dress damp. Emma struggled to move her arms, but rope chafed at her wrists behind her back. A thick coil about her chest pinned her arms to her sides, securing her to a roughhewn wooden support column.

To her left, on the far side of the room, a line of shelves held burlap bundles and a few small barrels. Closer on the right, a decaying mass of old wood-handled farm tools leaned against the dirt wall, their heads well rusted into uselessness. Coils of moldy rope hung on pegs above, next to a few cobweb-filled lanterns and one rotting saddle.

Kimber slumped at her left, head lolled against hers. Her little sister had been bound the same way, their shoulders touching. Pale green residue crusted around her mouth, as though she'd vomited watery pea soup and it dried.

Emma tried to wipe her mouth on her shoulder sleeve, certain a similar substance smeared over her face as well. *Dreamroot. If it gets wet again, it'll put me to sleep.* Her squirming woke Kimber, who moaned. It took the girl a moment to lift her head and take in her surroundings, after which she screamed.

"Kimber," said Emma. "Shh. It's okay. We'll be okay."

Her little sister spent a few seconds struggling so hard she broke out in a sweat. "No! Is not gon' be 'kay. We'as tied!"

As Kimber resumed squirming, Emma struggled to free her arms. She wanted more than anything to hug and hold on to her terrified sibling, but she could barely move. Not being able to embrace her sister changed fear into anger. Emma twisted her hands about, snarling and gasping whenever the rope bit her. "They won't hurt us. I won't let them."

After giving up and hanging limp, Kimber bawled.

"Shh." Emma leaned her head against Kimber's. "I'm right here. Don't be scared. Mama or Nan or Da will find us." *Ylithir, please guide them to us.*

"I'as scared." Kimber tried to sit up away from the pole, and let out a series of soft grunts while fighting the ropes around her chest. Her desperation to hug Emma caused her to cry out of frustration.

A few minutes later, Kimber gave up and sat still, sniffling while leaning against her.

Emma stretched her feet out, examining the rope. A dark substance smeared the knot between her ankles, tree sap or something like it. She pulled at her hands again, but the coarse, painful rope afforded almost no room to wiggle.

Kimber's sobbing melted to sniveling.

Emma looked down at herself. All the rope wound around her middle went outside her arms, but whoever'd tied her didn't seem to care too much if it let her breathe. Tightness gouged her elbows into her sides. She shimmied about, trying to slide down, but didn't get far.

Kimber pressed herself into Emma as much as she could, trembling.

"Don't give up yet. Let me see your hands," whispered Emma. She squirmed to reach to her left, fumbling blind for the cord around Kimber's wrists. It took a moment of straining, but she found it. Hard, smooth patches coated the knot, likely the same substance gluing the rope on her legs. "Oh, no."

"Wha?" Kimber's fingers squeezed around hers.

Emma looked about, searching for a rock or something sharp anywhere she could conceivably twist herself to reach, but spotted only blank dirt, bits of rotten wood, and a beetle or two.

The door clattered with the rattle of metal and keys.

Kimber gasped, shrinking against her.

Emma stared at the door. A dark shadow moved across the rectangle of daylight. She drew her knees to her chin, trying to hide behind her dress. The door creaked upward, swinging to the left, letting sunlight fall in on a worm-eaten wooden plank stairway.

A skinny man with straw-blond hair, clad in leather armor and a grey cloak, descended the stairs, ducking his head past the far end. The ceiling gave him an inch or so of clearance, making him appear huge.

He folded his arms, the flared bits of his leather gloves jutting out, and regarded the girls with a look of mild amusement. "You know hairs ya glad?"

Emma blinked.

"Brown bread," said Kimber, in a timid near-whisper. "Couple creeks."

"Ach." The man shook his head. "Wretched sot had it comin' bein' such an ogre to ya. Buck up, child. You'll not be hurt by anyone here."

"Please," whined Kimber. "Le' me gnomes. I nae rattle."

The girl's gone nutters. Emma squirmed, gritting her teeth as hairy rope stung her wrists. The coil refused to let her fill her lungs, so she sipped air in a series of rapid, short breaths.

"So..." The man stooped over Emma. "You're the one getting all the silk, are ya?"

Her mind raced. She could lie, threaten him, act terrified and hope they'd feel bad, or maybe play dumb, but she didn't trust what would happen if they believed it. It couldn't take long for Mama to find them. Widowswood Town had lots of dogs. Mama could ask one to sniff her trail. All she needed to do was keep herself alive until help showed up.

"Yes, sir."

"Good, good." He patted her on the head.

Emma bristled at being touched, but had nowhere to go.

"Here's what's going to happen. In a little while, you're going to go fetch us a nice fat bundle of it, from wherever it is you keep finding it. We'll make sure no harm comes to ya."

"Okay. I will. But you should let her go."

The man winced. "Terribly sorry, luv. Kinnae do. For one thing, she knows you're here. She a'say she no rattle, but everyone say 'at. Soon she's flown, she sings."

"No," whispered Kimber. "I donnae rattle. Gnomes... please."

"The other reason." The man lifted Emma's head with a finger under her chin. "So long as she's with us, we know you'll behave and do as you're told."

Kimber broke into sobs again.

"Oh, hush, child." The man fixed some of Kimber's hair out of her face. "If Emma doesn't behave, we wouldn't hurt you. We'd take ya back where ya b'long, raise ya a proper filch like's in yer blood."

"No," Kimber wailed, sniveling. She rocked about as much as the rope allowed. "Please... I don' wannae. I'as 'ave right gnome."

Emma jostled from the smaller girl's efforts to free herself. "If you're going to let us go after you get silk, take me now."

"Waitin' on the damn finger wiggler." The man spat to the side. "Blighter's late, as always. This be his show. If'n either of ya need somethin', scream a bunch and we'll come see."

Emma glared at him as he walked away and jogged up the stairs. The door came down with a deafening *slam* that made her jump and gasp.

"I'as scared," whispered Kimber. "I wanna go home."

Emma leaned left, touching heads. "Me too. Mama will find us."

Minutes dragged into at least an hour. The random voice of a man or nicker of a horse came from outside, along with the occasional laugh or clank of something metal. Kimber struggled, whimpered, and went still in a repeating cycle.

Despite sitting still, the ropes felt even tighter than when she'd awoken. The Banderwigh's cage had at least let her move around a little. Fear clawed into the back of her mind, and the tears came, streaming down her face. She resisted the urge to scream for her parents, but once the dam broke, she couldn't stop crying. Whenever she thought of Mama, guilt grew heavier. How scared and worried were they now?

Emma's weeping got Kimber bawling again. Every time the girl thrashed against the rope, it pulled at Emma's chest. Each tug made the sense of being trapped close in on her. Did she disobey again? They hadn't really left home too far. Had the faerie ever been real? Would these men have come into the house after them? *Probably.* She sniffled, pressing her face into her knees to wipe away tears.

"Was'a Banderwigh scary like 'dis?" Kimber looked over.

"No." Emma let her head lean back against the wood, and took a few deep breaths, trying to calm down. Tears dripped from her jaw. "This is scarier."

Kimber raspberried. "Naw. How 'dis scarier 'an a critter like 'at? Thieves ain' made o' darkness an' ice."

She spent a moment trying to get a finger on the nugget of rope between her wrists. The same hard resin fused it, frustrating any attempt to pick at the knot. "I knew it wouldn't hurt us. It wanted to keep us for a long time." Emma closed her eyes. *Ylithir help me.* "There's more frightful things than banderwighs."

Kimber trembled. Her face reddened and she started to cry again.

Emma cringed inside. *Oops. I just scared her more.* "I mean... the Banderwigh wasn't scary 'cause I knew how to thump him." She squirmed her legs back and forth, but the rope failed to give. "He was gonna do worse ta me an' Tam than thieves. These men won't eat our happiness and leave us empty like Hannah." She scowled at the dark bindings, hating them more than a cage that had no way to open. "They won't hurt us because they want something from me, and they know I won't give it to them if they hurt you."

"'Kay," whispered Kimber. Instead of bursting into tears, she huddled against Emma's side, trembling. "Ia's wanna go home."

"I do too." Emma tapped her foot on air while studying all the tools and supplies around them. There had to be *something* she could do.

IN THE DARK AND COLD

*E*mma sat still for a little while, until she could no longer tolerate the feeling of being trapped. She rocked side to side, hoping to stretch the rope or loosen something enough to slip out. If she could get off the post, maybe she could chew Kimber's hands free, or hop over to the old farm tools and find a blade. At least struggling felt like trying. Sitting there like a lump and crying felt like giving up.

Kimber wriggled as well, trying to get her heels under her. She pushed at the ground, but succeeded only in flinging sprays of dirt.

A few minutes later, they both stopped, out of breath.

"They'as not gonnae let us go." Kimber sniffled. "If they'as know you kin keep gettin' silk, they'as gonnae keep us f'rever."

Emma's tears ran down her face despite her trying to stay calm. "N-no. They're not going to keep us. They're just men, not monsters. There's no magic hiding us. Someone will find us. They can't want *that* much silk. I'll…" She stopped crying in an instant and grinned. "I know."

"What?" asked Kimber, mouth agape.

"When they make me get silk." Emma looked at the door for a second, and dropped her voice to a whisper. "I'll tell the Spider Queen that we've been kidnapped. The thieves won't know what I say to them. The emerald creepers can help."

"They'as do 'at?" Kimber's green eyes widened with hope.

"Maybe…" Emma smirked. "She *did* almost eat me."

"Wha' if she donnae give yas silk 'cause they'as forcin' ya?" Kimber grunted, shifting more upright to take a breath.

"They'll have to let us go then." Emma nodded. *Or cut our throats.* She trembled. "They only took me because I can get silk. If I can't get silk, they won't need me."

"If they donnae fink we know tae much."

Emma cringed. "We don't know anything."

Her thoughts ran away with how things could go. The spiders would help, and attack the thieves. They'd sneak into the... wherever she was, and sting the rest of the thieves and set Kimber free... or the queen would laugh and deny the silk. The thieves would threaten her with something like get silk or you'll never see Kimber again. She'd beg the queen to do something to help, but would she? Nan said spiders could be selfish. The wolves risked their lives to help her, but it didn't sound like spiders would do the same.

Nervousness got her trembling, and the chilly cellar didn't help.

She leaned against Kimber, waiting, hoping in the quiet dark. They'd been put to sleep by Dreamroot... who knows how far away from home the thieves took them. Emma couldn't decide if it would be worse to be only a five-minute walk from home and have no one notice her, or be fifty miles. She'd heard horses, so more than likely, they'd traveled a fair way.

The locking bar rattled. Emma gasped and went as still as she could. With a creak and a clatter, the door at the far end of the root cellar opened and a different man walked in. He looked younger than the first, with dark hair and a grey cloak over a drab green tunic. She figured him for maybe eighteen. He had two daggers and a shortsword, but no armor, and managed only the briefest glance in Emma's direction before he looked away.

Kimber sniveled and whined again. "Please let us go."

The man walked faster along the left wall, moving past them. Kimber leaned to her left to look at him, but Emma couldn't see him through the post. He rummaged about for a little while and returned carrying a bundle of burlap.

"Please..." Kimber whined.

The man kept staring at the wall, obvious in his effort to avoid looking at them.

Emma sensed guilt, and whimpered as well.

He stopped, halfway between them and the stairs. After heaving a sigh, he trudged over and halted a few inches from their toes. "You two thirsty or somethin'? Wanna blanket? Yer both shiverin'."

Emma strained to lean forward. "Please help us. You look sad. I know you're not mean like that other man."

"We's no' gonna rattle." Kimber wriggled. "I'as scared. Please lemme gnomes."

The man picked at the bundle, still refusing to make eye contact with them. "Look... You're just a pair of little kids. This ain't the kinda thing any of us like doing. None of the boys are happy about... this"—he gestured at them—"treatin' you like this and all, but there's a wizard throwin' kingscoin at us for this job and them's not the kindsa people you wanna get angry at yas."

"He won' know." Kimber bounced. "Please... I'as scared. Bring me druther, an' she may fines and sparkies."

Emma glanced at Kimber. "Can't you see she's so scared she's speaking nonsense?"

"Sorry." The thief sighed, his contrite expression made him seem almost sorry for them. "You sure you don't want some water or a blanket or something?"

"I should tell you." Emma puffed herself up against the ropes. "My Da is the captain of the watch at Widowswood."

"Oh, is that so?" The man chuckled. "Watch captain of a tiny little town out in the sticks? We're from Calebrin, kid. Ain't worried 'bout no farmer's militia."

Emma fumed and squirmed. "My Da's not a farmer! If I could move, I'd thump you for saying that."

"You'as wrong." Kimber's eerie calm stalled Emma's rage. "Tha' no bawisters here. Pa kin do anyfing he wants ta the likes o' you lot. You boys kidnappin' *both* his daughters. What you fink he gonna do a' ya?" She shook her head. "Ain' gon' be prison. He gon' lop yer heads right off."

The man grumbled. "We can handle a ragin' guard. Madder he is, better for us."

Emma slumped forward, crying. Half an act, she hoped pity would work better than fear.

"Dammit." He looked away from them. "Calm down, kid. None of the boys are goin' to hurt you. All we want is the silk. That's it. I'm not gonna risk havin' my spirit thrown all over the place on account o' getting masself killed by a wizard."

"What?" asked Emma, adding a long sniffle.

"Dead to a wizard, all sorts o' bad stuff happens. Restless spirits, ya know? Wraiths, haunts... I ain't spendin' the next five hundred years stuck wanderin' these damn woods."

Emma grumbled. She tried to stand to intimidate him, but her feet slipped out from under her before the rope around her chest let her move even an inch upward. "My Nan's a druid. A forest witch." She narrowed her eyes. "A wizard spell would kill you quick." She snapped her finger behind her back. "Druid poison would take days... and maybe Nan'll turn you into a pig before she kills you, so you're stuck as a ghost pig."

"Uhh... ehh..." He backed up a few paces before he ran for the stairs, almost dropping the bundle in his haste to get out of the root cellar.

The door slammed and the locking bar sealed with a *thunk*.

Kimber shifted toward her, face hidden behind curly red hair. "I'as fink ya scared him tae much."

"Yeah." Emma huffed, blowing hair off her eyes.

"Do you'as fink Nan'll turn 'em inta pigs?" whispered Kimber.

"I was just trying to scare him so he let us go." Emma fidgeted. "Nan will wrap 'em up in roots so Da can bring 'em to jail."

Kimber wiggled her toes. "I don'ae like jail."

"What?" Emma blinked. "They put you in jail?"

"Naw." Kimber shook her head, tossing her hair about. "Papa. I'as sleep inna alley 'hind tha jail till 'e git out. S'why we lef' Cal'brin City." She tapped her big toes together as she kept whispering. "Is big an' dark an' scary. I donnae wan' be a thief 'cause I scared o' jail." She went still and peered at Emma past a few curly strands of red. "Why don' these men a'scared o' jail. Why they take us?"

Emma narrowed her eyes at the door. "Because they're stupid."

"Yeah," whispered Kimber.

"And mean."

"Yeah," said Kimber. "Stupid an' mean."

Emma wasted another few minutes fighting a pointless battle against rope. "Don't be scared. We're still in the forest. Nan or Mama will find us."

Kimber bowed her head. "Wha if'n we not inna woods nae more?"

"We are." Emma studied the roots jutting out from the dirt ceiling. "They want silk, so they won't have taken us too far."

"You shoul'd nae 'ave scared tha' boy 'way." Kimber shivered. "Ia's cold, an he'as gonnae give us a blanket."

Emma huddled close to her. "Sorry. I'm cold too."

TALKING NONSENSE

*E*mma sagged limp, staring at the root cellar door as she struggled to breathe in spite of the tight coil of rope squeezing around her middle. The more she tried to sit still, the more she couldn't resist the urge to struggle. Being angry didn't help. She fumed in silence for a little while before she bowed her head. Kimber squirmed, still trying to work herself loose. Emma didn't see the point in fighting, but did it anyway. She frowned at the sap-glued knot between her ankles, daydreaming of Da bashing down the door and freeing them with a single swipe of his sword. Only the knowledge that these thieves had taken her to a real place and not some impossible room with an impossible cage allowed her to stop from surrendering to fear.

Tears kept flowing despite her best efforts not to cry.

Kimber squeezed against her, toes sinking into the dirt. "We'as stuck."

Emma bit her lip while digging at the hard patch on the knot binding her wrists. A bit flaked off. A tiny sliver of hope beat none at all, so she kept picking at it. "Don't give up."

"I'as scared." Kimber sniffled.

"They're just thieves. Not monsters. Nothing magic about them." Emma grumbled, again trying to wriggle up or down to ease the pressure around her chest. "It'll be fine."

"Em?"

She went still and looked to her left. "Hmm?"

Kimber managed a weak smile. "You'as nae a good fibber. Fank yas for lettin' me be your family, e'en if t'was only fer a bit."

"No." Emma strained against the rope, but failed to break it. "They are not going to hurt us. Don't talk like that."

"...like this one little bit," said an approaching man outside.

Two sets of scuffing boots approached the door.

Emma froze, barely breathing. The rope around her chest tugged and squeezed with Kimber's continued attempts to escape.

"Careful, friend." A second man made a low whistle. "Wrong person hears you airin' grievances about a chartered job, you gonna have bigger problems."

"It just ain't right involvin' wee children." The first man spat. Shadows broke the line around the door, a figure blocking the fading sunlight. "This ain't what we do."

Emma leaned into the ropes. *Please... Please...*

"You're gettin' all a tither over naught." A third man with a deep voice chuckled. "Them kids ain't gonna be harmed. Not like we usin' em as leverage er nothin' 'gainst the father. Ain't no unseemly deeds ta be done if somethin' ain't paid."

"We're goin' about this all wrong," said the first man. "Do either of you believe some little girl gathered a pile of creeper silk that big on her own? She's a damn messenger. Someone has her carryin' it, an' I bet she got nae idea what it be worth. We oughta be goin' after whoever's gatherin' it."

"Told ya havin' a kid o' yer own would make you soft," said Deep Voice. "Garris overheard the little one in that herbalist's place. She got it straight from the creepers."

Someone scoffed. "Balderdash. A little girl got anywhere near them things, she'd not come back."

"Hey... what all that about the forest witch stuff?"

Emma bounced. The third man sounded like the younger thief she'd scared off.

"Forest witch?" asked Deep Voice. "Boy, I thought you was older 'an that ta believe in such stories. Ain't no such thing as no forest witch, nor a 'curse of Widowswood.' Been out here in the weeds too long."

"Look, Ben... They're just a pair of wee girls. I"—the first man sighed —"think we should forget this whole thing, wizard and all. Nothing good will come of it."

"Yeah. We kin wait 'til dark an' set 'em loose in the woods. I think they'll keep quiet," said the young thief.

"Yes... yes, we will," whispered Emma.

Kimber nodded.

"And who takes the blame for that?" asked Ben.

"We all act surprised," said the first man. "Maybe they got out?"

"Rorick tied them knots," said Ben. "No one would believe a pair of kids got loose. Ten-year guildsmen can't worm their way outta his work without a blade."

"They're just children," said the young thief. "What are we doing?"

"Two thousand kingscoin, friend." A clap like a shoulder pat echoed twice. "For that much, them sprogs ain't goin' nowhere. Now, I understand ya. I do. If I thought for a minute them girls'd get hurt, I'd be the first one down the steps ta cut 'em loose. But, this is guild business, and a *lot* of money. I'm not puttin' my head on a spike over a pair o' guys who can't stand the sight o' a couple of tears."

Emma grumbled.

"It ain't right," said the first man. "I got one of my bad feelings 'bout all of it."

"He ain't ne'r been wrong before," said the young thief.

Ben laughed. "That's 'cause there's a wizard about. They're made of bad feelin's and fire. Don't forget it."

The crunch of boots on dirt moved away from the door.

"They'as nae gonna 'urt us," whispered Kimber.

"There's a wizard." Emma trembled. "They'll do whatever he tells them to do."

Emma struggled again, which got Kimber fighting her ropes as well. Some minutes later, they collapsed, exhausted.

"You'as gonna fink o' somethin'?" asked Kimber. "You'as got 'way from the Banderwigh."

"I'm thinking..." Emma studied the cord around her ankles while feeling at the rope between her wrists. It hadn't loosened at all. She looked up at the thick wooden post. One of Nan's roots could tear it down, but that might cause the whole cellar to collapse... and she probably couldn't summon a root that large anyway. "All I can do is make light and talk to animals." She sniffled.

"And beat up banderwighs." Kimber grinned.

Emma giggled in a whisper, despite wanting to bawl. Not caving in to sadness worked for a magical creature, but thieves wouldn't care how she felt. She picked at the knot between her wrists for almost an hour in silence.

"Eep! No! No!" yelled Kimber. She thrashed in a panic. "Get it 'way!"

"What?" Emma tried to reach behind her to hold Kimber's hand. "Calm down... what's wrong?"

Her little sister struggled so hard it almost seemed as if the post moved. "T-there's..." She wheezed.

"Kimber. Stop. Look at me."

The redhead went still, staring at her with tears rolling down her face, her mouth half open, her breaths tossing hair with each puff.

"Okay. What's wrong?" Emma furrowed her eyebrows. "Except for us being tied up in a root cellar."

Kimber whined. "Ia's sees a dirty rat!"

"A rat?" Emma shot upright as much as she could. "Where? That's perfect!"

"Wha?" Kimber looked horrified. "How's 'at?"

Emma tried to calm her racing heart. Three breaths later, she opened her eyes. "Strixian, pleeeease give me the Wildkin Whisper."

Tiny ethereal orbs of dancing light swirled around in front of her before seeping into her chest through the coil of rope.

"Where is the rat?"

Kimber pointed with her feet to the left.

Emma scrunched herself as far forward as she could and caught sight of a fuzzy black hairball among the burlap-wrapped provisions. She focused on it. "Hello? Mr. Rat?"

The critter whirled about and perked up on its hind legs, head darting left and right.

"Mr. Rat? Please..."

"Speaks? Humans speak?" It held its paws to its mouth as if in shock.

"Yes. I do. Will you please help us?" Emma bounced with glee.

"You'as say I talkin' nonsense." Kimber blinked. "You'as makin' squeaks. Anna rat lookin' at us! Eww!"

The rat scampered closer, sniffing at the air with one raised paw.

"Eeee..." Kimber recoiled, curling up. "Go 'way!"

"Don't be afraid of him." Emma let her feet slide forward, legs flat on the ground.

The rat crept closer, hopped up on her shin, crept past her knee, and perched sitting on her thigh. "Speaks the human, what it wants?"

"Can you please chew the ropes so we can get out?"

Kimber sat rigid. "I'as donnae wanna get rat bit."

"He won't bite us." Emma looked back to the animal in her lap. "Please?"

The rat groomed himself for a few seconds. "Wants in return something."

Emma bit her lip in thought. "Umm. I can bring you home with me and give you a nice warm place to sleep, and food?"

The rat raised both paws over his head. "Agreements."

He scampered down her leg and got to gnawing on the rope binding her ankles. The grinding *crunch, crunch, crunch* of rat teeth seemed far louder than it should. Emma stared at the door, trembling from her worry one of the thieves would walk down at any minute and catch the rat.

"If another human comes down the stairs, hide."

"Yes. Hides."

Emma squirmed at the whiskers tickling her feet. The rat chewed and chewed. Kimber stared in rapt wonder.

"Rat's doin' 'et," whispered Kimber.

"Yes."

After an agonizing few minutes, the rope broke open, and Emma pulled her feet apart. He climbed up and over her shoulder before scooting down her back. Tiny claws needled at her skin as he held himself upside down. The gnawing noise seemed to crawl up her spine and slither into her right ear. Every *crunch* of tooth on rope tugged at the topmost cord around her chest.

She kept staring at the door. *Please don't come down here. Please stay away.*

Eventually, the rope snapped and the entire coil around her middle went slack. She flexed her arms to the sides while squirming back and forth to widen it enough to slip loose. Kimber grinned. Emma scooted her butt forward and slid herself down out of the coil before falling over on her side. When the rat sniffed at her hands, she held still and waited for him to chew at the binding on her wrists. Soon, that rope failed as well, and she leapt to her feet.

"Yay!" whispered Kimber.

Emma hurried to the pile of decaying farm tools and found a small wheat sickle. While the rat gnawed at the rope on Kimber's ankles, Emma sawed at the bundle about her chest. Once she got her sister free from the post, she cut her hands loose.

She tossed the sickle aside and wrapped her arms around Kimber.

They hugged for a few seconds, sniffling and crying tears of happiness. Emma squatted and scooped up the rat, holding him nose-to-nose.

"Thank you Mr. Rat. You saved us." She set him on her shoulder. "Hold on."

"Me saved. Yes. I hero." The rat crawled around behind her neck and poked its head out under her right ear.

Emma crept over to the stairway. The door at the top resembled one belonging on the front of an old house, only laid flat on the ground. A chilly breeze rolled in the gaps between wood and dirt, carrying the scent of wet grass. She crawled up to the door, braced her back against it, and pushed with both legs, but it didn't move. Grunting, she relaxed gradually so it wouldn't make noise. If anyone outside saw the door move, everyone would know they'd escaped.

"Is a right windup," muttered Kimber.

"Why are you talking nonsense?" whispered Emma.

"Not nonsense." Kimber shook her head. "Is thief talk. So's people donnae know wha' they say. Gnome means home 'cause it rhymes, but 'gnomes' mean 'goin' home.' Ia's said it locked."

"No, you didn't. You said it's a windup."

"It locked. Lock rhymes wif clock. Clocks ya wind up." Kimber shrugged. "Easy."

Emma blinked. "That makes no sense at all."

Kimber grinned. "Nae s'posed tae."

"Shh." Emma crawled up to put her face near the door and peered out the gap.

From her angle, she could make out a tree line suggesting a clearing in the woods, and a bit to the left an ancient-looking house. The place would've been scary even if they hadn't been taken from home and locked in a cellar. Broken windows, crumbling walls, and black, falling shingles almost guaranteed a ghost or ten lived there.

Emma gulped. She shifted to the other side of the door, but couldn't see much more than sky and grass roots sticking out of the dirt around the wooden frame.

"Ain't gonna be me, I'll say that much," said a man outside.

Emma crouched. Kimber crawled up half on top of her and put her chin over her left shoulder.

"Wha'as they sayin'?" whispered Kimber.

"Shh," whispered Emma.

"Rorick's order is for at least six of us to go, and there's only nine here."

"I hate spiders," said an unfamiliar man. "I can't go. Even the little ones give me the heebies, and them green ones is the size o' dogs."

"What're we waitin' on anyway? The whole bloody town's gone inta the woods. Who the heck is that girl?"

"That girl is the key to a fortune," said Ben, the deep voice. "They know what they got."

"Forget the wizard. Let's take 'er now, get the silk, and be done with it."

"Gods take you! I am not goin' into Widowswood at night."

"Everyone quiet down," said Ben. "You're all goin' to have to get used to spiders. The Eyes are going to become the most renowned guild in all of Loth Moraine with this opportunity. We'll control all the creeper silk. Wizards will beg us to trade with them. That li'l girl might look like a child, but she's a pile of gold big enough to choke an archbishop."

Five or six men laughed.

Emma gulped. "T-they're not gonna let me go..."

Kimber's breath puffed warm at her ear. "I'as tol' ya so. We'as gotta 'scape."

"No chews door. Too large," said the rat.

Emma felt around the door for the locking bar. Halfway along the right side, a metal rod as big as Da's thumb went into a bracket. She stuck her fingers up to touch it and wiggled at it for a few minutes, but couldn't get it to move.

Kimber clamped on, trembling. "I don' wannae go to Calebrin. I wannae go home."

Emma backed down the steps and held her the way Mama always held Emma whenever she'd had a fright. Seated across Emma's lap, hands at her chin, Kimber cried in soft sobs. Emma stroked her hair, pulling it out of her face.

"Shh, Kimber. It's okay. We're almost out." She held up her rope-burned wrist. "Nothing can hold us."

Emma whispered to Uruleth, calling a little healing magic to mend their chafed and bleeding skin. Oh, how good it felt to be able to take a full breath again.

Kimber sniveled. "I wan' Mama..."

"Of course!" Emma gasped.

Her little sister lifted her head, tears replaced with confusion. "Wha?"

Emma eased her to the side, sitting her on the steps, and crawled back up to the door. "Mama... what does she always do?"

"Loves us... makes us food. Teaches us..."

"At the window?" Emma closed her left eye, and peered through the gap with the other, scanning the trees.

Kimber clapped. "Mama talk tae birds!"

I don't see any... too many leaves. She concentrated on the thought of birds, of Ralithir. She took a deep breath and focused on 'yelling' to them. "Can any birds hear me?"

"Shh," whispered Kimber. "Don't whistle sae loud. They'as hear ya."

"I need help," tweeted Emma. "Please come closer."

A handful of starlings emerged from leaves of brown and gold, hopping to the tips of branches. Amid a flutter of feathers, a medium-sized crow landed at the corner of the door and tilted its head to put one eye over the gap.

"Thank you," said Emma. "Will you please take a message for me?"

"I know you," said the raven. "You're the child of the child of Ralithir's chosen."

Emma's heart pounded with joy. "Yes! These people have kidnapped us. Will you please go find her and lead her here?"

"I will do this for you, daughter of the daughter of the Raven." The bird vanished in a blink.

Emma padded down the stairs and tackled Kimber into a spinning hug. Before their energy got too high, she pulled the girl around under the steps and made a 'shh' sign. "A bird is going to fetch Mama."

Kimber nodded.

Huddled against the earthen wall with her sister, Emma looked up at the underside of the steps, and waited. She eyed the bundles stacked along the right side wall, considering grabbing some burlap to hide under, but the sudden worry a thief would open the door as soon as she moved kept her still. The rat perched on her shoulder. She scratched under his chin, causing him to brux happily.

Mama, please hurry.

A FEW PICKPOCKETS

*T*he tromp of boots grew loud at the top of the steps. Emma squeezed Kimber, and held her breath. Once the thief walked away, she exhaled. After a moment of quiet, she relaxed a little more.

"Should hide in' aire." Kimber pointed at the mass of provisions piled against the wall. "Unner 'a stairs 'ey kin find us easy."

"If someone comes down here, we can run up the steps behind them before they turn around."

Kimber shook her head. "They'as gonna grab one of us. Kin see we'as nae tied ta the pole nae more."

True enough. The post with the empty coils of rope still hanging from it sat less than twenty feet away in a direct line from the stairs.

"But they have to come all the way down to get their heads past the roof. We can climb up the side and run."

Kimber scrunched up her face while thinking.

Cracka-Boom!

A brilliant white flash outlined the door at the same instant a tremendous peal of thunder rolled overhead.

Kimber screamed and clamped on to Emma. "Ia's a'scared'a storms!" She trembled.

Another crackle of lightning snapped the air outside, this one less thunderous, sharper. The higher-pitched strike echoed off the trees a few times.

A man howled in pain.

Emma pulled Kimber out from under the stairs and stood. "That's not a storm..." She shivered with excitement, happy tears welling in her eyes.

Kimber looked up at her as another deafening *crack* rent the air outside. The smell of ozone leaked in on the breeze blowing past the gaps around the door. Men shouted in a panic, and one or two cried out in agony. She eyed the dirt roof, turning her head as if to follow thunderclouds far overhead.

The whistle of an arrow preceded the *skiff* of it hitting dirt. A second later, a great *boom* rumbled in the earth, knocking clods of dirt down from the ceiling and making Emma jump.

"Run!" shouted a man.

Several voices joined in chorus, all screaming as if they'd seen a banderwigh. The terrified shouting of men and a woman or two faded into silence. The girls listened for a moment to nothing: no rain, no howling wind, and no thieves.

Emma hugged Kimber at the base of the steps for a moment before yelling, "We're here!"

The girls clung to each other in silence, listening for any sign of activity outside.

Dirt swelled outward on either side of the door. Emma pulled Kimber back a few steps. A pair of thorny roots as thick around as a man's legs wormed out of the earth and wrapped about the door, crushing it into a rain of splinters before tearing it up and away.

Nan's silhouette filled the square of exposed sky, dark raven-feather cloak fluttering in the wind. The scowl on her face scared Emma mute, but as soon as the old one saw her, Nan's usual warm expression returned.

"Nan!" Emma yelled, and ran up the steps.

Kimber started wailing before she'd made it halfway out of the cellar.

Emma crashed into her grandmother at a full sprint, caught under her left arm. Kimber collided next to her, but Nan didn't fall or even so much as take a step back. When the explosion of tears ended, Emma pulled her face out of Nan's cloak to stare up at her and sniffled.

"Emma... Kimber." Nan cradled them close. "Are you all right?"

Two men in grey cloaks, one wearing a leather-armored vest, squirmed and screamed, caught in a tangle of finger-thick thorny vines. The mass of whipping tendrils wrapped around their legs and most of their upper bodies, dragging them to the ground. Beyond them, cloaked figures sprinted away into the woods.

Two patches of grass burned with clusters of tiny fires, and one scorched area had a burnt glove sticking up from it.

The place the thieves had taken them looked like an old farmstead home surrounded by forest, and likely not lived in for many years. An overgrown field stood off to the right of a blackened two-story dwelling surrounded by the remains of a collapsed wooden fence. The well house had caved in as well, along with part of the stones. Emma gazed at the darkness beyond the windows and got the distinct feeling she shouldn't go inside.

One of the men caught in the squirming bramble yelped as thorns found something tender and pulled him down.

"It will hurt less if you stop struggling," said Nan.

The other man whined.

Emma looked up, wanting to tell what happened, but as soon as she saw her grandmother's face, she couldn't do anything but cry again. Nan patted her back in a soothing rub. Kimber went quiet, clinging.

"Don't look over that way," said Nan. "Are you hurt?"

"No, Nan. Just scared." Emma took a few rapid breaths to settle her nerves. She explained the faerie in the bottle, the dreamroot-soaked rag, and waking up tied in the cellar. "He helped us get out." She pulled her hair away from the rat. "I promised to bring him home and feed him."

Nan nodded. "And so we shall."

Tromping and crashing from the right preceded Da charging out of the trees, followed by seven of the Watch. The thieves who'd run off had long since vanished into the forest. The guardsmen converged on the two moaning figures in the bramble, as well as three or four others lying here and there in the grass.

Da headed straight for Nan.

"Here, Liam." Nan shifted so he could see the girls. "They're a little rattled, but unharmed."

"What are you doing rushing in here alone?" Da gave Nan a worried glare for a second before taking a knee and pulling Emma and Kimber into a hug. "Praise Belloch."

Nan harrumphed. "Don't get your feathers in a fluff. I can handle a few pickpockets."

"Da…" Emma looked up. "There's a wizard…"

His face paled. "You saw a wizard?"

"No. The thieves said they were waiting for him." She explained how the thieves had put them in the cellar and planned to force her to go get silk as soon as the wizard returned.

"Captain Dalen!" yelled Kavan. "You should see this."

Da made a face like he wanted to hit someone. He held his daughters for a half a minute, patted the girls on the back, and handed them off to Nan before trudging across the field to where Arnir and Haim worked to drag two men from the tangling vines. Nan flicked her cloak out and gathered Emma and Kimber within its warmth. Kimber smiled at her across Nan's stomach. The rat sniffed at Emma's ear, making her giggle.

"Shadow's Eyes," said Da. "Damn. What's left?"

"Three prisoners and four d—" Guard Haim glanced at Emma and Kimber. He held up four fingers.

Emma looked up, confused. "Shadows have eyes?"

Nan stroked her hair. "A thieves' guild, Em. From Calebrin." Her eyes hardened. "Those fools won't be quite so quick to return."

"Ia's wanna go home." Kimber sniffled.

"Me too." Emma beamed. "Gnomes."

Kimber kept crying, but grinned.

Da nodded to them. "I'll be along once we've cleaned this up. Please take them home. Beth's worried."

Emma's grin faded. "I'm sorry for scaring Mama."

"Don't you blame yourself, Em. This lot would've come through the windows if you didn't fall for their little faerie. No telling how long they'd been watching, waiting for you to be alone." Nan grumbled. With a hand at their backs, she herded the girls into a walk, heading into the woods. "Poor thing. I hope the stories are true."

Emma stopped clinging and took Nan's hand. "Which stories?"

"Faerie lanterns have been around for a long time. Some people have no respect for anything, no matter how innocent. They say being cruel to a faerie brings bad luck." Nan wagged her grey-caterpillar of an eyebrow. "*Very* bad luck."

Emma frowned. "She looked so sad. I wanted to help her."

"Poor faerie," whispered Kimber.

Head down, Emma walked among the dark of Widowswood for a second time, though this scenery felt far removed from the Banderwigh's nocturnal chase. Alongside Nan, the night forest comforted her, as if the trees themselves wanted to protect her. A touch over an hour later, the lights of home glowed warm and welcome. Mama paced about on the back porch, Tam likely asleep.

"Mama!" shouted Emma. She bolted forward.

"Mama!" yelled Kimber.

Emma held her hand out. Kimber grasped it, and they sprinted across the meadow side by side.

Mama rushed off the porch and caught them in a fierce hug a short distance from the house.

"I'm sorry, Mama." Emma snuggled tight.

"Mama..." whispered Kimber.

Her mother held them for a few minutes until Nan walked up. "Go on, Beth. Bring them inside."

Nan tugged at Mama until she stood, plucking Emma and Kimber off their feet. Without a word, she carried them inside and sat on the bed, clinging to them.

THE WIDOW'S WOOD

*E*mma curled up atop Da's lap in the large padded chair by the fireplace. Mama sat in its twin across the small throw rug, with Kimber asleep in her lap. Not to be left out, Tam stuffed himself under Mama's left arm, his legs entwined with Kimber's. Da traced his thumb back and forth over the red mark on Emma's wrist. He radiated so much anger she dared not make a sound. She knew he directed his fury at the thieves, not her, but the quiet tension frightened her nonetheless.

Little had happened the following day. Mama hadn't slept much and refused to let go of either of them all through the night. She eventually collapsed soon after Nan got to preparing the morning meal, and they let Mama sleep until lunch time. Da stayed home all day as well. Except for the occasional trip out to the privy, Emma had spent the whole day in one of her parents' laps. At some point in the afternoon, she'd ceased clinging out of fear, and held on to comfort them.

The rat occupied a small wooden box set on the floor to the left of the back door, packed with old cloth for nesting and a muffin all to himself. It took a bit of convincing to get Da to permit a rodent in the house, but after several minutes of the girls emphatically describing how the rat had helped them, he relented.

Da ceased worrying at her red mark and let her arm flop into her lap. "Em... it's too dangerous. I don't want you involved with the silk anymore. Your mother or Nan will talk to the spiders and set it right. You're too little to carry such a burden."

"Da," whispered Emma. "I made a promise. The queen was going to eat me. She said I was lying only to save myself."

"Spider not gonna eat you." Tam grinned. "Spiders don' like sweets."

Mama started to laugh, but clasped a hand to her face to stall tears.

Emma stuck her tongue out at Tam.

Nan brought over warm honeyed tea for everyone, setting mugs on a round table between the chairs. "Oh, I don't think those men will bother Emma again. There's not a one of them now who doesn't believe I'm real."

"You're not a witch," said Emma.

Nan waved dismissively. "Oh, what's a word? Perhaps I'm not a witch, but it's a scary word, and sometimes I like being scary. Especially if it protects my Emma." She raised both eyebrows. "You should have seen the looks on their faces when I flew in and changed back to human form."

Da almost smiled.

"I told them they had stolen someone dear to me, and the woods would know if they returned." Nan's eyes gleamed. A faint rumble of thunder crossed the sky.

Kimber gasped.

Da gave Nan an expectant look.

"Not me." Nan shook her head. "It's soon to rain. About time, too. We need it. Farms have been getting a bit dry."

"If they've a wizard with them, a few bolts of lightning aren't going to scare them for long." Da rubbed Emma's head, lulling her into a half-awake, contented smile.

"Perhaps…" Nan frowned, hands on her hips. "But you know the rumors of the woods."

"Story?" asked Tam.

"Yes." Da sighed. "I'm not willing to trust old wives' tales to protect my children."

"What's the rumor of the woods?" asked Emma.

Nan chuckled. "Well, people say that a long time ago, a young couple were married in a village deep in the middle of Widowswood. They enjoyed a pleasant life for a while, but something happened to the man. Everyone you ask will say something different: demons, money, other women, or perhaps he had always been a wretch."

"He hurt her," whispered Emma.

"Yes, Em. He killed her." Nan shook her head. "She had loved and trusted him with all her heart, and in her dying breath, she cursed his betrayal. Some people think her spirit has become part of Widowswood. The rumor claims men who wander too deep in the forest never return, and are never found, as she takes them. Some say 'tis why they call it *Widow's* wood."

Tam gasped.

Mama fidgeted.

Emma gave her a quizzical look.

"I've found bones, but"—Mama shook her head—"I've no way to know whose they were, or if the stories are true."

"The forest has many bones," said Nan. "Someone goes into the woods and doesn't return because they stumbled on an angry bear no one sees, they blame the curse. And so it grows."

"You sound like Emma now." Da smiled. "Or like she used to be."

"Liam," said Nan, "you should know by now that a mystical explanation is not the only one to any story. It doesn't mean it's not true. If the curse takes ten men and misfortune another ten, people say the curse took twenty."

"Is the curse real?" Emma pulled her blanket tight and tried to get her toes under it.

"Well." Nan shrugged, a trace of a smile on her lips. "I've never seen the spirit, but your father won't go into the deep woods alone."

"Only a fool would go into *any* forest alone," said Da.

"Am I a fool then?" Mama grinned.

"No, you're a druid." Da pursed his lips. "You know I meant someone without the gift."

Nan let off a sudden sharp chuckle sounding more like a startled bird.

Everyone looked at her.

"Those fools probably thought I was the Witch of Widowswood." Nan crossed the area in front of the fireplace and settled in her cushioned chair like a roosting hen pleased to feathers with herself. "Hmm. Perhaps I am?"

Emma covered her mouth with her blanket-wrapped hands and giggled.

"Em." Da kissed her atop the head. "For the next few days, I'd like for you not to leave the house." He lifted his gaze to Mama's chair. "That goes for you two as well."

Tam whined.

Kimber nodded. "Yes, Papa."

Nan scoffed. "Tellin' a wee druid girl not to go outside? Ye might as well put her back in a banderwigh's cage."

"I don't mind." Emma snuggled against Da's chest. "He just wants me to be safe, and it's only until the thieves are gone. I don't need to get more silk for two weeks."

"We talked about this," said Da. "I don't want you getting hurt."

Nan raised a hand. "I'll go with her. Let the child keep her word."

Emma lifted her head to smile at Nan, while Da kept running his hand over her hair. He didn't seem at all happy about the idea, but she got the sense he meant to argue the point later, when she couldn't hear it. Content to be protected, she snuggled against his chest and closed her eyes.

18

QUIET TIME

*E*mma perched in her Mama's lap, seated in front of *the cabinet.* Mama guided her through making one of the potions she always prepared for Da. She added a handful of fine dark brown powder, ground burlbark, to the crucible and added water.

Mama gestured at a jar of bright green slime. "Add a pinch of glistening moss."

"Yes, Mama." She reached in without hesitating and plunged her fingers into a minty substance, thick and goopy like cold snot. Her toes curled in disgust. "Eww."

Mama hid her smile in Emma's hair and kissed her head. "It won't hurt you."

The glistening moss peeled away like slime, a long goopy tendril trailing after her fingers. She held a hand under it to catch it in case it fell, but got it into the crucible without dropping any. After scraping her fingers on the edge of the stone bowl, she stuck out her tongue.

"You can taste it if you like."

Emma looked up at her mother in horror. "It looks like it came out of Tam's nose."

"You like jams and jellies don't you?"

"Yes."

She sniffed her fingertips, detecting sweet mint. A tentative poke of the tongue caused a pleasant coolness to spread across her mouth. "It's... sweet."

"Go ahead and stir everything together."

Emma licked her fingers. "Nan doesn't use this moss." She picked up the pestle and squished the mess in the bowl around, crushing everything together. "Is that why your potions taste good?"

"Part of the reason." Mama reached around Emma's sides and held her hands over the mixture. "Uruleth, grant me your strength and stamina."

A translucent cloud of pale green light formed within the crucible. The shifting energy reacted to Emma's stirring, becoming another ingredient blending in. The water, white gnarlknot root, dark burlbark powder, and the glowing magic congealed into an even, dark green liquid with a faint hint of light within.

Mama leaned forward, chin over Emma's shoulder. "You're learning quite well."

Emma poured the mixture into an empty bottle. "What does this do?"

"When your father drinks it, it makes him a little stronger and a little tougher."

"Oh." Emma smiled. "Would it make me as strong as a bear?"

"It would make you stronger than a little girl ought to be, but you wouldn't be as strong as your father." She corked the bottle and gathered some Nymph's Breath and Liferoot. "We need to make him a few elixirs in case he gets hurt."

Emma nodded.

She mixed three potions with the same ingredients, each infused with a Mythandriel spell from Mama. Inside the house, the bright green glow emanating from the liquid was obvious. Perhaps in the sunlight, one could miss it. Emma furrowed her eyebrows at them, wondering how Da could've possibly *not* believed in magic. Mama had been giving him these potions as long as she could remember, and they *glowed.*

With that thought grinding around within Emma's head, Mama lifted her off her lap and set her standing.

"I'm going out for a bit."

The dire tone hidden behind her cheerful expression made Emma squint up at her. "You're going to hunt the thieves?"

Mama bit her lip, looking guilty. "Well, I suppose you're getting older, Em. Yes. I'm going to prowl about for a bit. I hope for their sake I don't find any."

"There's one who wasn't mean to us." She described the younger man who'd wanted to let them go. "Please don't hurt him."

"Em. I'm not going out there to kill everyone I see dressed like a thief." She winked. "More to keep up the myths of the woods. Scare them away."

Emma nodded.

"Do you think you can tend to your chores today? If you're still frightened, I don't mind if you rest."

"It was scary, but I can do my chores. Nan's here." Emma smiled.

As Mama changed into her traveling clothes, Emma brought the rat a fresh slice of bread. She spent a while chatting with him, scratching his back, and making sure he'd gotten comfortable before setting about dragging the basket of dirty clothes and linens out to the back porch. Kimber helped run buckets back and forth from the pump to fill the basin. Nan tended the kettle, adding a few pots of boiling water to the basin of cold.

Emma waited, watching steam waft up from the washbasin until Nan gestured to go ahead. She took a pillowcase and pushed it underwater, cringing at the heat until her arms got used to it. The soap Nan made for the clothes felt like grabbing a handful of pudding, but it smelled of lavender. Kimber ran over to help, and soon the girls fell into a conversation about faeries while scrubbing clothes and sheets. Emma admitted not knowing a whole lot about them, having not believed they existed for most of her life. Now that she'd seen one, she'd become quite curious, and they made up stories and guessed about how faeries lived.

Tam raced about, demanding to go out and play. Nan occupied him with a spinning top for a while. Before long, the girls went out to the back porch so they could hang the wet laundry. Emma scowled at the forest, daring a stupid thief to show himself. She almost wanted to watch what Nan would do to him, but at the same time, wasn't quite sure she wanted to see it. The glare on Nan's face when the cellar door opened held anger the likes of which she never imagined her grandmother capable.

The moment had been frightening, but the memory made her feel loved.

"Like a mama bear," whispered Emma.

"Hmm?" asked Kimber, up on tiptoe to hang one of her dresses.

"I was rememberin' how Nan looked angry when she found us." Emma smiled. "Like a mama bear when someone gets too close to the cubs."

Kimber adjusted the dress on the line and dropped to stand flat. "Mama bears donnae make lightning."

"No." Emma cringed at the thought of the hard sticking up out of the burned grass. "They don't."

Once they'd hung the laundry, Emma took her broom out to the front porch while Kimber ran about inside with a smaller one. She hesitated at the door and looked back over her shoulder at Tam, who whined about wanting to go play in the meadow.

"Nan? Why do we have to sweep the porch? Can't you make the breeze clean it?"

"That is a good question, Emma." Nan winked, held up a finger, and muttered something. Stick Knight and Shrub Dragon moved on their own and engaged in a duel.

Tam gawked, paralyzed with awe.

Nan walked over to Emma and put a hand on her shoulder. "The spirits provide their assistance when we need them to. You should always make sure you need something before you ask."

Emma looked down, thinking, lifting and dropping her toes for a few seconds. "Do I need to talk to animals when I just want to say hello? Or only like the rat when I really need help?"

"Can you talk to animals without asking for Strixian's help?"

"No."

"Can you sweep the porch without asking Andreth to stir up the wind?"

Emma smiled. "I understand."

"Here and there, they don't mind a little laziness… but you shouldn't make a habit of it." Nan gave her a light pat on the bottom. "Understand?"

"Yes, Nan."

Emma headed outside to the far right corner of the porch. After a quick glance around at the cloudy sky and no sign of anything unusual, she hummed happily to herself while sweeping.

A LITTLE SUNLIGHT BROKE THROUGH THE RAINY CLOUDS SOON AFTER chores had finished. Emma ran about in circles across the damp meadow behind the house, chasing Kimber. They both clutched dolls, making them fly like faeries. Tam, wanting nothing at all to do with faeries, darted left and right with his wooden sword, protecting the girls from 'goblins.'

Flying became a faerie tea party for a little while before they lost interest. Nan walked them to the creek a short distance into the woods, where they swam and splashed. Kimber found the courage to walk hip deep into the water, but retreated when Tam tried splashing her. With her grandmother close by, Emma didn't bother worrying about thieves. For the better part of an hour, she only worried about having fun.

"Come, children. It's time to go in." Nan handed them back their dresses, and Tam his tunic.

Dripping wet, Emma ran laughing to the back door.

Soon, Tam flopped by the fireplace with the once-again normal Stick Night and Shrub Dragon locked in their constant battle. Emma and Kimber helped Nan prepare dinner, baking potatoes as well as a plump roast beef.

Emma sprinkled the meat with seasonings at Nan's instruction, still mulling over a little guilt at eating an animal she could now speak to. Wolves ate sheep and deer, or rabbits, or whatever else they could catch. *Can wolves talk to deer?*

"It's the natural order of things, Emma." Nan added some black pepper. "I see that look on your face. The true essence of this bull has returned to the forest. It may return as a bull, a chicken, perhaps even a tree or flower. Iskarun aids in that."

"The insect spirit?" Emma grunted with the weight of the pan and carried it to the oven.

Nan opened the lid and took the pan from her before putting it inside. "Insects continue the cycle. They consume the remains of the dead and allow life to continue." She made a circular motion with both hands.

The girls sat with Nan at the table while the food cooked. The old one set about teaching them to read. By the time Da walked in, Emma had written her name four times. Kimber took a little longer, but managed to write her name as well. She held up the paper and cheered.

Da smiled at them and hurried around to hug them in turn, before removing his armor. "How's the day found you, mum?"

"Quiet as a mouse." Nan raised an eyebrow. "Or a rat."

"Indeed." Da laughed.

Emma slipped out of the chair. "I forgot to feed him." She ran to fetch a bit of bread, then hurried to the rear hallway.

The rat lounged in his bed like royalty, half on his back with his belly open to the air. Only crumbs remained of the muffin from the previous day.

She knelt, and asked Strixian for the Wildkin Whisper. "Hello."

"Happy greetings." The rat rolled onto his legs and reached up for the bread. "I thankful."

Emma handed him the bread slice and pet him for a little while as he nibbled. "You saved us. This is your home now, too." *All I can do is make light and talk to animals.* She grinned. *Maybe it's not so weak.*

The front door opened. Mama walked in, looking tired.

"Thank you again." Emma pet the rat twice more and bounded to her feet. She sprinted over to Mama, standing by the cloak pegs to the right of the door to wait, and leapt into a hug as soon as her mother hung her cloak. "Welcome home!"

"Any luck?" asked Da.

"Not a trace." Mama leaned her staff on the wall. "That smells wonderful."

"Emma's making a roast," said Nan, not looking up from her knitting.

Mama took her seat at the table and yawned. Emma ran to grab the great wooden pitcher and went out back to the pump to fetch water. She struggled with the ponderous container, shuffling into the house and hauling it up onto the table. By tilting it forward, she poured everyone a cup, giving Mama the first one.

"A few starlings told me a man in a dark robe returned to that house. He did not stay long, and they described him as quite upset." Mama took a long drink and gasped. "I've been walking all day. I think I'll take to bed with the children tonight."

"Shall I read you a story as well, Beth?" Nan chuckled.

"Go ahead, Mother. I'll not be awake to hear it."

"Pff," said Nan.

They both laughed.

"Perhaps about time, then." Nan sniffed the air. "Dinner's ready."

"Seems the thieves have lost interest. The three we found at old Pieran's place weren't in the mood to talk. They're on their way to prison in Calebrin, not that they'll stay long."

Emma looked at him. "They're gonna let them go?"

"Barristers." Da grumbled. "Sometimes the law works the wrong way when money's involved. That guild of theirs has some sway with the local magistrates. At least it seems Nan gave them quite the scare."

"They'as a'scared o' wizards," said Kimber. "Nan's better'an a wizard."

"Why thank you, child." Nan set the roast on the stovetop and bowed.

"I'm sure none of them expected the Forest Witch to come down from the sky hurling lightning." Mama flashed an expectant grin.

Nan threw a towel over Mama's head from behind, setting her into a fit of laughter.

"What do you take me for, a wizard?" Nan grumbled. "The lightning came from the clouds."

Da grinned. He reached under the table and extracted Tam by one ankle, held him aloft for a few seconds while tickling his stomach, and set him in a chair.

Emma laughed. She leaned forward in her seat, swinging her legs. Her home, filled with warmth, the laughter of her family, and the smell of a good meal, put silk thieves far out of her mind.

19

DOUBTS

D a took up a post in his large chair by the fireplace, poring over his work ledger. With the Feast of Zaravex over, and the beginnings of hope that the thieves might be too worried to return, he finally seemed to relax back to his old self. He nursed a goblet of wine while reading and making the occasional adjustment to something on the page.

Emma sat in the bathtub, hugging her knees to her chest. Water rippled around her body a few inches under her armpits. She tucked her feet on either side of Kimber, who sat in front of her. Tam knelt in front of Kimber with his back to her. Mama handed each girl a dollop of soap and sat on the floor behind Emma, who mushed the flower-scented lump into Kimber's head and worked it into a lather as Mama did the same for her.

Kimber washed Tam's hair as the boy splashed.

"You know, Beth... I've been thinking." Da set the goblet on the small round table. "Em's getting a bit old for a family bed. I know it's how you grew up out here in the woods, but by her age, I had my own room back in Calebrin."

"We're not *in* Calebrin." Mama smiled.

"How old were you when you got your own bed?" asked Emma.

Mama acted as if it took effort to remember. "Seventeen."

"Weren't you wed to Da then?" Emma reached a hand out of the water and scratched her head.

"This one's smart." Mama patted her on the head.

"Plus we've got another daughter." Da smiled at Kimber. "Do you plan to pile them on top of each other like boards when they're Hannah's size?"

"Em?" asked Mama. "What do you think?"

She liked having her family close, especially whenever the spider dreams haunted her. However, being mushed into the wall every night she could do without. "I feel safe with everyone close. I don't want to be alone at night."

"Well." Da tapped a finger to his chin. "I've been thinking of adding on to the house. Get our bed to a proper master bedroom. Perhaps add a pair of new rooms. We could put two beds in one for the girls. If they feel like sharing now, they can. When they get older, they'll have their own."

"Something to think about." Mama laughed.

"Liam," said Nan. "The feast of Zaravex planting ideas in your mind?"

Mama coughed.

Da found the ledger fascinating.

Emma cupped water in her hands and rinsed Kimber's hair. She stood and lathered soap about herself head to toe. When she finished, she soaped up Kimber's back before turning around to let her return the favor. After a few minutes, Emma sat and rinsed off, splashing the barely-warm water up over her chest, arms, and face. Mama washed Tam, this time not making the mistake of letting go of him when it came time to get out of the tub.

She wrapped him in a towel and held on while the girls dried themselves off.

Emma gathered a towel around herself and followed Kimber to the fireplace to let the heat dry her hair. The rat approached and crawled into her arms. She'd asked him to hold his forelegs out to the sides and wave if he wanted to say something to her, so she knew to ask Strixian for the gift. Tonight, he seemed content to be held, no words needed.

Kimber edged closer, clutching her towel tight about herself. She eyed the rat, looked at Emma, glanced at the rat again, and swallowed. After a few minutes of watching Emma skritch and pet him, she reached over a tentative hand and touched two fingers to his head. The rat rolled into her caress, adoring the attention.

Da grumbled and shook his head.

Emma looked up at him. A few droplets of water fell from her hair and landed on her knee. "Da?"

Nan glided between the children to the hearth. She pulled an iron poker from the brass bucket and jabbed at the fire, added a log, and prodded at it again.

He finished writing something and peered over the book at her. "Yes, Emma?"

She sat up into the wave of warmth coming off the fireplace, basking in the scent of wood smoke. "Why do you try to act like there's no magic?"

The rat leaned up and licked at her hair, drinking the water gathering in droplets at the ends.

Da glanced at his ledger, flicking at the corner of the page with his thumb, his expression somewhere between apologetic and worried. Emma bowed her head, sorry for having asked. Nan cleared her throat, returned the poker to the bucket, and settled in her chair. The rat licked at Emma's ear, making her scrunch up her shoulder and grin.

Her father shut the book and set it on the table before gesturing for her to climb into his lap. She plucked the rat from around her neck and held him to her chest as she walked the two steps to Da's chair. He pulled her into his lap, gave her a long, reluctant stare, and sighed.

Kimber sprang to her feet and ran over, scrambling to keep her towel. Da held his left arm out and let her crawl up. She leaned her head on his shoulder and smiled at Emma.

"You've been here in this house your entire life." Da put his arm around Emma's back and squeezed her. "The rest of my family still dwells in Calebrin. As a boy, I grew up surrounded by stories of the grandeur of the gods, and the practiced art of magic as learned by wizards."

Emma let the rat slip from her hands and crawl up her leg to the knee, where he perched, sniffing at Kimber who still didn't quite seem sure if she should be afraid of him.

Da smirked at the rodent. "My mother, my sisters, father, and younger brother all have a certain opinion of the way things are."

"Snooty," muttered Nan.

Tam supplied Shrub Dragon's roar as he pounced on Stick Knight. Kimber leaned to her left, running her fingers through her hair to help dry it.

"Be that as it may," said Da. "They have a rather low opinion of... 'nature magic,' if you will. Mum thinks it's contrary to the will of the gods, and those who use it are dealing with dark powers."

"Sorcerers," said Emma. "Not druids."

"They're the same sort of people who see no difference between a knight and a hiresword," said Mama from the table. She returned her attention to her knitting.

"If gods donnae wan' us tae do et, they would nae 'llow it." Kimber blinked. "They'as *gods*."

"Da, Mythandriel *is* a goddess." Emma broke into giggles as the rat sniffed at the sole of her left foot and licked her big toe.

"Among elves, yes." Da nodded. "Our people recognize a specific group of deities and—"

"Everything else is forest witchery?" Nan wiggled her fingers along with 'forest witchery.' She raised her eyebrow. "They still think Beth ensorcelled you, don't they?"

A sick feeling stirred in her stomach. Emma pulled the damp towel tight about herself and looked up with a mournful stare. "Da? Are you ashamed of me for being a druid?"

"No, Emma." He held her tight for a few seconds and kissed her head. "I am not ashamed of you." His voice gained volume. "I'm not ashamed of your mother or of your grandmother. It's high time I admitted that to myself." He slapped the armrest. "I'm not really sure if I tried to believe the ways I'd grown up thinking, or if by pretending none of it existed I somehow fostered goodwill from the other side of the family."

Mama put her knitting down and walked over, her expression hopeful. "Liam?"

He looked up to her, lifting his hand from Emma's shoulder to take hers. "Yes. You're right, Beth. It's been nothing but pigheaded of me to close my eyes to it and cling to that old stodginess." He smiled between Mama and Emma. "If they aren't willing to accept my wife and daughter, I have no further need of them."

"You don't have to shut out your blood." Mama stooped to kiss him over Emma's head. "I know your words have meaning. Whatever face you must wear for them, don't let me be the wedge in your family tree."

"Come here, boy" As soon as Tam climbed into his lap between the girls, Da hugged all three of them together. "*This* is my family tree." He ushered the kids back to their feet. "Now put on your night clothes. 'Tis time for bed."

Tam darted straight out of his towel to the shelf where his nightshirt waited.

Emma carried the rat to his box before hurrying after her brother. She traded her towel for a nightgown and crawled into bed, sitting in the corner with a pillow at her back. Kimber and Tam leaned against her, fidgeting with excitement as Nan dragged a chair over for story time.

THE WHIMS OF WIZARDS

*N*an took her seat at the side of the bed and opened the same black-bound book she'd read from last time. Emma squinted at it with a mischievous grin, still doubting her grandmother needed it. The old one began the story with Princess Isabelle upon her horse, riding through the forest of M'ur Ellonae. She traveled day and night, stopping only to sleep for a little now and then when the horse needed rest. Each time she slept, she held the Hearthfire Potion close, using it like a heat stone to keep her warm in her blanket. After four days, she returned to the place where the frost demon had lured Sir Aemon into her icy trap.

The travel part of the story hadn't been as exciting as the rest. Emma's mind wandered off in the direction of thieves. She'd been extra careful since escaping, but hadn't seen anything suspicious in the following days. The sight of the men who'd been so scary when she'd been tied to a post running and screaming from Nan like small boys caught doing mischief took much of the fright from the memory. Da had warned her trading in enchanted spidersilk would be dangerous. Both Mama and Nan used their magic to protect themselves. While talking to animals and making light proved quite useful, she understood what Nan had meant about boys wanting to go straight to calling storms. Emma stared down at her hands, quite incapable of making even a small spark.

Then again, calling lightning while fixed to a pole in a root cellar probably wouldn't have been smart. Even if she knocked a thief out, it wouldn't have helped her escape. Nor could she have aimed that magic with her hands tied behind her back. Emma grinned at the sudden idea of firing lightning bolts from her big toe. She raised her leg under the sheet and pointed her foot at an imaginary thief.

"The ice around Sir Aemon glowed blue in the light of the moon," said Nan. "Although Isabelle had been trapped in a dungeon when such fate had befallen him, she felt the weight of guilt upon her heart. Weeks had passed, and yet she found herself no closer to curing the king."

"There's gonna be a dragon." Tam nodded. "That's why she needs the knight first."

"Nae dragon," whispered Kimber.

Emma lowered her leg and gave both her siblings a stern 'be quiet' look.

"Princess Isabelle took the Hearthfire Potion from her pouch and cradled it. It gave off a warm red light that grew brighter as she neared her frozen protector. She held the bottle up to his lips, and water ran from his chin. When the ice shrank away from his face, she raised the end, pouring the whole potion into his mouth. For a second, nothing happened."

"O'nae," whispered Kimber. "It didn't wo—"

Tam covered her mouth.

"Soon, a red glow shone from inside his chest"—Nan tapped her heart —"and *whoosh!*" She flung her arms open. Kimber and Tam tried to lean back, squishing Emma into the wall. "A bright flash of magic knocked her on her bum. When she could see again, she found Sir Aemon's hand reaching to help her up."

Kimber clapped. "Do'a they gettin' married?"

Tam put his hand over her mouth. "Nan's tellin' it."

The redhead narrowed her eyes at him.

Emma giggled.

Nan winked. "They still have much to do. You see, Sir Aemon didn't remember being frozen and had no idea that almost a month had passed since the ice demon had lured him. To him, the ice demon had simply vanished. Neither of them knew if the king, Isabelle's father, still drew breath."

Emma shivered. *The king can't die... Isabelle would be so sad.* She eyed the door, where Mama and Da had gone out onto the porch. The thought of losing her Da made her cry.

"Em?" Asked Nan.

"I don't want the king to die. Isabelle needs her Da."

Nan smiled. "The princess was in tears too, for she feared the same thing. The king had been weak before she left, and she'd already spent time she could have been searching for Nymph's Breath trying to save Sir Aemon."

"Princesses don't save Kni—"

Kimber put her hand over Tam's mouth. "Donnae."

He dove across Emma at Kimber. The two wrestled on top of her, each trying to make the other shut up. Emma tolerated it for a few seconds until Tam's knee got her in the gut.

Emma hooked her arms around their necks and pulled them close. "Be quiet and settle down or she'll stop tellin' the story."

"I'as sorry," whispered Kimber.

Tam pouted at his lap. "Sorry."

Nan cleared her throat. "Sir Aemon wanted to take her back to the castle right away. He believed the story false, and that the wizard's true purpose had been to send Isabelle out into the wilds in hopes she never came back. Isabelle refused to abandon her father, still believing the Nymph's Breath could break the icy curse. 'What good can you possibly do?' asked Sir Aemon. 'You're a princess, and barely fifteen.'"

Emma bit her lip.

Nan shook her head. "Princess Isabelle whirled on him with fire in her eyes, and—"

"Real fire?" asked Tam.

"No, my boy. She was angry. It's a figure of speech." Nan put on an expression of fierce determination. "Isabelle walked right up to him and said, 'I saved *you*, didn't I? Perhaps I am stupid, after all.' When he protested, she pointed at all the ice on the ground behind him. Sir Aemon at last admitted he'd been trapped. 'Go back to the castle then, and play nursemaid to my father. I shall recover the Nymph's Breath and return with it… or not return.'"

Emma grinned. She saw herself as Isabelle, fierce and brave, and ready to storm off into the Elven Forest alone to save her father's life. She clutched Kimber and Tam close, squirming with excitement.

"Sir Aemon, of course, could not let his princess rush off alone, and so he relented."

Tam mouthed the word 'dragons' without giving voice to it.

Nan chuckled. "For all their fears, it took them only a day or so to find the Nymph's Breath once they'd entered M'ur Indril... and alas, no dragon guarded the plant."

"Aww," mumbled Tam.

Emma blinked. "We have Nymph's Breath here. In the cabinet."

"You are correct." Nan smiled. "In fact, ours is from M'ur Indril, too. It's not terribly far for a raven to fly, you see. West into the land of Namriel."

"Elf words?" asked Tam.

"In our language, M'ur Indril means 'The Endless Wood'. The forest is hundreds of miles long."

Emma gasped, trying to imagine the sorts of wonders one might find there. Her mind ran away with tall rocks covered in ivy, waterfalls sliding past elven carvings, and trees so enormous they would make her feel like an inches-tall faerie.

"Princess Isabelle plucked a strand of Nymph's Breath, as it hung down far enough for her to reach from horseback. Not knowing how much she'd need, she collected a few and bundled them with care. Now, the dangerous part of her journey began." Nan narrowed her eyes, hunching forward.

The children all gasped.

"Isabelle was no potion maker. She knew very little about them at all. However, she *had* heard wild stories about a local forest witch who everyone claimed stole children for her own."

"Like a banderwigh?" asked Kimber.

"Oh..." Nan waved dismissively. "They made up all sorts of stories. She baked them into cakes, turned them into rabbits and birds, cast magic on them so they'd be children forever and never grow up." Her eyebrows wagged.

Tam sniffled. "I wanna grow up. Knights can't be small."

"Some stories even claimed the forest witch would keep little girls and play with them like dolls until she got bored of them, then bring them back to their village many years after their parents had gotten old and died, but the girls hadn't aged a day."

Emma squinted, making the same face she used to make when she didn't believe one of Nan's stories. The door opened as Mama and Da came back inside. Mama adjusted her disheveled bodice, and Da's hair appeared mussed. He returned to his chair and ledger while Mama resumed her knitting at the table.

Nan ruffled Emma's hair and winked. "Well, Princess Isabelle had heard all of these stories, and worse, so she certainly feared for her life. Sir Aemon vowed to protect her from any witch, but Isabelle had seen how well his sword and shield handled the demon. The girl had little trust that he could stop the forest witch from keeping her forever, but she took the chance."

"She had to," said Emma, urgency in her voice. "Her father was dying."

Nan turned a page. "They traveled for several days, stopping at villages and asking after the witch. Eventually, they stumbled upon a dark and scary forest, full of dangerous creatures and loathsome beasts."

Tam drew in a breath, but Kimber covered his mouth. He sputtered and giggled.

"No, Tam. Alas, no dragons." Nan shook her head. "They braved the depths of the forest and stumbled upon a little cabin in the middle of a copse of gnarled, twisted trees. Beside a small stream, they found a woman with wild black-grey hair and wilder eyes."

Nan opened her eyes as wide as she could while making a face as if she'd been stung on the backside by a dozen bees.

Emma giggled.

"The woman looked not old, but not young either, and eyed the bright-blonde princess with suspicion. Without a bit of fear in her, Isabelle dismounted her horse and strode up to the forest witch. She begged for a moment of the woman's time and told a sad story of a cursed king, and a beloved father. Sir Aemon kept his hand on his sword, not trusting the witch. He believed the stories, and expected her to make Isabelle vanish at a mere touch."

"Almost time," said Da.

"Aww," whined Emma. "Please, Da, a little longer?"

He glanced at Mama with an impressed face. "Since when did our little Emma become so taken with stories? Do you not think them boring?"

Emma shook her head so hard her hair flew about.

"Very well, a little longer." Da tossed his journal on the table. "I should tend to the bathwater."

Da lugged the tub out the back door. Mama smiled at Emma for a few turns of the knitting needle.

"The forest witch invited them inside and agreed to help. She offered them onion bread and mead, though Sir Aemon didn't trust it. He mistook tales of faerie bread for witch's bread." Nan winked. "When a small, dark-haired girl emerged from a curtain, Sir Aemon turned as white as snow, as though finding a child in the witch's home proved all the stories true."

"Were they true?" asked Tam.

"No." Nan chuckled. "The forest witch had a daughter, and though she was but a little one, a year or so younger than you are now, she'd taken an odd fascination with the art of potion making."

Mama smirked at Nan, shook her head, and let off a weak sigh. Despite her mother being seated well behind Nan out of sight, the instant she smirked, the old one smiled.

"It took but two hours to make the potion. By then, Isabelle had eaten her bread and drank her mead... much to the worry of Sir Aemon."

"She'as poisoned her?" Kimber shivered.

"Sometimes, child, bread is only bread." Nan chuckled. "And stories are stories. Tales spun 'round a dozen hearth fires are quite often far different than the truth that created them."

Kimber nodded.

"Princess Isabelle thanked the forest witch for her help and promised to reward her, once she'd hurried back to her father. Poor Isabelle was frightened. She didn't know what to do if the wizard returned. Sir Aemon bade her stay hidden in a village near the castle, lest the wizard steal her mind and take control of her body. Or worse, freeze her in ice like Sir Aemon."

Emma gawked. Kimber clung to her.

"Once again, Princess Isabelle thought more of her father than her fear, and set off for the castle, her home."

Nan closed the book. "Alright, children. Tuck in."

Da tromped back in with the empty tub, which he set beside the cabinets. He came over to the bed to say goodnight.

"Da, can a wizard really steal someone's mind?" asked Emma.

"Well, the ones I've seen don't usually bother with being fancy. They just throw fire and lightning. Now, sorcerers on the other hand..." He muttered, "Belloch, protect me," before raising his voice again. "They spin all manner of evil. No more thoughts of sorcerers or mind-stealing wizards. Off to sleep with you."

Emma smiled. "Night, Da."

After good night kisses went around, Emma lay flat on her back with Kimber clinging to one side and Tam the other. Her sister fell asleep in mere moments, making Emma feel a touch of jealousy. Tam fidgeted for a short while longer before he too succumbed to sleep.

Emma closed her eyes, daydreaming of Feldurin the elf riding a pure white horse at her side as they set off on some grand adventure.

21

EMERALD MESSENGER

*E*mma awoke in the deep hours of night. Kimber's arm wound about her middle, the girl's breath puffed warm at the back of her neck. Tam's fingers clutched her nightdress at her hip, the boy likely clamped around Kimber. Somewhere behind her, Da snored. Emma stretched her legs. Coarse linen slid across her foot. Tam didn't stir, so perhaps Kimber had moved or pinched or squeezed too much. Emma didn't have to run to the privy, and the bed hadn't gone cold. Unable to figure out what woke her, she didn't bother opening her eyes, and settled into her pillow again.

"Use the chamber pot," she muttered.

No sooner did Emma resign herself to return to sleep, than a stick prodded her cheek. She slid a hand up out from under the bedding into the cold night air, and brushed at her face, emitting a soft moan.

Poke.

Emma opened her eyes, and found herself nose-to-face with an emerald creeper a smidge larger than a housecat hanging on the wall over her head. Instant terror paralyzed her from head to toe. The creature's leg span had to be twice her shoulder width. It clung to the wall, upside down, as calm as could be, and poked her in the cheek with a single foreleg a third time.

She couldn't force a scream out of her lungs. Sitting up would move her face *closer* to it, even if for a second. Emma pushed off the wall and rolled over her sister and brother in a blind panic. She scrambled across Mama's back, who lay half on top of Da with her head at his chin, and dove to the floor on her hands. The fuzzy green spider leapt from the wall to the bed and followed her.

A whining scream slipped out from her nose. She crawled backward on the floor, the creeper within inches of her toes no matter how fast she scurried. When she could no longer move backward as her shoulders hit the fireplace stone, she continued trying to push herself into the solid hearth. Cold seeped into her nightdress from the rocks.

The huge spider crawled closer and tapped her on the left foot twice. She whimpered and curled into a ball, trembling. Swaying side to side, the spider stared at her, as if waiting for something.

It... It's... Her head swam with dizziness. She took rapid, deep breaths. *It's not biting me...*

"Easy, Emma," she whispered. "Calm. Calm."

Four breaths later, her brain woke up.

"Strixian, please grant me the Wildkin Whisper." She gulped as the tiny lights swirled around once and faded into her body. "H... hello?"

The spider waved its forelegs at her. "I bring a messsage from the queen. I regret that I ssscared you. Why are you afraid of usss?"

Emma couldn't stop trembling, but forced herself to uncurl. "I don't know. I just am. Are spiders ever afraid of anything and don't know why?"

"Gryphonsss." The spider twitched its leg. "Large birdsss. Inssstinct. You sssay humansss are afraid of usss the sssame?"

"I am more than most." Emma forced a weak smile. "Sorry."

"I undersssstand. If you had not ssspoken with our queen, we would think you food."

She stared into its eight red eyes and imagined herself stuck to the web again. Before panic set in, she concentrated on how she felt in Da's arms. "Yes. I know. I don't want to be food." *Not for spiders, or for goblins either.* "Why did the queen send you? It's dangerous for you to leave the forest. Other humans would try to hurt you."

"Yesss."

Emma gradually extended her left hand, trying to overcome her fear, but couldn't quite decide where to attempt to pet an emerald creeper.

The spider rose on its legs and brushed its body against her fingertip. She whined and managed a nervous smile.

"The queen sssendsss me to warn you. Humansss have made cloth homesss near our nessst. To the north and wessst. They are hunting usss." The spider tilted itself forward, as if bowing in mourning. "Five of my brothersss have been killed."

Emma blinked. "Oh, no."

"They ssstrike from far away with tiny flyirg ssswords. The queen doesss not pursssue them, fearing a trap. Ssshe is angry, but doesss not blame you." It pointed one leg at her face. "You are recccently hatched of your egg, sssame am I. We do not fight unlesss we are forcccced. The queen demandsss help in accordanccce with the promissse."

"I will help. I'll do everything I can." She put a hand over her heart. "It's the thieves..."

"Thievesss? No, they are humansss. Soldiersss, though they have one egg-layer, perhapsss their queen."

Emma shook her head. "Thieves are a type of human who take things that don't belong to them."

"I do not undersssstand. Humansss have egg-layers and soldiersss, do they not?"

Emma's fear of spiders receded to frustration. Some battles *were* pointless. "Yes. Yes. They're bad soldiers. A different nest, and they don't like my nest."

"I sssee. The queen sssends her thanksss, for whatever you can do for usss, little egg-layer."

She furrowed her brows. *I am not a bird!* "You should go home before someone sees you. People will try to hurt you out of fear."

"Inssstinct." The smallish emerald creeper bowed once more, and zoomed across the room, scurried up the wall to the loft, and squeezed out the tiny window at the peak of the angled roof.

She stood, and grumbled at the annoyance of having to pee when she wanted to go back to sleep. Emma contemplated the chamber pot, but as Da said, those were meant for private bedrooms, and emergencies. As much as the privy at night scared her, she couldn't bring herself to use the pot. After a deep breath, she braved the arduous march out back, and returned as fast as possible. She made sure the door lock clicked, then hurried back to her soft, warm bed.

Kimber lay sprawled flat, in the same pose Emma had shoved her into by rolling over her. Red hair fluffed every which way, her mouth hung wide open, and she almost, but not quite, snored.

Emma covered her mouth to stifle a giggle. *She'd sleep through the middle of a swordfight.*

After crawling into her spot by the wall, Emma pulled Kimber's arm over her. Tam sensed the motion and cuddled up to them. Her mind too foggy to dwell on a way to help the spiders, Emma drew the blankets up and snuggled once more in her warm bed.

22

PROMISES, PROMISES

*E*arly morning sun warmed Emma's face, dragging her awake. She sat up, yawned, and rubbed her eyes. Her dreams had been filled with strange sights: At first, she hung in the root cellar, trapped in a spidersilk cocoon affixed to the post while the Banderwigh chased thieves around. Next, she rode a huge spider like a horse up walls and over ceilings, before realizing she'd shrunk to the size of a faerie. Her mind's conjuration of what a wizard must look like, a tall, withered old man with a beard down to his knees and glowing white eyes, grabbed her little faerie-sized self and put her in a bottle, which he hung from a tree branch.

Thousands of spiders crawled up the trunk toward her. Emma screamed at the swarm, fearful they'd somehow get into her bottle and devour her. She'd pounded on the glass, but couldn't get out. The spiders engulfed her prison, cutting off the light. Sobbing, Emma curled up on the bottom, screaming for Nan. At the *pop* of a cork, she looked up to see smiling, happy spiders waving at her. Too frightened to move, she remained still as they gathered her out of the bottle and carried her home.

Emma awoke feeling confused, and more tired than before going to bed. For a good two minutes, she stared at the wall trying to figure out how a spider could smile.

Kimber and Tam had already changed into their day clothes, Tam in a sky blue tunic long enough that Mama didn't insist he wear pants, and

Kimber in a pale pink dress that left her shoulders bare save for two strips of fabric embroidered with flowers.

Da returned from his morning trek to the outhouse and settled into his chair at the table. Emma changed into the blue dress Nan had made her, tied the cloth belt snug, and hurried over to help Nan slice apples and cheese. Mama selected a loaf of bread from the pantry, and soon they all sat around the table eating.

Emma looked up at Da every few bites. She wanted to say something about the spiders, but each time she got up the nerve to break the pleasant silence, she chickened out. Mama smiled at her. Emma grinned and gnawed on a bit of tough bread.

"So who was your little visitor last night?" asked Mama.

"You saw him?" Emma blinked.

"The rat?" asked Da. "Please don't tell me the rat was in the bed."

Emma took a deep breath and let it out. "Da, a spider brought a message last night. There are humans in, umm, cloth homes?" She scratched her head and blinked. "Tents! There's people camping in the wood near the spider nest, and they're hunting them. We need to do something. The queen's angry."

"They're just spiders. Leave it be." Da put a slice of cheese atop a piece of apple and tossed them into his mouth.

Emma cringed. Cheese and apple needed to be eaten *separately* and not mixed. "Bleh."

"It might be those thieves." Mama frowned.

"If they're near the nest, they're nowhere near town. That was quite a walk." Da sipped water, still chewing. "If it's true they've got a wizard, it'll—"

"It's true." Mama dropped a nibbled bit of bread on her plate. "The birds saw a man at old Pieran's place that had the look of a wizard about him."

"All the more reason to keep our distance. I wouldn't want to raid that encampment with less than twenty men, and that's six more than we've got here."

Nan gestured at Da. "You don't even know if the wizard returned. Most of their ilk wouldn't suffer the discomfort of a tent in the deep woods when they can have a fine inn room and hot meals."

"Are wizards that scary?" asked Emma.

Da grinned. "Not if you can reach them. Need twenty men so you have two or three left standing by the time they get close."

Emma gasped.

"Exactly." Da nodded. "I'm not risking my men's lives over some spider queen... and need I point out, again, that this spider queen was going to eat you?"

Emma squirmed in her seat, brushing the memory of sticky silk from her arms and legs.

"Perhaps there *is* something we can do that doesn't involve a reckless charge?" asked Mama. "Do remember, Em, you can't be responsible for everything that happens in the woods."

Nan raised an eyebrow. "Listen to your mother. It took her twenty-four years to learn that lesson."

Mama scoffed.

"Let me see." Nan set her hand (and the bread in it) on the edge of the table, tapping her finger. "Deer poachers, that one fool who summoned a shadow troll... the Talethian Empire's scouts who fell through the faerie circle in Neverwood and wound up here, the root blight, the—"

"Mother..." Mama frowned.

Kimber grinned.

Tam held a pair of large purple grapes to his eyes while making a face at Emma and a (sort of) dragon noise. She grinned. He dropped the grapes on the table, laughing.

Da paid extra attention to his food, not looking at either woman.

"But Mama, I *promised* the Spider Queen I would help."

"If I'as stuck inna giant web"—Kimber held her arms and legs out in an X—"I's promise anna'fing tae get free."

"That's what she thought I was doing... lying." Emma's eyebrows drew close. "I didn't lie."

Mama smiled with a sigh. "Spiders aren't like other animals, Em. They're selfish and opportunistic."

"Like humans?" asked Emma, sitting taller.

Da laughed, and Nan coughed into her hand.

Mama shook her head. "As soon as those spiders believe you can't offer them anything, don't think they won't turn on you. I'm surprised you can even talk to them."

"Ylithir, Beth." Nan offered a sagely nod. "The wolf is an opportunist. I suspect he's taken a liking to her."

"There were quite a few rather *large* wolves about when that... umm." Da waved his bread about. "Cursed fellow with the axe chased her."

Emma frowned at him. "The guards were going to hurt them. You have to tell them not to. The wolves are nice to me. They saved me from the goblins, too."

A worried expression crept over Mama's features. She turned her head to Nan. "You don't think Iskarun has spoken to her?"

Nan cringed. "No. She's taken to wolves and rats, not beetles and bees."

"I'll ask my friends to have a look about. This will be easier if we know what we're facing." Mama ate a bit of cheese.

"Even if Mayor Braddon believes this story of talking to spiders, and even if we had the entire Watch working to keep hunters away, *someone* will risk it because that silk is so darned expensive. The amount Emma brought to Marsten could've bought ten of these houses, and paid the workers to build them."

Mama coughed.

"Ahh, but it's only valuable if someone wants it." Nan chuckled. "If no enchanters are in need of it, it's not worth much more than our humble cobwebs."

Da shook his head. "I don't want that creature blaming our daughter for something happening when people we have no control over hunt spiders. Let nature take its course. Those thieves haven't set foot in town for days. Marsten's got some rather pricy mercenaries who I doubt they're interested in tangling with, and Nan scared their ghosts right out of their bodies."

Emma stared down at her plate. "But I promised."

"If one of those thieves had a knife at your neck, ready to slit it… and he offered to let you go if you promised not to tell anyone you saw him, would you tell me or your mother, or Nan?"

Kimber gasped and clutched both hands to her throat.

Emma started to nod, but snapped her gaze to meet his. "That's different. That's a person doing bad things. The spiders are just being spiders."

He grumbled.

"And they have lots and lots of silk they don't even need." Emma's voice grew louder. "Please, Da? They're *killing* them for silk and they don't have to."

Da shook his head and pursed his lips. "She wasn't happy with me for killing that bander-thing after it chased her to the ends of Widowswood with an axe, now she wants to save all the spiders." He glanced at Mama. "She *is* your daughter."

"What's that supposed to mean?" asked Mama with a hint of a smile.

"You've both got more this"—he tapped a closed hand over his heart —"than this." He tapped two fingers to the side of his head.

"If I remember correctly, the stubborn need to keep true to one's word comes from *your* side of the family." Mama tossed a grape at Da.

He caught it and held it up in two fingers, examining the dark purple-red sphere in a beam of sunlight. "I'll think about sending some men to check it out."

Nan raised a piece of apple to her mouth. "Perhaps you should bring Em, so she can tell the spiders to leave the guardsmen be." She flared her eyes at him and ate the apple.

"No, Mother." Mama grasped Tam's hand as he tried to stuff a grape up his nose. "I'd rather Emma not go near the spiders until we know what their true intentions are."

"So it's settled then," said Da. "You ask your birds, I'll see about some volunteers. If those are the same thieves, I'm sure the men will be quite keen to meet the miscreants who laid their hands on Em."

Emma fidgeted at her dress. He hadn't said no, but it didn't really feel like a yes either. She peered through her hair at Mama without raising her head. Mama and Nan both did many things without Da knowing. He didn't care to witness druids' magic, so they left him out of it. *The Spider Queen knows I'm just a child. I can wait a little while.*

Maybe.

23

EMMA THE SENTINEL

*E*mma tugged the chair a little to the left under an empty part of clothesline before climbing on it to hang one of Tam's tunics. Kimber handed her up another, followed by the long cloth strips of the boy's skivvies. She repositioned the chair and added two of Mama's nightdresses to the line, then made her way along, tossing Da's tunic and breeches over the rope. His skivvies, she handled with a tiny pinch at one corner and threw over the rope like a dead snake that'd bite her if she stayed too close.

With the basket empty, Emma climbed down from the chair and wiped her damp hands on her dress. She gazed into Widowswood, searching with eye as well as heart. The forest still emanated comfort and protection. If a spirit did exist within the trees, perhaps it had taken a liking to her.

Mama had left soon after morning meal and headed into the woods. Da went toward town as he always did, but didn't seem as though he meant to investigate the woods. Emma moved to the porch edge and sat, feet on the top step, and bent forward to put her chin on her knees. Gazing at her toes offered little more help than the woods had.

Kimber sat next to her. "Wan' me tae git tha' brush?" Her little sister fussed at her hair, using her fingers to comb it.

Emma smiled into her dress. "I'm thinking."

"Oh." Kimber continued fussing with Emma's hair. "Do'et hurt?"

"Yeah, a little." Emma laughed and sat up.

If Mama found the thieves, she'd want to do something to help Emma. She had no doubt her mother had sensed how sincere she'd been in her desire to help the spiders and keep her word.

"It's so stupid to kill them when they have all that silk everywhere." Emma held her arms wide. "It's too quiet. Where's Tam?"

Kimber pointed at the door. "Nan's readin' him ae knights wif dragon story."

Earlier had been the closest she'd ever seen her parents to disagreeing. She suppressed a snarl. *I'm not gonna let those stupid thieves make Mama and Da fight.* She stood. "Stay here. I'll be back in a little bit."

Emma bounded down the two steps to the meadow and walked amid grass ranging from knee to shoulder-high. She passed the spot where Nan had showed them the light spell and came to a stop a stone's toss from the edge of the forest. She leaned back, closing her eyes and adoring the feeling of the wind at her face and the grass between her toes.

After a few breaths, she sank to kneel and thought of Ylithir and Greyfang. *I will find the thieves and I will lead Da there so he can put them all in prison. Will the wolves walk with me?*

A small hand squeezed her left shoulder. "Em? Wha'ya doin'? Tae close'a th' woods. Donnae ya' learn?"

Emma meditated on her desire to communicate with the pack and with Ylithir. Kimber knelt behind her, wrapping her arms around.

"What ye doin'?"

"Talking to the wolves." Emma opened her eyes and stared into the forest. "I have to keep my promise. I'm not a goblin. Mama and Da are gonna fight over what to do."

"Da said a'nae."

"He said he'd think about it. That's not exactly 'no.'"

Kimber squeezed her arms tight and rested her chin on Emma's shoulder. "Ae t'ink 'bout it is Da talk for 'nae.'"

"Mama went into the forest. Mama and Nan do things all the time without telling him. He doesn't like to see magic."

The majestic form of the alpha wolf emerged from the trees a distance ahead in the forest. His mate, Moonfang, trailed him, eyes glowing like pale yellow coals set within fur as black as pitch. Fleeting glimpses of the wolves fighting to protect her from the Banderwigh flickered in her mind, and her heart swelled with gratitude.

Emma cast the Wildkin Whisper. "Greyfang, Moonsong." She bowed. "Thank you for coming."

"Your father is superstitious, Emma." The deep, silken voice of Greyfang washed over her. "From his days as a cub, his parents weaned him on stories of forest witches and curses."

Kimber mouthed 'wow' without lending it voice. To her, Emma and the wolves made indecipherable howls, yips, and grunts, but the sheer size of the creatures had left her staring, mouth open.

"I promised the Spider Queen I would help. There are bad people in the forest killing her children."

"You are a child yourself, Emma." Moonsong drew close and nuzzled her. "You do not belong in war."

Emma looked up at the wolves, reaching to stroke both their muzzles. An overwhelming sense of love radiated from her, for her pack. "I want to help. I only need to find them, so I can tell my Da where to go. Have you seen Mama in the woods?"

"She has gone to the spider's nest," said Moonsong. "She does not search for humans."

"Will you protect me?" Emma stood. "I have to help the spiders because I promised. I know it is dangerous, but"—she thought back to Princess Isabelle finding courage—"it's what I have to do, even if it's scary."

Greyfang regarded her for a long moment, his ice blue eyes showing little clue of his thoughts. "Very well. We shall offer our aid once more."

"Thank you." Emma hugged him about the neck, having to stand on tiptoe.

"Eep," whispered Kimber. "You'as talkin' tae them?"

Emma turned to her. "Yes. Please go back to the house. I'm going to find the thieves so I can show Da where they are hiding."

Kimber grabbed her arm and pulled. "Donnae go! If'n the thieves catch yas, they tie yas to a tree again." She sniffled.

"I'm not going to get that close. The wolves can smell them. Thieves can't sneak up on them. The pack will protect me." Emma hugged Kimber. "I'll be home before Da gets back."

Kimber sniffled back tears. After stumbling over a few words she couldn't quite spit out, she whirled around and sprinted across the meadow, heading for home.

Emma moved to Greyfang's side. *Ylithir, please protect the pack. Please run with us.*

Greyfang lowered himself and Emma climbed onto his back.

He waited long enough to watch Kimber disappear into the back door, safely inside, before darting into the trees. Emma clamped on with her arms and legs, squinting at the onrush of wind in her face.

Moonsong yipped out, beckoning to others: Runs in Shadow, another jet-black wolf, appeared from nowhere and ran to Emma's left. Stalks the Wind trailed in from the other side, keeping pace with his mother. Howls at Rain leapt into view ahead, standing still until the pack reached him, and bolting up to a full sprint behind Greyfang. Half Tail and Three-Fang, a pair of pale grey-furred males, joined up from the right, taking place near Moonsong. Bites the Root, the final name Moonsong called out, thundered in from far off to the left. At the distance, Emma thought him bigger than Greyfang, but he seemed younger than his size implied.

Eight wolves, plus Emma, raced past the foliage, as silent as ghosts. Other howls and yips broke the silent forest here and there, along with snaps and thuds. More followed, though they remained out of sight.

With the wolves around her and the energy of the forest within her, Emma felt powerful enough to thump all the thieves. She hoped to find that man who'd first threatened to take Kimber back to Calebrin if Emma didn't do what they wanted. As terrified as she'd been of him while lashed to a post, she hoped to see his face when Greyfang growled at him.

Emma leaned down, putting her mouth by the wolf's left ear. "The Spider Queen said they have a camp close to the spider's home, north and west."

He nodded. "We will find their scents."

She kept herself tight to Greyfang's fur. He led the pack, keeping a steady pace into the woods. The rest of the Wolves fanned out to both sides. Emma smiled at them, glowing with pride. Widowswood was her home. *Her* forest. The silk thieves did not belong here, and she would not let them hurt creatures under her protection. She considered asking the wolves to scare the thieves away, doubting any of them had the nerve to draw a weapon on Greyfang. At his size, even Mama's feet wouldn't touch the ground if she rode him.

No. I don't want them to get hurt, either. She set her jaw in a determined glare. *Da will bring the thieves to jail.*

Seeing a large fallen tree coming up, Emma hunkered down and grabbed two handfuls of fur. Greyfang leapt the great mossy log with ease, sailing into the air and stretching himself long. Emma came close to letting out a shriek of glee, but held it in. If the thieves heard her coming, they would either hurt her or flee before she could return with Da. The wolf landed hard, knocking the breath from her chest. She held on tight, and within seconds, he resumed his stride. A moment later, the pack turned as one, a grey, black, and rust-brown V knifing through the trees. Branches whipped past overhead and startled deer scrambled for cover, one charging headlong into a tree amid its panic.

Eventually, patches of white dotted the constant blurry green. Spider silk. The wolves eased to a brisk jog, noses to the ground.

"Humans," said Three-Fang. "This way."

The elder wolf tossed his nose in the air, indicating a direction to the right.

"I smell them." Runs in Shadow trotted in that direction, growling.

Greyfang surged ahead, slowing to a light jog once he'd resumed his place at the lead. Bites the Root raced back and forth, sniffing at everything. His overabundance of energy and eagerness to help reminded her of Tam. The sight of him zigzagging combined with his fuzzy coat, made him resemble an oversized puppy, at least to Emma. The thieves would see a massive pale-grey fiend with huge teeth.

If they saw any of them.

"Here," whispered Stalks the Wind. "Over the ridge."

Greyfang slowed to a walk and eased up to another fallen log, this one so old it had become part of the ground, covered end to end with shelf mushrooms. The pungent smell of fungus and moss brought a smile to Emma's lips. *Her* forest welcomed her.

The decaying wood formed a retaining wall at the top of a sharp downhill grade. Dirt, roots, and broken branches covered the ground between her and the site of an old abandoned village. Hints of pathways lined with stones remained, outlining where huts had once stood. Six tents, two large ones on the left, and four smaller ones on the right, sat under a covering of branches and leaves. Perhaps from a distance it would've made them difficult to spot, but as close as the wolves had brought her, they were obvious.

Both of the large tents took up about the space of a one-room cabin, while the others might have enough room for a pair of bedrolls. Between the two large tents, nine horses milled about, tied by the bridles to the side of a small wagon, a short length of stacked-stone wall, and a tree.

Two men in familiar grey cloaks sat on either side of a cook fire at the farthest end of the camp from where she crouched. A corner of the nearest of the large tents flapped up in the wind, exposing wooden trunks, suggesting it held provisions or equipment.

"We have found them," said Greyfang. "Let us return to guide your father and his soldiers here."

"Yes." Emma grinned at the horses. "But I have an idea."

24

SILVERBELL

*E*mma slipped down from Greyfang's back and stood beside him, her head not even up to the height of his shoulders. She smiled at the wolves gathered about and pointed at the horses.

"I'm going to untie them and ask them to gallop to Widowswood. That way, the thieves can't run from Da."

"The horses will become restless if we draw near," said Moonsong. "I hear humans sleeping, but the sun is out."

"They hunt at night," whispered Three-Fang. "The two who burn wood protect the rest."

Emma crouched low and crawled to the far left end of the rotting wood. Jelly-like moss squished under her feet, cold and slimy. The smell of earthen dampness grew stronger. She didn't mind the chill ooze mushed between her toes—it came from *her* forest. "If the horses will make noise, you should wait here. I'll sneak in and set them free."

"Danger," said Moonsong. "This is unwise."

"Perhaps, but it is of Ylithir's mind." The angle of Three-Fang's eye tufts suggested a chuckle. "Sneaky."

"May well he walks with you, cub," said Greyfang. "We will wait here."

Emma nodded. "Linganthas, please guide my step."

She crept over the wood and wobbled down the hill. No thorns found her soles, and twigs bent without snapping under her feet. Linganthas eased her passage around gnarled roots eager to trip the unwary and kept her silent. At the corner of the nearest large tent, she crouched low and listened to horses nickering and shifting, and the distant scrape of forks on tin plates.

Both men eating might see her if they turned. The four horses tied to the wagon, she could free while hiding *in* the wagon. The next three had been tethered to a fragment of former stone-walled house. She could hide behind the stacked rocks and duck if one of the thieves moved. The last two, tied to the tree, had the least cover, but the second large tent looked close enough for a quick dash given the need.

Emma crawled to the far corner of the first large tent and peeked around at the thieves having a meal. They sat on small logs, one with his back to her, the other three-quarters facing away. Both had their hoods down, though neither looked familiar. Their overall clothing, at least what she could see of it, reminded her enough of the thieves Da called Shadow's Eyes. She grinned to herself. *Nan really did scare them away.*

The most risky part of her plan lay ahead: covering about six feet of open space between the first tent and the wagon. Within a few seconds of observing the men, a wolf howled in the distance to the northeast. The sound made both men turn their backs to her. Emma darted forward and jumped up and over the tail end into the wagon. A few empty burlap sacks and a handful of stray oats greeted her inside. She crawled over to the first horse.

"Hello."

The animal's ears twitched back twice. "You talk?"

Three more horses perked up.

"Human girl? She's talking?" asked a mare.

"I never imagined," said a male horse.

The last horse fixed to the wagon bared its teeth in an effort to smile.

"I have to ask you to do something important. I'm going to get you loose from this tack. Can you all go to Widowswood?"

"We're already in Widowswood," said the mare.

"I mean the town." Emma pointed roughly east. "If you go there and wait for me, I'll bring you a bushel of apples."

All nine of the horses nodded.

Emma eased herself up and reached over the side of the wagon to untie the first bridle. "Don't walk away until I've got you all untied. If they see me, I'll have to run away and the rest of you are stuck."

They murmured in agreement, nodded and bared gums at her.

She edged to the second bridle and undid it from the wagon.

"Somethin' spookin' the horses?" said a distant man.

Emma dropped to the wagon floor and curled up against the sidewall.

"Naw, probably just that wolf we heard." Footsteps approached. "Nothin' over there."

"Awright."

The thuds of a man walking fell quiet. Soon, he yawned and grunted. Emma waited a twenty count and leaned up to peek. Both thieves again sat by their fire, one tending to a kettle. She hurried to undo the third horse and ducked again when one of the men let out a long, loud yawn.

After another ten count, she risked looking again. Neither glanced in her direction, so she untied the last horse from the wagon.

Emma nodded at them, then climbed over the driver's bench. She crouched like a cat on her hands and toes for the span of a breath before leaping to the ground. Three quick steps put her behind the crumbling remains of a hut wall made of stacked stone. A depression in the earth a little ways to the left hinted at where the fireplace had been. She rolled on her back; here, she could get to the reins tied around the gaps of missing stones without peering over the top.

She made short work of the three, rolled onto her hands and knees, and scurried to the tree. As soon as she grabbed the leather reins for the first of those horses, one of the men yelled a bad word.

"The horses are loose," said the thief.

"Uh-oh." The horse who'd taken one step back turned his head to look at them. "Sorry."

With that, the seven free horses took off in random directions.

Emma fought to free the eighth horse, who bolted as soon as the leather came loose. She hissed and waved her hand in an attempt to soothe the burn of the reins pulling out of her grip so fast. Someone ran toward her on the other side of the large tent. Fearing discovery, she darted for the second one. Emma dove to the ground and crawled under the canvas, emerging between a pair of heavy wooden trunks she could've lay down inside with room to spare. She pulled her foot in under the tent not a half second before a man ran past. He didn't slow, so Emma allowed herself to breathe. *I'll hide here among the boxes until—*

On all fours, she froze at the sight of a shimmering white-blue light on the ground and the sound of a man breathing in his sleep. Emma cringed, expecting to get caught. When the man's light snoring continued without interruption for a few more seconds, she raised her head and looked around at the rear portion of a tent set up like an inn room.

A plush red and gold rectangular carpet covered most of the ground, except for a small patch of dirt by the trunks. A man in loose-fitting black and grey robes slept on a bedroll along the right wall, next to a scattering of books. They lay open, pages covered with strange markings and diagrams, some of which emitted light. A pair of candles as big as her arms perched in red wooden holders carved in the likeness of dragons.

Two impressive gold rings adorned the sleeping man's one exposed hand, the other hidden amid bedding and clothes. A short portion of belt held four small pouches and a long, thin case from which a wand protruded. Dark brown hair half-covered a face much younger than she'd ever imagined such a person could be; the man didn't even look as old as Da.

"Oy, what the bloody?" asked a man outside. "What's with the horses?"

A splintering *crunch* preceded a yelp of surprise and the clatter of several pieces of tinware falling over. Hoof beats pounded the ground, fast becoming distant.

"It's the witch!" rasped another man. "She's come for us!"

"Fool," said a familiar deep voice. "Lew did a shoddy job of tying the reins. 'Tis no witchery afoot."

Emma's jaw hung open. Trembling started in her shoulders and spread down to her feet. *The wizard.* She scooted back toward the tent wall, intending to leave before he spotted her, certain the ruckus outside would've disturbed him. She reached for the canvas, but her gaze shifted left to the source of the flickering light.

A wooden table opposite the bedroll stood next to a single flimsy chair. Upon it sat an empty plate, a fork, and the same faerie lantern she'd seen hanging from the tree. The tiny woman inside slumped at the bottom, her back against the glass. She no longer emitted the bell-like tones, but her light also seemed much weaker. Perhaps she rested?

Or neared death.

The lantern sat five or six steps away. Five or six steps *closer* to the wizard. A man who could kill sixteen men in the time it took them to charge across a field. A man who could steal her mind and make her do whatever he wanted. The Faerie seemed miserable, her silver butterfly wings crumpled around her, stuck in a metal and glass cage she could barely stand in. The way her shoulders shook left no doubt in her mind the little creature sobbed.

Stop thinking!

Emma eased herself upright and tiptoed up to the table. She braced one hand on the near edge and reached out for the lantern. The faerie lifted her head, glowing sparkles of tears falling from her cheeks, and froze at the sight of Emma. She matched Nan's description of the Astari elves in all ways but size, being slender and delicate. Emma shot a quick look at the wizard.

He still slept, hadn't even moved.

Men outside complained about the horses, though their voices sounded distant, as if they'd tried to chase. Emma clasped the ring at the top of the lantern while holding one finger to her lips.

Hands pressed to the walls of her prison, the tiny woman nodded eagerly. With hope brightening her face, her radiant light also grew.

The lantern surprised Emma with its weight. She let out a grunt of exertion when she lifted it, but the little noise didn't disturb the wizard. She leaned back, extended one leg behind her, and tiptoed in reverse, not taking her gaze off the sleeping man until her back touched the tent wall. She sank to her knees and clutched the lantern to her chest.

After remembering to start breathing again, Emma lay flat on her stomach and slithered under the flap of canvas. Men grumbled only a few feet to her left, likely standing by the crumbling stone wall. She kept as still as she could, and put her body on top of the lantern to hide the light.

"I'm gonna give Lew somethin' ta remember this little job by, damn fool."

Another man let out a wheezy chuckle. "Bad luck follows wizards as sure as the day follows night. Somethin' spooked them horses."

"You heard wolves, eh?" The first man tossed a stone back atop the wall. "Furry blighters probably saw a tasty little buffet all lined up."

Please go away. Emma shivered from nerves, trapped between thieves and a sleeping wizard. They grumbled for a moment longer, but mercifully walked away. She pushed up from the grass, gathered her feet under her, and darted straight forward into the trees. Her path didn't take her back to the wolves, but it did keep a large tent between her and the camp.

As soon as she had half a dozen trees to hide behind, she skidded to a halt and flopped seated on the ground with the faerie lantern between her knees. The little figure inside still seemed miserable, but no longer lay in a defeated slouch.

Emma studied the tiny prison, poking and twisting at the ring and the bronze caps on either end. Six thick crystal panels formed the 'windows' of a hexagonal chamber, separated by metal spars about the width of her finger. Both bronze caps glowed with inscribed arcane markings, lime green against the dark metal. It reminded her of the Banderwigh's cage, in that it seemed to have no way to open.

The faerie looked about seven inches tall, but couldn't stand up straight. Bits of light, spots on her chest and a tiny skirt made of leaf-shaped fragments of energy, clung to her body with no apparent support. Compared to Emma, the little creature's skin was dark: she had a similar rich tan to guard Kavan, and fine silver/white hair all the way down to her feet. Wings like those of an enormous butterfly crumpled against the glass, jammed into the small chamber without care. Here and there, fine cracks seeped blood.

"Oh, no." Emma cringed. *She must be in pain.*

Faint rustling in the woods suggested the wolves moved around closer to her.

Plink, plink. The faerie got her attention by knocking on the glass. Her mouth moved, but whatever she said (or screamed) didn't make any sound. Emma pointed at her ear and shrugged. The faerie hung her head for a second before pantomiming grabbing something in two hands and bashing it against the glass.

Emma nodded. She set the lantern down and scampered about in search of a rock.

Greyfang and Moonsong emerged from the trees a short distance behind her.

"Emma. We need to take you from this place at once," said Greyfang.

"I have to help this faerie." She found a stone the size of a potato and ran back to kneel over the lantern.

The faerie waved at her as if to beckon her to continue, then curled in a tight ball near the bottom.

Emma lined up the narrow end of the oblong rock with the top portion of the glass, as far away from the faerie as she could get. She took the stone in two hands and smashed it down with all her strength.

Upon contact with the glass, the rock sent a bright yellow eldritch spark skittering away across the forest floor. Emma held the stone up over her head and brought it down again, but it bounced away without harming the lantern.

"I'm not strong enou—" Emma blinked. "Great Uruleth, please grant me your strength."

Warm energy spread down her back, a tingling sensation followed in her arms and legs. Grinning, she raised the stone over her head, and tapped all her desperation to free the little innocent faerie as well as her desire to go home.

Crack!

The glass panel exploded in a shower of glimmering, bright yellow eldritch sparks. A wave of warmth hit her like a pillow wielded by a giant. Emma sailed over backward, plowing a trail of clean dirt through a mass of fallen leaves. For a few seconds, she stared up at the sky past the treetops, without a clue as to why the world spun around in circles.

Moonsong nuzzled her until she sat up. Greyfang stepped up beside her and bowed his head, setting the limp faerie down in her lap. Emma gasped with worry. She placed the faerie on her back and gently flattened her smooth, silken wings. The miniature chest rose and fell, reassuring her the faerie hadn't died.

"Come, Emma." Greyfang nipped at her dress behind the neck, as if trying to pluck up a kitten.

"Wait." Emma held her hands over the faerie. "Uruleth, please hear me. Please give me the power to heal this faerie."

A cloud of dark green light swelled up between her hands and seeped into the small body. The faerie arched her back, twisting left and right as the cracks crisscrossing her wings mended. In seconds, the wings stiffened and came alive with a subtle white light, no longer limp and wrinkled like used handkerchiefs. As the last of the healing magic absorbed into her, she opened eyes that glittered like tiny, glowing sapphires.

She blurted something in a strange language and zipped up to hug Emma's cheek. Hundreds of flecks of white energy rained from her fast-fluttering wings, which again emanated a soft continuous bell-tone. The faerie floated a few inches in front of Emma's nose and kissed the tip. She rattled on in the same high-pitched strange language, speaking so fast one word ran into the next in a continuous, warbling tone. A second later, she burst into tears, but seemed happy beyond measure and hugged Emma's face again.

"We have to leave, right now," whispered Emma.

The faerie beamed at her. "Sorry. Forget you common not speaking. Neema my name is. In lantern trapped I was for many years. Die I wanted, for I could not bear it. Grateful very to you is this Silverbell faerie."

"What's this?" yelled a man's voice.

Emma gasped and looked up as if she'd been caught stealing.

The wizard stood at the corner of the tent, glaring at her with a cruel frown, framed by a short goatee and moustache. Twenty or more pouches of various sizes dangled on his belt. Fine lines of glowing silver energy appeared and faded at random within the material of his oversized black tunic and pants. While he'd slept, his garments seemed to be robes. This man looked nothing like she'd imagined a wizard to be. If not for the two wands and glowing strands of magic moving within the fabric of his tunic, she'd have taken him for a thief—a rich thief, but a thief nonetheless. Despite his not taking the form of the robe-wearing long-bearded demon with magical white eyes, the sight of him frightened her mute.

Neema screamed in terror and shot into the forest as if fired from a crossbow, leaving a hanging trail of silvery light.

Emma leapt to her feet and reached for Greyfang. Her fingers managed to touch fur an instant before an invisible force wrapped around her and sent her hurtling at the wizard. The bizarre acceleration stopped as hard as it started, knocking the breath from her chest. Whatever magic had moved her left her standing within grabbing distance of him. Intangible weight surrounded her feet, pinning her to the forest floor.

She stared at the handle of a slender silver and black longsword hanging from a belt cinched by a buckle in the shape of a human skull. On his right hip, a leather sleeve held two wands, one red and one black, both tipped with bejeweled caps of gold.

Emma gulped and lifted her gaze to make eye contact. One leather-gloved hand stroked a neatly trimmed goatee, as though the man couldn't quite decide what to make of her. She tugged at her legs, but her feet remained adhered to the ground, as impossible for her to move as solid stone boots.

The wizard's expression darkened, and her heartbeat thundered in her head.

A SIMPLE WEEDMAGE

A t growling from behind her, Emma gestured for the wolves to wait. If what Da said about wizards had any truth, she didn't want them to die because she had been stupid. She tapped into the feeling of protection the forest still radiated and puffed out her chest. Though she couldn't unstick her feet from the ground, she set her fists on her hips and glared up at him.

"The emerald creepers are under my protection. You should go home."

His growing frown became a smile of amusement. "Oh, is that so, little one?"

She folded her arms. "Yes. This is my forest. You and your thieves are not wanted here."

Four men in grey tunics and brown leather armored vests rounded the tent, gathering to the wizard's left. They looked at Emma with a mixture of confusion, fear, and annoyance.

Greyfang, Moonsong, Three-Fang, and Half Tail stalked out of the forest behind her, all growling low in their throats.

The thieves backed up a few paces each.

"By the gods, look at the size of that one..." One man pointed at Greyfang.

"Unnatural," whispered another.

Moonsong let out a low, long howl.

Answering howls emanated from the forest on all sides of the camp.

The wizard backed up as Greyfang and Moonsong flanked Emma.

"Whatever you did to me, make it stop." Emma grunted and tried to pick her feet up. "And go away before I ask the wolves to eat you all."

"*That's* the forest witch?" asked a thief. He pointed at Emma while making a face as if someone had slipped a raw fish into his pants. "I'd expected something a bit… older. More wrinkly."

"Maybe this is one o' them kids she stole and turned inta some kinda little evil witch-demon-imp?" asked a thief with light brown hair and a scar over his left eye.

"I'm not evil," said Emma. "You are. You're the ones who're killing innocent spiders."

The thieves exchanged perplexed glances. One snickered.

"Child…" The wizard raised a hand. "You have some manner of arrangement with the town, yes? That simpleton in the apothecary shop is spreading some nonsense about no one is permitted to hunt spiders. I understand you procure a regular portion of silk for him? Surely a little girl has no need of all that money."

"What money?" asked Emma.

The wizard raised an eyebrow. "You are far more shrewd than you appear. The last little parcel of silk you delivered was"—he held his hands about three feet apart—"quite sizeable. Easily five hundred kingscoin. Even if Marsten was cheating you, that's at least a hundred a month for little, ehh 'innocent' you."

"The other man said two thousand." Emma squinted.

Men yelled in alarm on the far side of the tent.

"Wolves!" shouted one man.

The rapid thuds of someone running passed from left to right on the other side of the tent. "They're bloody everywhere!"

"Why aren't they attacking?" yelled a woman.

"Don't ask that," whimpered a man.

"The witch! The witch has come to kill us. She's going to cut our hearts out and—"

A loud meaty *smack* preceded the *thump* of a body hitting the ground.

"Everyone stay calm," said the deep-voiced man.

Low howls from wolves mixed with panicked pleas to the gods to protect them from the forest's curse.

"I am not taking money." The magic holding her in place weakened. She dragged one foot back a few inches. "I'm trading silk so the spiders *and* people don't get hurt. If you leave Widowswood right now, I will ask the wolves not to harm any of you. I will not allow you to kill spiders in my forest."

Emma balled her hands in fists and stared at him. The trembles in her arms came from fear, but she hoped it at least *looked* like anger.

"Surely you are attempting some manner of jest, girl?" He let off a patronizing laugh. "I'd not take a threat from a simple weedmage seriously, much less a child version of one? Unless you'd like a lesson you'll not soon forget, you are going to behave yourself and do as we tell you to do."

"D—my father says the enemy who defeats you is the enemy you underestimate." She reached out to either side and put her hands atop the wolves' shoulders.

"Oh, come now, girl. You expect me to turn tail and run at the tantrum of a little shrub dweller. While you're out here rolling about in the dirt, we control entire cities. Our influence stretches well into Sondaren, and we're soon to expand beyond even that."

The magic faded the rest of the way, replaced by a sensation of pins and needles from her knees to the tips of her toes. She eyed the camp and glanced behind her. Runs in Shadow didn't seem to be anywhere. Perhaps Moonsong had sent her pup home so she would not have to watch him die.

Emma fumed. "I do not care what you do outside of my forest."

"You could become quite a wealthy woman someday," said the wizard.

"Oy, boss… why ye tryin' ta wheedle her 'round. Just do the"—the thief wiggled two hands' worth of fingers in Emma's direction—"thing again."

The wizard pursed his lips and pointed at Emma. "Don't move." He whirled on the thief and brought his hands together, fingertips steepled. "Do you possess enough of a mind to ration the difference between an automaton and a thinking, reasoning person?"

"Aye," said the thief.

"*Vas koransil Il'dalthri. Il'vadoor m'athra nur,*" chanted the wizard. He waved his hand at the thief on the far right end.

The man's eyes glowed with red light for an instant, and his posture slackened.

"Unstack and restack that wall." The wizard gestured at the rubble to which the horses had been tied.

The ensorcelled thief plodded over to the wall, moving with all the grace of a hand puppet, and picked up a rock. He pivoted to the side, dropped it, and grabbed another stone. Every motion came jerky and a second or two slow, as if a giant controlled a man-sized puppet on strings.

"While I could do the same to our little friend here"—the wizard gestured at Emma—"having her wits about her would make her a far more productive ally." He whirled back and fixed her with a threatening stare. "Do you not agree, little Emma? Wouldn't you much rather remain yourself?"

She stared at the mindless thief. Rock after rock thumped into the dirt.

"Or would you rather spend the next several years curled up alone in a little black space at the back of your dreams?"

Emma thought of Da saying wizards were easy to fight if you got close enough. She focused her voice to the wolves. "He wants to hurt me. Get closer."

The wizard raised an eyebrow, the thieves blinked at her. To them, she'd spent a few seconds making wolf noises.

Greyfang and Moonsong ambled forward, keeping themselves on either side of her.

She fought to keep her voice calm. "I am trying to be nice, but I don't think that's working. I won't ask again. Take your thieves and get out of my forest."

The wizard laughed. He gestured at her while glancing at the thieves. "*This* is what I am reduced to. Being threatened by a whelp of a weedmage?" His expression hardened. "No."

Furious, Emma took a step *at* the wizard. "You may not find a little girl threatening, but you should be afraid of my pack. Now, *go away!*"

Greyfang and the rest of the wolves lurking in the woods nearby all growled in unison.

The thieves edged backward. Two looked around as if in search of an escape route.

"Cowards," said the wizard. "They're just wolves. Kill them." He pulled the red wand from its sheath. "Kill them all and make boots."

26

MERE WOLVES

"*N*o!" screamed Emma. She charged, throwing herself at the wizard's right arm.

A gout of roaring fire swelled into a ball the size of her head at the tip of the wand, and shot off into the woods, missing Moonsong by inches before blasting a hunk out of a tree in a shower of smoking splinters. Emma gasped and flinched from the wave of heat on her face.

Growling, the Wizard made a fist with his left hand. Emma stared defiantly up at him. He shook his head and sighed. Rather than hit her, he shoved her away hard enough to spill her onto her back, legs in the air.

Greyfang and Moonsong rushed at him.

The camp filled with snarling wolves. More than twenty smears of grey and black erupted from the underbrush. Men, and one woman, shouted in fear. Emma recovered to her knees as Greyfang and his mate knocked the wizard to the ground, sinking their teeth into both his forearms.

He screamed like a peasant girl finding an emerald creeper in her bed.

A curvy blonde woman in a tight leather vest and leggings covered in dagger sheaths backed away from two huge black wolves. Though she had a shortsword pointed at them, the look on her face said she had no intention of using it. One man loosed an arrow from a shortbow, and a yelp of wolven pain sounded from out of sight behind the tent.

Emma leapt to her feet and growled, pointing. "Him!"

Three wolves changed course, going for the man she indicated. He rushed his next arrow, missing a black wolf by a foot or two. Half Tail hit him from behind, biting the back of his knee as the other two bowled into his front. The thief went down in a mass of swirling grey fur and gnashing teeth. Here and there, thieves took hesitant swings at circling wolves, the attacks missing by too much to seem like anything more than attempts to keep the animals at bay.

Emma filled her lungs, about to yell for the wolves to flee, but froze as Greyfang and Moonsong zoomed away to either side with startled yelps. They slid to a halt some thirty yards distant and struggled against magic binding them to the ground. Moonsong thrashed, snarling and snapping with desperation as if her cub faced imminent death.

Salvaging a few scraps of dignity, the wizard got to his feet and adjusted his tunic. After tugging his sleeves into place, he muttered a few strange words and flung his arms out to his sides. Both wolves calmed, stared at him for a second, and collapsed asleep.

"I could have killed them, girl." He flared his eyebrows. "And I still may, unless you do as you are told."

She sprinted away, but he caught up in a few strides, clapping one hand onto her back with a shove that flung her to the ground. Emma spat out a few leaves and scrambled upright. He grabbed a fistful of her dress, knuckles digging into her breastbone, and lifted her onto her tiptoes.

"Now listen here, sprite. Little girls should behave themselves, and I am at the limit of my patience with *this* little girl in particular. I'm not about to be made the fool by a dirt-covered shrub witch, much less a child."

Emma punched, kicked, and struggled. The man weathered her assault, his sneer deepening.

Uneasy wails from thieves mixed with dire growls from wolves.

She looked at the still-sleeping alpha and his mate, angry tears streaming down her cheeks. Emma couldn't let him hurt her friends. She grabbed his hand in both of hers, trying to pry his fingers away from her dress. "Let me go! Get off me!"

He chuckled

Snap.

The wizard looked up from Emma, and made a face that said 'oh, now what?' at something behind her.

"I'm no child," said Mama. "And you are threatening my daughter."

Emma twisted around, gawking at her mother striding out from the forest, green cloak flaring around her, Stalks the Wind at her side. Behind them, a pair of emerald creepers with bodies as big as old hogs glided forward without a sound.

Mama mumbled under her breath, calling upon Linganthas. She raised both arms high, and the entire area of the camp erupted with a tangle of writhing, thorny vines. Thieves cried out in pain as the finger-thick tendrils of wood shredded cloth and boot leather to bite flesh.

"Linganthas guide my step," whispered Emma, still pulling on the wizard's fingers.

The patch of roots grew, sweeping past her like a miniature tidal wave of writhing brown plant matter. Fabric ripped; the wizard stifled a groan. Scratchy tendrils passed around her legs and feet like the kneading paws of an affectionate cat, but didn't snag on her dress or pierce her skin.

"Linganthas, I call upon your wrath." Mama thrust her right arm forward, projecting a thin whipping vine at the wizard.

He dropped Emma to raise his hands, whispering, *"An'drasil niim."*

The vine Mama threw struck something invisible inches in front of the wizard's fingertips and deflected off to the side, slicing his tent clear in half.

Emma landed flat on her back, barking like a kicked goose as the air burped from her lungs. The thorny patch she'd fallen into slithered around her, not hindering her motion. Seeing stars, she rolled to her feet, the sharp pointy roots scraping over her from head to toe. They didn't grab or cling, instead feeling like a comforting back scratch. Once upright, she sprinted away from the wizard.

"Mama!" Emma's eyes sprang with tears as soon as she wrapped her arms around her mother, but she kept them quiet, her face hidden so the wizard would not see.

"I can't ruddy get out," screamed the female thief. "It's the witch!"

"Argh!" shouted a man over a repetitive clanking of metal on wood. "They ain't cuttin' either!"

One man wailed in agony.

The wolves didn't press their attack, standing sentinel in clusters around each group of trapped humans. One wolf had an arrow sticking out of his left shoulder, but seemed unaffected by it.

The wizard struggled, stuck in place by the roots. Shredded to tatters below the knee, his loose cloth pants fluttered in a light breeze. Trails of blood ran down the exposed skin above his tall boots. He hissed in pain.

"My daughter and her wolves would have slaughtered you along with your invaders. You are fortunate that she asked them not to harm anyone." Mama pointed her quarterstaff at the wizard. "You *don't* want to see what happens when a grown druid gets on your bad side. Only because my daughter is watching have I not filled your lungs with wasps and turned your blood to serpent's venom. Leave this forest never to return, or I shall feed you all to the spiders."

One thief happened to glance at the gargantuan creepers behind Mama, screamed, and fainted.

"You..." The wizard looked around at the struggling thieves hemmed in by wolf and root. "Pathetic cowards, the lot of you!" His right hand shot up, a gleam of blue light flashing over one of his rings.

Mama sucked in a breath. "Ling—"

Crack!

A thin bolt of lightning connected his outstretched finger to Mama's chest in an instant. A concussive blast knocked the breath from Emma's lungs. Mama flew off her feet and landed a short distance away, smoke or steam coming from her gaping mouth. Tingling electrical energy made Emma's hair stand up and flung her to the ground as well.

Emma stared at Mama, paralyzed with dread.

Her mother didn't move.

27

EYES CLOSED

"*M*ama!" Emma screamed. "No! Mama!"

Bawling, she scrambled over to where her mother lay and collapsed on top of her. The wizard muttered something else, but Emma ignored him. She sniffled and got up on her knees, hands outstretched over her mother's chest.

"Uruleth…" She broke into sobs and sniffled. "U-Uruleth, please—" She choked up and couldn't stop crying.

Greyfang's howl brought silence to the din of combat. Moonsong shook off the unnatural sleep and rose to her feet. A blast of fire puffed at the ground near the wizard, scorching a clear spot in the brambles, freeing him. He looked up at Mama with murder in his eyes and drew back his hand.

Before two words left his lips, Greyfang crashed into him, knocking him to the ground, snarling and tearing. Moonsong ducked and weaved, trying to get fangs on his neck.

Emma sniffled and tried to focus on calling Uruleth's healing magic. Again, she held her hands over her mother's heart, but couldn't force her voice past the enormous lump in her throat. Tears blurred the forest into a twisting mass of browns and greens. She grabbed Mama's cloak in two fists, but the harder she tried to push aside her terror and guilt to focus on the spell, the heavier the weight upon her heart became. Mama didn't seem to be breathing anymore. If she hadn't run off alone, Mama wouldn't he hurt. She blubbed, crying too much to speak even a single word.

Emma closed her eyes while clinging to Mama. *I have to call on Uruleth.*

Snot streamed from her nose as she coughed and gasped for air, searching for calm.

"Uruleth—"

Greyfang's pained yelp made her jump.

Again, he and Moonsong rocketed away, their claws dragging gouges deep in the earth and tangling vines. The bloodied wizard left them snarling in place and stomped up behind Emma. Enraged, she grabbed the dagger from Mama's belt, but he seized her by a fistful of hair.

Emma screamed as he hauled her to her feet. He grabbed her wrist and squeezed until she dropped the knife.

"Now, whelp, I shall show you the true meaning of obedience." By the grip on her hair, he twisted her head around, forcing her to look him in the eye, and pulled her up off her heels. She screamed again from the pain wrapped around her skull. The wizard held his other hand above her face, staring rage down upon her.

She wriggled, punching and kicking at him. He clutched her hair tighter until she ceased fighting and could only wobble there on her toes, whining at the painful grip.

"*Vas koransil...*" Dull red light glimmered in his eyes.

All the sounds of fighting slid far away, as if she listened from the end of a pipe. Dizziness came out of nowhere. Numbness crept up from her toes and fingers.

No! Mythandriel, give me your light!

"*...Il'dalthri...*"

The weight pressing in on mind grew heavier. The world started to fall away, leaving her in darkness.

"*...Il'vadoor...*"

Emma desired the light, as bright as the sun, as bright as Mythandriel would grant her. She thrust her hand in his face and cried out in angry panic.

A brilliant burst of pure white light exploded from her palm with a soft *pop*. Her fingertips had to be mere inches from his nose. The wizard released her hair in an instant; he backpedaled, grabbing his eyes in both hands while wailing in panicked, breathless shrieks.

Emma stumbled and fell on her bum.

Greyfang and Moonsong both strained to pull themselves free from the magical binding.

"Mama!" yelled Emma. She rolled onto her hands and knees and crawled back to her mother, who still hadn't moved. After a momentary glare at the two massive spiders who as yet had not done a thing but watch, she raised her hands again. Her heart pounded in her head. She had to calm down or she'd never be able to speak to Uruleth. Emma clasped her hands to her heart, trying to calm down while staring at Mama... and the satchel on her hip.

I'm so stupid!

She dove across Mama and reached into the satchel. It took her only seconds to find a glowing green healing elixir far more potent than her little spell.

Mythandriel, please don't let Mama die. Pleeeease!

"My eyes!" The wizard shuffled back another step. He lowered his hands and blinked while trying to look around, though he still behaved as if he couldn't see anything. "Little wretch. You're going to hurt for that."

"Run," yelled a thief.

"I bloody can't," shouted another.

"Where? Into the wolves? Daft fool," said the deep-voiced man. "Kill them."

The woman in leather raised her hands at the pair of wolves menacing her. "Nice wolfies. I don't want to hurt you, okay?"

Emma pulled the stopper and sniffed. Mint. *Yes. Definitely life energy.* She upended the bottle into Mama's mouth. Bright green light glowed from within, amid a bubbling rush like boiling water. A weak flare of matching glow filled her nostrils for a split second.

"Argh!" yelled the wizard, still blinking. "There you are, you little wretch..."

Emma whipped her head up and looked back. The wizard stormed closer, once again reaching for her. Greyfang and Moonsong trudged toward him as if mired in deep, sticky tar. She refused to leave her mother defenseless and run, instead shooting a glare at the two massive creepers. "Help! Don't just stand there!"

The wizard grabbed her arm.

Emma bit him on the wrist, snarling.

He drew back his hand in a fist.

The spiders raised their chelicerae, hissed, and charged at a frightening pace given their size.

"Gah!" yelled the wizard. He released Emma and scrambled backward, nearly tripping in his haste. The golden-brown tan in his face fled to a pallor.

Emma froze as the massive spiders bore down on her. She couldn't help herself and shrieked in sheer terror. The spiders raced by, their undersides high enough over her that only a hint of contact met the top of her hair.

The mage screamed. He raised his hands, conjuring fan-shaped sprays of fire, which brought the spiders to an abrupt halt. One circled left, the other right, waving their forelegs and mouthparts in a menacing dance. He spun in place, throwing small gouts of flames from his fingertips, but the spiders only reared back before leaning in again. He seemed to be trying to call more than little puffs, but stammered over the words.

One spider made a horrible sound, like a demon-possessed cricket chirping. A barrage of urticating hairs rained down on the wizard, each as big around as arrow shafts. Many stuck in his arms, legs, and chest. He howled in pain, guarding his face with his left forearm while struggling to keep the fire jets going. He backed into a still-intact patch of the thorn vines Mama had summoned, which wrapped around his legs up to the thigh, making him wail again.

"Mama!" Emma grabbed her mother by the shoulders and shook. "Mama!"

Greyfang, slowed by magic, trudged closer to the mage with a glare in his eyes that said he intended to tear the man to pieces. Emma twisted to look toward the growling. She didn't want him to get hurt, nor did she want to watch him eat the wizard. Before she could decide what to shout at him, a labored wheeze laced with the scent of minty smoke drew her attention to her mother, who coughed once and sucked in a massive gulp of breath.

Flares of orange firelight pulsed behind Emma, along with screeching and snapping from angry spiders.

Mama's eyes rolled around with disorientation for a second before her gaze focused on Emma. She exhaled a little smoke, took in a huge breath, and lapsed into a coughing fit. Emma fell on her, clinging. A roar of flames and a burst of heat came from behind. Mama pushed her down and stood in front of her.

The spider raining hair-daggers on the mage let off a keening screech that would've shattered glass. Most of the fur on its left side vanished, and one of its legs broke off under a prolonged stream of flames. Pale green fluid boiled away from the stump.

Emma gawked in horror.

"Linganthas, I call upon your fury. Lend me your power." Mama snarled and made a grabbing gesture in the direction of the wizard.

A single brown root, as thick as Da's arm, burst from the ground and whipped around the wizard's throat. It tensed, trying to lift him, but the tangle patch refused to yield his legs. His face darkened. He clawed at his neck for a second to no effect, then gestured at Mama while making frog-like noises.

"I thought I remembered wizards needing to speak to use their magic. I suspect that is a mild problem for you now." Mama glared at him. She tightened her fist and the root around his neck creaked, making his eyes bulge. "You should've listened to my daughter. Now, you've made me angry. Emma, close your eyes."

The giant root-tendril ripped him out of the tangle patch, lifting him into the air a few feet. The pain of the thorns shredding down his legs manifested in a spastic flailing of his arms and his face turning purple, his screams unable to escape his crushed throat. Mama whipped her arm down, and the root obeyed.

Emma averted her eyes.

A heavy *whump* accompanied the crackle of a thousand-thousand twigs snapping. Emma pictured the writhing mass of smaller vines coiling around every inch of him, trapping the wizard in a cocoon of needles. Both spiders surged forward, their chelicerae thrashing. The wizard's gurgles and struggles faded to stillness.

She looked up.

Greyfang and Moonsong broke free from the magic, but skidded to a halt. They skirted the huge spiders, as if they too didn't care to be close to such creatures. With the wizard helpless, they trotted over to Emma.

The conflict between thieves and wolves simmered with uneasy whimpers and menacing growls.

Emma stared at the wizard, who lay sprawled motionless on the ground. After a few seconds, the rising and falling of his chest became evident. *They paralyzed him.* She clung to Mama from behind, peering around her. Both spiders set to the task of cocooning the wizard in silk.

"By Mythandriel, receive the gift of life," whispered Mama.

A shimmering aura of dark green light surrounded the wounded spider. Wisps of energy coalesced at the stump of the severed leg, which regenerated, growing an inch or so every minute.

At a wave of Mama's hand, the thorny patch receded from the mage, allowing the spiders free access to their meal.

"They're going to take him back to the queen, aren't they?" Emma wasn't sure how she felt about the idea. Her worst nightmare had come true, for someone else. She *did* know she would be much safer with him gone.

"Yes." Mama turned to face her, took a knee, and wrapped her arms around her.

A small, burned hole in Mama's shirt, at the middle of her chest, hovered inches from Emma's eyes. Remorse weighed down her tongue and stole her voice. Overwhelmed with joy at Mama being alive, she clung and sniffled.

WORRY AND RECOMPENSE

*M*ama smoothed a hand over Emma's hair in a continuous motion. Emma pressed herself into a tight embrace, eyes closed. All the fear from the past few minutes condensed into a stone of guilt. The thieves continued to grunt and emit uneasy noises. A twig snap or yelp of pain signaled their continued war with the bramble patch.

"You shouldn't have run off alone, Emma."

Emma looked down. "I'm sorry, Mama. I was only going to find this place so I could bring Da here. I got an idea to let the horses go free so they couldn't run away. That man had a faerie locked in a lantern." She leaned back to make eye contact. "I couldn't leave her there... I just couldn't."

Mama looked equal parts angry and terrified. "What should I have done if that wizard had hurt you? By Mythandriel, what were you thinking running into the woods alone?" She fussed over her, checking for injuries. "Are you hurt?"

"I didn't go alone," said Emma in a small voice. "Greyfang and Moonsong, and the whole pack was with me. All he did was pull my hair."

"My apologies," said Moonsong, head down. "I should have scruffed her and brought her to you when she decided to enter the humans' camp."

Greyfang approached. "Ylithir has favored her. Perhaps all has happened as he foresaw."

Mama ran her hand over the alpha's head. "You fought for her as though she were your own cub. For that I am grateful."

"She is as such," said Moonsong. "Ylithir has spoken to us."

Emma put an arm around the black wolf, hugging her and Mama at the same time.

"Kimber asked Nan to find you, but she couldn't leave her and Tam alone in the house. Her bird found me when I left the Spider Queen's nest. Your sister was terribly frightened you would be hurt."

Emma sniffled and stared at the ground. "I only wanted to help. You and Da were fighting over what I promised the spiders. I didn't want you to fight." She wiped her eyes. "I wanted us to be happy."

"You should have talked to us, not run off."

"Yes, Mama." She nodded. "I'm sorry for being stupid."

"Emma. You're not stupid." Mama kissed her atop the head. "That is the problem." She chuckled with tears in her eyes. "You're too smart. And too caring, and you don't think enough about what could happen to you. What you did was *foolish*, not stupid."

Emma wiped her cheeks of tears. "Nan said you couldn't talk to the spiders…"

"I believe they are not true spiders. As if I couldn't guess that from their size. They are smarter, much smarter than the tiny ones."

That means Ylithir has *chosen me.* Emma bit her lip, a warmth spreading across her chest.

"Come, Em. Some of your pack are injured." Mama took her by the hand and walked her to the edge of the bramble patch. She cleared her throat and raised her voice at the thieves. "Listen here, you lot. Drop your weapons and you will walk away with your hides intact." She glanced at the large cocoon of silk where the wizard had been. "Don't test me."

The thieves went quiet.

Nine wolves with injuries ranging from small cuts to deep stab wounds approached. Emma kept a vigilant watch on the thieves while Mama tended to the animals. Green light shimmered around wolves over the next several minutes. As each healed wolf walked away, Emma hugged them, offered thanks for their help, and apologized for causing them to be hurt.

Crunching came from the east. Emma, as well as most of the thieves, looked in that direction.

Da marched out of the thick underbrush into the clearing, followed by ten of the Watch. The thieves broke into panic, fighting to tear themselves free of the sharp vines fusing them to the ground. One man snapped loose only to fall face first into the mass. Roots wrapped him in seconds, and he wailed like a scalded babe. Many shouted in protest that they hadn't done anything illegal. The woman among them put on an innocent air, acting terrified and making pleading faces at the guards as though she needed someone to save her.

Emma looked down at the writhing vines hovering within a finger's width of her legs. Sharp thorns brushed and caressed, but didn't draw blood. "Mama, how long will these vines last?"

"They will move for a little while. When the magic fades, they will become normal plants."

Da headed around the outside of the tangle patch and stopped at the closest point to them. He looked at Emma with a disappointed smirk. "What have you to say for yourself, Emma?"

"I was worried you and Mama would fight. You don't like magic stuff. I was foolish." She hung her head.

"She shouldn't have run off, even with the wolves, but her reasons were admirable. She'd planned only to scout the camp for you." Mama explained the faerie lantern. "Still, I expected better from you, Em. I would have come with you if you had asked."

Emma kept quiet, crying silent tears.

Da struggled to walk into the brambles. Mama gestured at him, and the patch withdrew from around his legs. He stumbled over and put a hand on Emma's shoulder.

"Perhaps this deserves the paddle. What do you think?"

Emma bit her lip. "I don't think that is a good idea."

Mama tried (and failed) to hide a smile.

"Oh, and why is that?" asked Da.

Emma looked up at him. "Because you would feel sad and guilty for making me hurt."

Da's amused face fell to a look of shock and guilt. He started to talk twice, but stopped both times after a fragment of a word.

Mama rubbed Emma's back. "She's not wrong. You haven't paddled her but once, and that was at least four years ago."

"No." Da sighed. He looked down at her. "Perhaps no paddle could be more punishment than the way you feel right now, but this time is not the same as what happened with Marsten."

"Yes, Da. Mister Marsten needed help right away. I shouldn't have come out here."

"Correct. So, for the next two weeks, you are not to leave the house without me, your mother, or Nan. You're going to remember that you are still a *child*, and be responsible like one."

"Yes, Da."

"Furthermore, with the exception of any emergencies involving your rat, I don't want you using magic for the term of your punishment."

Emma gasped.

He raised a finger. "Unless you, umm"—he twirled his hand in a circle —"somehow wind up in another Marsten situation and someone's going to be hurt if you do not."

Head down, Emma nodded. "Yes, Da."

"And finally…"

She looked up, cringing.

"We hope you will think next time before you do something so reckless," said Mama.

"Finally"—Da cleared his throat—"for the next two weeks, you will again be responsible for cleaning the chamber pot each morning." Emma made a sick face. "And… if you drop *this* one in the privy, I'll tie a rope about you and lower you right in to retrieve it."

"Da!" Emma gawked. "Y-you wouldn't!"

"You'd best not drop it then." He chuckled.

Emma looked to Mama for help.

"Will you at least let her call a light spell so she can find it?" asked Mama.

"I'll consider it." Da winked.

Please be teasing… Still sick to her stomach, Emma clasped her hands in front of her and looked down. "Yes, Da. I'm sorry for making you worry about me."

A muted moan emanated from the man-sized bundle of spidersilk. The huge creepers lifted the enwrapped wizard and carried him off into the woods.

"Well," said Da. "The man finally got his silk. From the looks of it, quite a fortune."

"Perhaps what Mother said about faerie lanterns bringing bad luck is true." Mama scowled at the cocooned wizard. "Arrogant fool."

"Faeries…" Da huffed, his eyebrows up. Some things would take longer for him to accept.

Mama pointed at the tree, and the one remaining horse. "Go and wait by that tree while I help the Watch collect the thieves from the tanglevine.

I trust you will be able to wait by a tree without running off to save a small village from a stone giant?"

Guilt poked her in the gut, but she smiled. "Yes, Mama. Can I free the horse?"

She patted Emma on the head. "Please do. He's been whining forever that you've forgotten him."

Emma hugged her Da, hugged Mama, and ran up to the horse. The stallion flapped its lips at her. She opened her mouth, but closed it.

"Mama?" yelled Emma.

Her mother looked over her shoulder.

"Please tell him I can't talk to him because I'm being punished and not allowed to use magic."

Mama smiled. A second later, she emitted a faint whinny and clicking noise.

The horse nuzzled Emma as she undid the bridle. Once she freed him, he trotted off into the woods.

She sat on the ground with her back against the tree, watching the guards and Mama free the thieves from the root snare. Eventually, the roots stopped moving and hardened into a knee-high tangle of natural brambles. One by one, the Watch interrogated the captured thieves. A few who had been present at the farmstead where Emma had been held captive were dragged off in irons, though more than half who hadn't been involved with that were sent away. Hunting spiders violated no law but Emma's.

Two weeks without using magic.

Emma sighed. Her cheek mushed up against her fist as she sulked. Knowing she deserved it didn't mean she had to like it.

SMALL FAVORS

*D*a carried Emma all the way through the forest back to their home. He didn't say anything about how worried he'd been, but he didn't have to. The firm grip holding her said everything words couldn't. No sooner did her feet touch the front porch than Kimber crashed into her with a tearful hug, knocking her back into Da.

He picked them both up and carried them inside.

Tam zoomed over, running circles around them, cheering, "Em's back!" over and over.

Da set them down, seated on the edge of the bed. "I've watched grown men who couldn't stand up to a wizard. Tonight and tomorrow, you rest. No chores."

"It's all right, Da. I can help."

He ruffled her hair. "Your punishment hasn't changed, but you're still a child who's had a scare. Rest."

"Yes, Da." She bowed her head.

Da moved off to help Mama and Nan hurry to prepare something to eat for supper. Nan's disappointed look hit her harder than a paddle could have. Emma stared at her toes.

"I'as glad you's nae dead." Kimber shied away from her, refusing to make eye contact.

"I'm sorry for scaring you."

Kimber nodded. "Donnae mind. Forgiven."

Tam climbed up on her left side. "You thumped the thieves! Wanna story..."

Emma looked up at Da. He didn't look pleased. "Not now."

The boy whined at her.

"Thanks for telling Nan." Emma took Kimber's hand. "I'm not angry with you for tattling."

Kimber looked up, astonishment on her face. "Trues?"

"Yes."

Her sister grinned. "I'as scared. Donnae wantin' yas tae get 'urt."

Emma hugged her.

Nan walked over and folded her arms. "Emma... I'm disappointed in you."

"Yes, Nan." She sniffled and burned guilt into the floor with her eyes.

"Next time, stay hidden and send a bird to your mother."

"Mother!" yelled Mama.

Da sighed at the ceiling.

Nan clucked her tongue. "It seems you've got quite a bit more to learn, but not about magic."

"Yes, Nan," said Emma to her feet.

"All right then." Nan tapped her on the head. "Come eat. We'll worry about that later."

Emma stood.

Nan pulled her into a hug, patting her on the back. "Don't give me a scare like that again, ya hear? This old bat can't take it."

Emma giggled with tears in her eyes and followed Nan to the table. "I promised the horses a bushel of apples."

Da blinked at her before staring at the ceiling. "She's so free with my coin, is she?"

Nan chuckled. "In a few years, you'll think a bushel of apples a bargain."

He groaned and sat in his chair, a hand over his eyes.

Nan produced an apple out of thin air. "Worry not of your promise, Emma. I'll attend to those horses."

Emma nodded and frowned a little. If the one horse hadn't moved, she might've been able to sneak away... but she'd still have gotten in trouble for going out there at all. She sighed, sank into her seat at the table, and smiled. "Thank you, Nan."

"BLARGH!" YELLED NAN.

Emma shot upright in bed, staring past the tent her feet made in the blanket at the shelves for a few seconds in bewilderment, startled awake by her grandmother's shout.

"Well…" Nan muttered something incomprehensible.

Emma looked to her right. Mama stood near the table, a hand over her mouth, gawking.

All the cabinets gleamed with a high polish that hadn't been there the night before. The pantry Nan opened overflowed with provisions. Threadbare spots in the fireplace rug had been mended. The dirty laundry bin lay empty, the shelves full of clean and folded clothes and bed linens… and the chamber pot shined clean. Every inch of the house sparkled: chipped walls repaired, gouges in the table legs polished out, even the doorknob glimmered in the sun.

Nan opened the other pantry. It too, overflowed. The breads looked unusual, a rich golden brown. The scent of fresh baking reached Emma's nose all the way across the house. Blinking, she crawled over a still-sleeping Kimber to the opposite side of the bed and dragged herself to her feet. Once standing, she closed her eyes and yawned.

"Oh, my," said Mama.

Nan put her fists on her hips and turned to face Emma. "Young lady, did you help a faerie?"

"Faeries don't exist!" said Tam, mimicking the same face Emma had so often worn.

The word 'faerie' pulled Kimber out of sleep. She opened her eyes wide.

Emma, still foggy-headed after the abrupt change from sleeping to awake, ground her hand at her right eye. "Why are you asking that like I did something bad?"

Nan leaned toward her, eyebrows up. "Well did you?"

"Yes. That's why I got stuck at the thieves' camp." Emma recounted how she found the Silverbell faerie in the lantern and smashed it to free her. "The wizard scared her. She ran away as soon as he came outside of his tent."

"Wha?" Kimber scrambled out of bed and grabbed Emma. "Yo'as found a faerie light? Aww! I wan' ta see 'er too."

"It's not like a firefly in a bottle. I had to set her free."

Kimber sighed with disappointment, but nodded. "I'as know. Jes' wan' see a faerie."

"Well, apparently"—Nan gestured at the pantry and the house—"they are quite grateful."

"Why do you sound unhappy?" Emma stifled a yawn and walked up to Nan.

Mama tapped her fingers, muttering as if deep in thought. "It's been so long I can't remember. Do we need to ward the house?"

"Silverbell?" asked Nan.

Emma nodded.

"No... they're not mischief makers. They're rather civilized. May as well be Astari elves in miniature." Nan scratched at her chin. "However, if we don't thank them... things will get chaotic."

Emma furrowed her eyebrows. "We have to thank them for thanking me?"

"Yes."

Kimber blinked. "Tha's donnae make sense."

"Faeries." Nan smiled. "It makes sense to them."

"What do we do?" asked Emma.

Mama pulled a beautiful bit of bread from the pantry and sniffed it. "Is this safe to eat?"

"I believe so. Gifts of gratitude are seldom laced with trickery." Nan took it from Mama, smelled it, and handed it back. "It's fine, and it'll stay warm until we eat it."

Emma leaned up to sniff at it. The bread carried a hint of ginger and sweetness. Her mouth watered. "Can we have that for morning meal?"

Da walked in from the back door. He didn't react to the immaculate condition of the house and headed straight to Emma. After picking her up in a spinning hug, he set her back on her feet and gave Tam and Kimber a similar good morning.

Nan opened another door and clucked like a startled chicken as a basket of apples toppled and spilled out all over her, bouncing away across the floor. The kids scrambled to collect them. Tam chased three under the bed. Once they'd been gathered, Nan sent Emma out to grab logs for the oven. Mama got a fire going, then everyone settled down to eat.

Emma picked up a thick piece of the still-warm bread and bit into it. Sweet ginger and spice with a hint of molasses filled her senses. Despite the size of the loaf, it seemed more like a treat than a bread. Da's eyes widened as soon as he tasted it, and he devoured his first slice in four bites. Emma disregarded the apple wedges for the moment, deciding to savor the bread.

"To thank faeries for their kindness, you'll need to set out some little treats tonight." Nan paused to nibble at her bread. "I know just the thing, but I'll have to go fetch some berries."

Emma grinned and attempted to mumble, "Yes, Nan" around a mouthful of the wonderful bread.

Da sent a glance of mild disapproval at Nan.

"Well, Liam. It's your choice if you'd rather not. 'Tis no more magical than baking. Of course, if you fancy every scrap of clothing in the house to be up in trees tomorrow morning or everyone's hair braided together—"

"All right, all right." Da smiled at Emma. "Well, I suppose she did save a wee one's life."

EMMA SPENT MOST OF THE AFTERNOON WORKING ON READING AND writing. With no chores to be done since the faeries had left the house in a state of perfection, she decided to stay inside. Kimber and Tam laughed and squealed out in the meadow. She wanted to join them, but it seemed like something she ought not to do while on punishment. Mama sat with her once she noticed what she'd started, and taught her more letters and words.

Spending time with Mama didn't much feel like punishment at all.

A while later, Kimber and Tam burst into cheers.

Emma looked up from her paper a few seconds before Nan walked in, trailing a swirl of raven feathers. She carried a long sprig of bright green vine, loaded with pink and violet round berries. Kimber and Tam chased her in, running circles around her.

"That's enough for now." Mama gathered the papers and inkwell. She ruffled Emma's hair. "You should attend to your baking."

"Yes, Mama." Emma scooted from her chair and hurried over to the counter.

She stood in patient silence as Nan collected flour, molasses, eggs, and a small jar of vanilla oil.

Tam reached up to grab a berry, but Nan caught his wrist. "These are not for small boys, Tam. Humans shouldn't eat these berries."

"Are they poison?" asked Tam.

"Not entirely. Effectively yes, but." Nan sighed. "They're Faeberries."

Kimber withered in on herself, all joy gone in an instant.

Nan perched on a stool near the counter and pulled the boy into her lap. "You've seen the men leaving Eoghn's Inn sometimes, barely able to walk."

He nodded.

Emma pulled Kimber into a hug.

"Just one of these berries would do the same to a boy your size. And they would make you see and feel things that aren't there." Nan gestured around. "The walls would seem to move. You might hear voices coming out of chairs and pillows. It's quite frightening."

He stared at the berries as if they would eat him.

Kimber sniffled. "I'as donnae like faeberries."

Nan raised an arm. Emma guided Kimber into Nan's embrace. "These berries are not for anyone in this house. To the faeries, and elves, they're little different than sweet."

Kimber nodded, wiping her tears.

Emma wanted to throw another rotten apple at Old Man Drinn for how he'd treated Kimber.

Soon, Nan hovered behind Emma, teaching her how to make small teacakes and tiny muffins. Some berries, she mashed into a preserve, which topped about half the cakes like tarts. Others, they added whole to small loaves. A bit of juice on her fingers got her feeling woozy and a little sick, and added a blur to everything in the room. New leaves seemed to start growing from Mama's staff. Emma stared at it, bewildered, until a sensation like a hundred spiders walking all over her made her squirm.

Nan muttered something to Mythandriel and patted her on the head. The odd feeling passed, and all the new growth on Mama's staff disappeared. "Careful, Emma. They're strong."

"They smell yummy."

"Oh, they are. Why do you think the faeries love them so much?" Nan chuckled.

Kimber tugged on Emma's arm. "Please donnae eat 'em."

"I won't," said Emma, alarmed at the imaginary things she'd seen merely from getting the juice on her skin. Her sister seemed to expect anyone even touching the berries to become mean and start hitting her. She grinned. "Maybe we'll see the faeries come to have their treats?"

"Ooh!" Kimber perked up, all sorrow gone. "D'ya fink?"

Emma bit her lip. "Maybe."

Nan took the baking iron full of doughy lumps and set it in the oven. She sent Emma out back to collect more wood, and soon the house filled with the pungent-sweet smell of faeberry. Emma wondered if the faeries would smell it from wherever they lived, and how it would be possible for them to eat such things. Some of those treats were twice the size of a faerie's head. *Hmm. Maybe they share?*

She went out to the back porch and sat on one of the two chairs, feet tucked up under her, watching Kimber and Tam resume running about the meadow. Beneath a dark blue and cloudless sky, Widowswood stood quiet save for the occasional trill of a bird. Emma thought back to strange lights she'd always thought to be huge fireflies—back when she didn't believe in faeries. Emma closed her eyes and daydreamed about little elven people watching them from the woods.

AFTER SUPPER, EMMA SPREAD A CLOTH ON THE BACK PORCH NEAR THE steps. Upon it, she arranged the faerie treats. Nan set a cup of mead nearby, along with a handful of thimbles for the faeries to use as glasses. Tam kept his distance, seeming fearful of the baked goods.

Emma hurried back inside to change into her nightdress, as did Kimber. She kept one eye on the windows by the back door, hoping to see a flicker of light. Nan gathered a blanket and carried it into the alcove full of Da's packs, spare weapons, boots, and riding gear.

Kimber followed, dragging Emma along by the hand.

"Now, you must remember to be quiet." Nan opened the blanket and the children crawled in. She bundled it closed around them. "No matter what you see... or do not see, remain still. If you frighten them, they might become angry."

Emma nodded.

Nan stood up, hands on her hips. "There is a chance they will not return before your father insists you take to bed."

Kimber made a soft whine.

"If you keep quiet enough, perhaps he won't notice you're not in bed." Nan winked.

Emma covered her mouth to mute a giggle.

Nan returned to the main room. The children huddled together, wrapped in a blanket with their faces at the glass. Eventually, the sun sank away, leaving Widowsood in the dark. A chill wafted from the glass, making Emma pull the blanket up to her nose. Kimber slid around behind her and draped herself over Emma's back. Tam sat in front of her, the top of his head at her chin. She wrapped him in her arms, holding him for warmth... and to keep him from charging out the door as soon as something appeared.

Minutes dragged into hours.

Emma's eyelids grew heavy. In the comfortable warmth of her siblings' embrace, she slid into sleep. Tam squirmed under her weight.

"Em!" whispered Kimber.

She snapped awake and glanced at Kimber, who thrust her arm out, pointing at the window.

An orb of silver-white light trailed out of Widowswood, following a meandering path toward the house. Kimber gasped in awe. When it reached a point about halfway across the meadow, the figure of a little person inside became clear. Kimber squeezed her hard, bouncing with glee.

"Shh," whispered Emma. "Hold still. Don't scare her."

The faerie dipped out of sight in the rolling meadow, but popped up over a shallow hill seconds later. She glided to land on her feet at the edge of the porch. Metallic silver butterfly wings stretched half again her height to either side, glowing with magical light.

Emma almost didn't recognize Neema. She seemed far more majestic. A day freed from the lantern must have allowed her energy to recover, or perhaps other faeries had healed her.

Neema tiptoed up to the spread of treats, picked one up, and sniffed it. She glanced at the window and smiled.

A cry of excitement leaked out from Kimber's nose.

"Shh!" whispered Emma.

Neema's wings flashed into a blur, and she darted from the porch to the windowsill. She waved at Emma before zipping to the left. The back door opened on its own, and the seven-inch woman flitted over to land seated on the interior sill.

"Wow," whispered Kimber. "Is'a real faerie."

"For freeing me, thanking you, Emma." Neema reached a hand up.

Emma held out one finger, which the faerie shook. "Sorry if we're too loud."

Kimber looked at Emma. "Can I'as touch 'er?"

"Ask Neema," said Emma.

The faerie giggled and flew to land on Kimber's shoulder. One wing fluttered against the girl's cheek.

"Eee!" squealed Kimber, scrunching her shoulders up. "Tickles!"

"Do not disturb please my friends," said Neema. "Time will it take for them to trust you."

Emma nodded. "I understand."

Tam stared aghast at the faerie, barely having breathed since she appeared. He shivered when she looked right at him. "A-are you gonna steal me?"

Neema laughed. "Nope! Not *those* kinds of faeries is Silverbell." She stuck her tongue out.

With that, the little one hugged Emma's head once more and zipped outside. The back door closed by itself.

Moments later, somewhere between twenty and forty faeries, men and women alike, streamed out of Widowswood. All had metallic silver wings, as well as garments made of pure light. Their hair color ranged from silver-white to bright pink, lemon yellow, lime green, and various shades of brown and even black.

Emma, Kimber, and Tam huddled low and quiet, watching the faeries enjoy their cakes and mead. They stayed for only a few minutes, and carried most of the baked goods away into the forest—though none of the mead remained.

Once the last traces of magical light receded into the trees, Emma shifted around and stood. Kimber hung on her back, feet off the ground.

"To bed," said Emma.

Kimber giggled and clapped, releasing everything she'd been keeping quiet. The grin on her face looked as though it would last for months.

Emma pulled Tam upright, and the three of them walked in a blanket-covered group to the bed.

TALISMANS

Calm blue sky peeked through gaps in the trees overhead. Widowswood came alive with the calls of birds and the rustles of boar, deer, and small unseen animals. Emma walked at Nan's side, gazing up into the branches in hopes of spotting a faerie, bird, or squirrel. A sharp pain poked her in the foot. She gasped and hopped on one leg. Nan looked down at her, smiling. She'd kept true to Da's wishes, and not asked Ylithir for the Dryad's Step. *Another twelve days.* Emma grumbled inside her head as she plucked a spiky burr from her sole.

Nan winked. "Go on, Em. I'm sure your Da won't mind something so small."

"I shouldn't." Emma shook her head. "I promised." She sighed and frowned. "I'm in trouble, and I'm not supposed to use magic. If I can keep a promise to a spider who wanted to eat me, I can keep a promise to Da."

"He knows you're already coming with me to help prepare a ritual." Nan winked.

Emma looked down to watch where she stepped. "Do you think it will work?"

Nan scoffed. "Of course it will. Now, you will need to speak to them to help me. Your father knows this."

Emma nodded.

Nan pointed out various useful plants and herbs as they walked. They spotted a cluster of Alabaster Throne mushrooms gathered around the base of a great pine tree, broad, flat caps of coppery brown atop a nine-inch stalk. Soon after, the edges of a large stream seemed to glow with a copious spread of Bluebell flowers that caught the sunlight.

Emma found a moss-covered fallen tree that served as a bridge and held her arms out for balance while walking across. For a short distance at the middle, she stepped in ankle-deep water where the bend of the old log dipped below the surface. Nan followed in kind, navigating the wooden bridge with ease that seemed unlikely for her age. At the opposite bank, she pointed out emerald moss.

A pair of huge grey longfoot rabbits sprinted from the bushes, disappearing into the underbrush amid snaps and thumps as they charged in reckless panic. Emma laughed at the sight of them bouncing off trees, rolling, and colliding with each other in their haste to get away.

Perhaps an hour after they'd entered the woods, they reached a spot where traces of spidersilk hung here and there in the trees, lofting on a gentle wind. Once they neared the nest, Emma concentrated and asked Strixian for the Wildkin Whisper. Da had given her permission to help Nan with this task, and she couldn't do that without talking to spiders.

Emma led the way into the tunnel, walking upon pillow-soft silk around the bend to where a sentry waited. She steeled herself, clinging to the memory of them protecting her from the wizard to dampen her fear.

"Hello." She curtsied. "My Nan would like to speak with the queen."

"The Raven comesss." The spider tilted his body forward in an attempt to bow. He scurried in reverse, waving at them to follow. "Welcome."

Emma made faces as the silk grew stickier the deeper they walked, but it never got to a point where she had to struggle to lift her feet from it. The queen rose from her perch in the wall and descended along the strands of an enormous web.

Nan took on a regal posture, nose raised a little more than usual. "Greetings to you, queen of the emerald creepers."

"To what do we owe the pleasssure of your visssit, Raven?" asked the Spider Queen.

"Not long ago, my granddaughter stumbled into one of your snares. I am here because you did not harm her. The arrangement she has made with you has created risk that I cannot abide. She is a small child, and unable to manage the danger her role in this creates."

The Spider Queen shifted with agitation. "Ssseekkss to break our agreement?"

"No," said Emma. "My parents said I can't trade silk because people will hurt me to get it. Like your little spiders obey you, I have to obey them."

The queen made a rattling hiss. It didn't translate to words as much as a feeling of annoyance.

Nan raised a hand. "I have come to offer you a more long lasting protection in keeping with Emma's intention. She wanted to stop humans from harming your children. I wish to stop humans from harming my grandchild."

"What do you propossse?" The giant spider took two steps closer to Nan, her body tilted with curiosity.

"I will call upon the spirits to enchant an area around your home. Anyone not in harmony with the woods will be unable to enter this place. My curse will make them walk around this nest without realizing it, protecting you and your children."

"What do you demand in return?" asked the queen.

Nan smiled. "Two things."

The hairs on the Spider Queen's abdomen quivered. Eight red eyes blinked at once.

"First, I would ask the assistance of one of your smaller children to help place a series of talismans high in the trees."

"Sssecond?" asked the queen, seeming to calm a little at such a trivial request.

"That you no longer hold Emma responsible for preventing trespass here while she remains a child. I will teach her how to create this ward so she can repair it should it ever come unwound."

Emma clasped her hands in front of herself and stared down. "I promised I would protect your spiders. I did something dangerous and almost got hurt."

"She risked her life for your children," said Nan. "Until she is grown, I cannot allow that to happen again."

The Spider Queen rotated to swing her massive face in front of Emma. "I did not think humansss capable of sssuch actsss. Your kind hatesss and fearsss usss. You have my ressspect." She twisted back to Nan. "I acccept your termsss."

Emma exhaled with relief at no longer standing two feet away from a mouth large enough to swallow her whole.

Nan gestured at a spider with a body the size of a medium dog. "He will be able to help."

The queen nodded.

"Yesss?" asked the 'small' spider.

Nan smiled. "Climb up on Emma's back and come with us for a little while. We will bring you back in a few hours."

"What?" Emma stared up at Nan.

"Spiders tire quickly, and you will be walking far."

Emma wasn't sure what to be more frightened of: a spider touching her, or being alone in the woods again. "I'm not supposed to be outside alone." She went stiff as the smaller spider, its head only level with her waist, scurried around behind her. *No, no, no, no.*

At the first touch of a spider leg at her back, she whimpered.

Nan took her hand. "Why are people afraid of spiders?"

"They don't want to be bitten," whispered Emma. She closed her eyes as another spider leg pinched at her dress.

"Do you think he will bite you?"

"No," said Emma in a small voice.

"Then what are you afraid of?"

Emma opened her eyes as twenty some-odd pounds of spider pulled up onto her back. She grunted and took a step to the side under its weight. "I..."

"Have had bad dreams of them ever since you saw a dead one on a wagon. You needn't be afraid of them. They are your friends now."

"You're right." Emma breathed in rapid, shallow sips of air. Nan made sense, but forgetting five years of sheer terror didn't come easy. She forced herself to nod.

Nan offered a bow of respect to the Spider Queen and headed for the tunnel.

Emma waved at the queen. "I don't know when I'll be back to visit, but if something happens, you can send another messenger."

"Be sssafe, little egg-layer," said the Spider Queen. With that, she rotated away and ascended the web back to her cubby.

Stooped forward, Emma trudged up the shaft behind Nan, trying not to think of the knife-sized sharp fangs hovering behind her head. The spider clung to her like a backpack. Nan stopped only a few steps from the nest entrance and slung her bag off her shoulder. She sat on the ground, pulled it open, and removed a wooden bowl, a metal bowl, hairs, powders, and a handful of charcoal nuggets.

Emma fought the urge to abandon her dress to get away from the spider, and stood still, but for a tremble she couldn't stop in her right leg.

Nan removed a smaller bag from her large sack, and handed it to

Emma. "These talismans need to be placed in a circle around the nest. Walk north"—she pointed—"one hundred steps. No, you have little legs. One hundred forty."

Emma laughed.

"Stop there and ask the spider to carry one of the talismans high into the tree and secure it with silk. It's fine if he wraps it in a sack."

Emma nodded. "Yes, Nan."

"Ask Linganthas for guidance so you know where you are, and walk around in a circle." Nan made a mark in the dirt and drew a large circle around it. "Think of these talismans like posts in a fence making a ring around the spider's den."

"Yes, Nan." She glanced north. "Is it safe?"

"It is. You will not be so far away that I cannot hear you or see you." She winked. "Now go and do your task, for I have my own to work."

"Aren't you going to show me how work the enchantment?"

Nan chuckled. "I've already done too much to start now. I will show you the process from the beginning soon enough."

Emma nodded and headed off to the north, counting her steps. After reaching a hundred and forty, she stopped and opened the bag. Talismans of wood, straw, and twine filled it, reminding her a bit of Stick Knight in a grass skirt if he carried two swords instead of one. She counted nine in total and pulled one out to examine. A faint sense of unease radiated from the wood. Nan had already imbued it with some kind of magic. While it didn't scare her, it radiated an energy she didn't want to tamper with.

"Will you take this up into that tree, high enough for a human not to see it, and bind it to the wood with silk?"

"Of courssse." The spider climbed off her and accepted the talisman before scurrying up into the branches.

Emma slouched with relief. She knelt after a few seconds of enjoying not touching a giant spider, and closed her eyes. "Linganthas, I call upon you to guide me. Please let me know my place in these woods. Help me protect the Spider Queen and her children."

She meditated on the desire to understand a circle around a dot. A faint sense of a tug at her inner energy came and went, though little else happened that she noticed. At the weight of the spider climbing onto her back once more, she opened her eyes.

The forest didn't appear any different, but a direction called to her. She grunted and stood. An inexplicable sense that the creepers' nest lay off to her right hovered at the back of her mind. Confident in her direction, she walked. In her mind, she pictured nine dots around a circle, spaced out as evenly as possible.

Emma made her way to each point that *felt* right and sent the spider up a tree to secure the talisman. Focused on the spacing and keeping the circle as round as she could, she lost track of worrying about thieves or goblins. Eventually, the spider descended from the ninth tree and once again climbed on her back.

She headed for the middle of the circle she pictured, no longer much noticing the extra weight of her passenger or her fear of spiders.

Nan whirled about her pair of bowls, surrounded by long streams of ethereal energy, each tipped by a bright orb. She waved her walking stick overhead, chanting in tones rather than words. A cluster of raven feathers adorned a shaker in her left hand, which she rattled in time with her dance. Her shawl and cloak glided after her, fluttering in a wind that only existed to Nan.

Emma approached within a few steps of the circle created by the orbiting strands of energy. The spider climbed down to stand beside her. She appreciated the lack of burden, but at the realization she didn't mind the spider being close, blinked. When that shock wore off, she sat cross-legged next to the emerald creeper and watched.

Nan danced about the bowls first in a circle, followed by a figure eight, and then a circle going the other way. She held her arms out to the sides in the manner of wings, shaking the rattle and waving her cane. Some minutes after Emma took a seat, Nan appeared to notice her. Her motions picked up speed and the size of her path collapsed inward until she stood between the bowls, spinning in place.

Energy flowed out of the woods, sweeping over Emma from behind and gathering in the place by the bowls. The air around Nan radiated power that left Emma as awestruck as Kimber seeing the faerie. Nan leaned back and raised her arms over her head in a slow rising gesture while emitting a low, throaty chant.

At the instant shaker and cane touched, nine comets of pale white light raced off in a starburst. Emma spun to watch one go by, assuming they headed out to the talismans. Nan regarded the pattern with a pleased smile and whirled about one last time, landing on her knees. She breathed heavy, like someone who'd just run a long distance.

Emma rushed to her side. "Nan, are you all right?"

"Yes, child. The magic is draining. I will likely be lazy for a few days." She chuckled and gestured at a large wooden figure on the ground between the bowls. "Take the last talisman. Give it to the queen, and tell her to keep it safe in the nest. It is the focus of my druid's curse. If it breaks, the magic will fade."

"Yes, Nan." Emma crawled over to where the bowls sat in the pine bed.

Charged air prickled at her skin with the tingles of an icy wind, passing through her dress as if it didn't exist. A larger talisman, a crude human figure carved from a twelve-inch tall log, lay on its back between the metal and wooden bowls. Sticks wedged into holes on the sides gave it arms, and Nan had painted eyes and a grimacing mouth on the rounded head.

Emma stood and carried it into the nest, followed by the small spider. She jogged down the pillow-covered cave, no longer worried or scared about the presence of spiders.

Once more in the great chamber, she waited for the queen to descend.

"This talisman is the heart of the magic. Any human who would do your children harm cannot find this place so long as this does not break." She handed it up.

"Yesss. I can sssenssse the power within it. The Raven isss strong." The Spider Queen grasped the talisman with her mouthparts. She handed it to a sentry, who carried it up to the cubby, and turned back to Emma. "You have ssshown me that not all humansss care purely for their own interessstsss. Little egg-layer, you are a friend to my kind. Go in peaccce."

Emma reached out and touched the queen's foreleg. "Thank you."

The Spider Queen reversed, walking backward at first and rotating as she ascended the web to her cubby.

"Be safe." Emma waved at the entire chamber full of spiders and strode back up the tunnel with a smile on her face.

Nan met her at the entrance, the sack once more draped over her shoulder. "The spiders are pleased?"

"Yes. She said she can feel the magic in the talisman." Emma fell in step at Nan's side, holding her hand. "How long will it last?"

"If no one locates the talismans and breaks them, perhaps many lifetimes."

Emma nodded.

"Ahh. I am looking forward to a soft bed and a big cup of hot tea."

They walked in smiling quiet for a short while before an idea zipped into Emma's head like a drunken faerie.

"Nan?"

"Yes, Em?"

"What happened to Princess Isabelle after you made the potion for her?"

Nan laughed. "Oh, I imagine she's still in the palace at Andor."

"Andor?" Emma looked up at Nan for a second before returning her gaze to the ground to watch for more burrs.

"The castle city far to the east." Nan smiled.

Emma blinked. "You mean *Queen* Isabella?"

"Perhaps." Nan sent an innocent smile into the treetops. "What do you think?"

"But..." Emma gasped. "The wizard who cursed the king was *real*? Is he still out there?" She squeezed Nan's hand.

Nan shook her head. "You'll have to wait, my dear. We haven't gotten to that part of the story yet."

Emma glared up at Nan, amused and annoyed in equal parts. When the old one burst into laughter, she caught it, and giggled along.

Soon, the comforting shadows of Widowswood fell away to open grassland and the sight of home at the bottom of a long, sweeping hillside. From here, Kimber looked like a little red-haired faerie zooming around the meadow behind the house. Tam, a smaller light brown spot, chased after. Farther down the spread of verdant green, the town of Widowswood teemed with activity. Rooftops and windows glinted in the sun, other children ran hither and yon as horses and adults went about their day.

"Ahh," said Nan. "No more trips into the woods, and no more worrying of spiders for a while. I don't know about you, but I am looking forward to some peace and bloody quiet."

Mama appeared from behind a house, walking up the dirt path from town proper, also headed home.

"Yes." Emma beamed and waved to Mama, then looked up at Nan. "I am too."

fin

The adventure continues in Book 3 - Emma and the Silverbell Faeries!

A druid's work is never done... even if she's ten years old.

With the Silk Thieves no longer a threat to Widowswood, Emma enjoys the solace of home and the peaceful routine of her chores. She is happy to be with her family, but still hasns't quite forgiven herself for making them worry about her.

One afternoon, Neema, the Faerie she freed from the wizard's lantern, returns seeking her help. Her people are dying, and she's convinced Emma can save them, and do it in only a few minutes.

The plea proves hard to resist, and Emma soon discovers cursed animals are attacking the faeries. Even though some Silverbells have perished, they are hesitant to kill the creatures. Their queen hopes Emma can find a way to save both animals and faeries alike.

Far from her family in a strange magical forest, Emma feels too small for the task set before her, but cannot abandon the faeries to their fate— even if it means she may never find her way home.

ACKNOWLEDGMENTS

Thank you for reading Emma and the Silk Thieves!

Additional thanks to Orion Rodriguez for editing and Ricky Gunawan for the wonderful cover art and interior illustrations.

ABOUT THE AUTHOR

Originally from South Amboy NJ, Matthew has been creating science fiction and fantasy worlds for most of his reasoning life. Since 1996, he has developed the "Divergent Fates" world, in which *Division Zero, Virtual Immortality, The Awakened Series, The Harmony Paradox, and the Daughter of Mars series* take place. Along with being an editor at Curiosity Quills press, he has worked in IT and technical support.

Matthew is an avid gamer, a recovered WoW addict, Gamemaster for two custom RPG systems, and a fan of anime, British humour, and intellectual science fiction that questions the nature of reality, life, and what happens after it.

He is also fond of cats.

Visit me online at:
    Facebook: https://www.facebook.com/MatthewSCoxAuthor
    Pinterest: https://www.pinterest.com/matthewcox10420/
    Goodreads: https://www.goodreads.com/author/show/7712730.Matthew_S_Cox
    Email: mcox2112@gmail.com

OTHER BOOKS BY MATTHEW S. COX

Divergent Fates Universe Novels

Division Zero series

- Division Zero
- Lex De Mortuis
- Thrall
- Guardian
- Harbinger

The Awakened series

- Prophet of the Badlands
- Archon's Queen
- Grey Ronin
- Daughter of Ash
- Zero Rogue
- Angel Descended

Daughter of Mars series

- The Hand of Raziel
- Araphel
- Ghost Black

Virtual Immortality series

- Virtual Immortality
- The Harmony Paradox

Divergent Fates Anthology

(Fiction Novels - Adult)

The Roadhouse Chronicles Series

- One More Run
- The Redeemed
- Dead Man's Number

Faded Skies series

- Heir Ascendant
- Ascendant Unrest
- Ascendant Revolution

Temporal Armistice Series

- Nascent Shadow
- The Shadow Collector
- The Gate to Oblivion

Vampire Innocent series

- A Nighttime of Forever
- A Beginner's Guide to Fangs
- The Artist of Ruin
- The Last Family Road Trip
- The Phantom Oracle

Standalones

- Wayfarer: AV494
- Axillon99
- Chiaroscuro: The Mouse and the Candle
- The Spirits of Six Minstrel Run
- The Far Side of Promise anthology
- Operation: Chimera (with Tony Healey)
- The Dysfunctional Conspiracy (with Christopher Veltmann)

Winter Solstice series (with J.R. Rain)

- Convergence
- Containment

- Catalyst

Young Adult Novels

The Eldritch Heart Series

Evergreen Series

- Evergreen
- The World That Remains

Standalones

- Caller 107
- The Summer the World Ended
- Nine Candles of Deepest Black
- The Forest Beyond the Earth
- Out of Sight
- Evergreen

Middle Grade Novels

Tales of Widowswood series

- Emma and the Banderwigh
- Emma and the Silk Thieves
- Emma and the Silverbell Faeries
- Emma and the Elixir of Madness
- Emma and the Weeping Spirit

Standalones

- Citadel: The Concordant Sequence
- The Cursed Codex
- The Menagerie of Jenkins Bailey
- Sophie's Light

www.ingramcontent.com/pod-product-compliance
Lightning Source LLC
Chambersburg PA
CBHW032118170626
46808CB00006B/1995